W9-ACI-580

OMNIVM LVX CIVIVM

BOSTON
PUBLIC
LIBRARY

A MORBID TASTE
FOR BONES

WITHDRAWN
No longer the property of the
Boston Public Library.
Sale of this material benefits the Library.

by the same author

DEATH MASK
THE WILL AND THE DEED
DEATH AND THE JOYFUL WOMAN
FUNERAL OF FIGARO
FLIGHT OF A WITCH
A NICE DERANGEMENT OF EPITAPHS
THE PIPER ON THE MOUNTAIN
BLACK IS THE COLOUR OF MY TRUE-LOVE'S HEART
THE GRASS WIDOW'S TALE
THE HOUSE OF GREEN TURF
MOURNING RAGA
THE KNOCKER ON DEATH'S DOOR
DEATH TO THE LANDLORDS!
CITY OF GOLD AND SHADOWS
THE HORN OF ROLAND
NEVER PICK UP HITCH-HIKERS!

A MORBID TASTE FOR BONES

Ellis Peters

WILLIAM MORROW AND COMPANY, INC.
NEW YORK   1978

CODMAN SQUARE

JUL   1981

PZ3
.P2165 Mo
1978x

Copyright © 1977 by Ellis Peters

Originally published in Great Britain in 1977
by Macmillan London Limited.

All rights reserved. No part of this book may be reproduced
or utilized in any form or by any means, electronic or me-
chanical, including photocopying, recording or by any information storage and retrieval system, without permission
in writing from the Publisher. Inquiries should be addressed
to William Morrow and Company, Inc., 105 Madison Ave.,
New York, N. Y. 10016.

Library of Congress Catalog Card Number 78-60992

ISBN 0-688-03374-1

Printed in the United States of America.

First Edition

1   2   3   4   5   6   7   8   9   10

CHAPTER ONE

On the fine, bright morning in early May when the whole sensational affair of the Gwytherin relics may properly be considered to have begun, Brother Cadfael had been up long before Prime, pricking out cabbage seedlings before the day was aired, and his thoughts were all on birth, growth and fertility, not at all on graves and reliquaries and violent deaths, whether of saints, sinners or ordinary decent, fallible men like himself. Nothing troubled his peace but the necessity to take himself indoors for Mass, and the succeeding half-hour of chapter, which was always liable to stray over by an extra ten minutes. He grudged the time from his more congenial labours out here among the vegetables, but there was no evading his duty. He had, after all, chosen this cloistered life with his eyes open, he could not complain even of those parts of it he found unattractive, when the whole suited him very well, and gave him the kind of satisfaction he felt now, as he straightened his back and looked about him.

He doubted if there was a finer Benedictine garden in the whole kingdom, or one better supplied with herbs both good for spicing meats, and also invaluable as medicine. The main orchards and lands of the Shrewsbury abbey of Saint Peter and Saint Paul lay on the northern side of the road, outside the monastic enclave, but here, in the enclosed garden within the walls, close to the abbot's fish-ponds and the brook that worked the abbey mill, Brother Cadfael ruled unchallenged. The herbarium in particular was his kingdom, for he had built it up gradually through fifteen years of labour, and added to it many exotic plants of his own careful raising, collected in a roving youth that had taken him as far afield as Venice, and Cyprus and the Holy Land. For Brother Cadfael had come late to the monastic life,

5

like a battered ship settling at last for a quiet harbour. He was well aware that in the first years of his vows the novices and lay servants had been wont to point him out to one another with awed whisperings.

'See that brother working in the garden there? The thickset fellow who rolls from one leg to the other like a sailor? You wouldn't think to look at him, would you, that he went on crusade when he was young? He was with Godfrey de Bouillon at Antioch, when the Saracens surrendered it. And he took to the seas as a captain when the king of Jerusalem ruled all the coast of the Holy Land, and served against the corsairs ten years! Hard to believe it now, eh?'

Brother Cadfael himself found nothing strange in his wide-ranging career, and had forgotten nothing and regretted nothing. He saw no contradiction in the delight he had taken in battle and adventure, and the keen pleasure he now found in quietude. Spiced, to be truthful, with more than a little mischief when he could get it, as he liked his victuals well-flavoured, but quietude all the same, a ship becalmed and enjoying it. And probably the youngsters who eyed him with such curiosity also whispered that in a life such as he had led there must have been some encounters with women, and not all purely chivalrous, and what sort of grounding was that for the conventual life?

They were right about the women. Quite apart from Richildis, who had not unnaturally tired of waiting for his return after ten years, and married a solid yeoman with good prospects in the shire, and no intention of flying off to the wars, he remem-bered other ladies, in more lands than one, with whom he had enjoyed encounters pleasurable to both parties, and no harm to either. Bianca, drawing water at the stone well-head in Venice —the Greek boat-girl Arianna—Mariam, the Saracen widow who sold spices and fruit in Antioch, and who found him man enough to replace for a while the man she had lost. The light en-counters and the grave, not one of them had left any hard feelings behind. He counted that as achievement enough, and having known them was part of the harmonious balance that made him content now with this harboured, contemplative life, and gave

6

him patience and insight to bear with these cloistered, simple souls who had put on the Benedictine habit as a life's profession, while for him it was a timely retirement. When you have done everything else, perfecting a conventual herb-garden is a fine and satisfying thing to do. He could not conceive of coming to this stasis having done nothing else whatever.

Five minutes more, and he must go and wash his hands and repair to the church for Mass. He used the respite to walk the length of his pale-flowered, fragrant inner kingdom, where Brother John and Brother Columbanus, two youngsters barely a year tonsured, were busy weeding and edge-trimming. Glossy and dim, oiled and furry, the leaves tendered every possible variation on green. The flowers were mostly shy, small, almost furtive, in soft, sidelong colours, lilacs and shadowy blues and diminutive yellows, for they were the unimportant and unwanted part, but for ensuring seed to follow. Rue, sage, rosemary, gilvers, gromwell, ginger, mint, thyme, columbine, herb of grace, savoury, mustard, every manner of herb grew here, fennel, tansy, basil and dill, parsley, chervil and marjoram. He had taught the uses even of the unfamiliar to all his assistants, and made plain their dangers, too, for the benefit of herbs is in their right proportion, and over-dosage can be worse than the disease. Small of habit, modest of tint, close-growing and shy, his herbs called attention to themselves only by their disseminated sweetness as the sun rose on them. But behind their shrinking ranks rose others taller and more clamorous, banks of peonies grown for their spiced seeds, and lofty, pale-leaved, budding poppies, as yet barely showing the white or purple-black petals through their close armour. They stood as tall as a short man, and their home was the eastern part of the middle sea, and from that far place Cadfael had brought their ancestors in the seed long ago, and raised and cross-bred them in his own garden, before ever he brought the perfected progeny here with him to make medicines against pain, the chief enemy of man. Pain, and the absence of sleep, which is the most beneficent remedy for pain.

The two young men, with habits kilted to the knee, were just straightening their backs and dusting the soil from their

7

hands, as well aware as he of the hour. Brother Columbanus would not for the world have let slip one grain of his duties, or countenanced such a backsliding in any of his fellows. A very comely, well-made, upstanding young fellow he was, with a round, formidable, Norman head, as he came from a formidable, aristocratic Norman family, a younger son despatched to make his way in the monastic ranks as next-best to inheriting land. He had stiff, upstanding yellow hair and full blue eyes, and his modest demeanour and withdrawn pallor tended to obscure the muscular force of his build. Not a very comfortable colleague, Brother Columbanus, for in spite of his admirable bodily equipment he had some while since proved that he had a mental structure of alarming sensitivity, and was liable to fits of emotional stress, crises of conscience, and apocalyptic visions far removed from the implications of his solid skull. But he was young and idealistic, he had time to get over his self-torments. Brother Cadfael had worked with him for some months, and had every hope for him. He was willing, energetic, and almost too eager to please. Possibly he felt his debt to his aristocratic house too nearly, and feared a failure that would reflect on his kin. You cannot be of high Norman blood, and not excel! Brother Cadfael felt for any such victims as found themselves in this trap, coming, as he did, of antique Welsh stock without superhuman pretensions. So he tolerated Brother Columbanus with equanimity, and doctored his occasional excesses philosophically. The juice of the paynim poppies had quieted Columbanus more than once when his religious fervour prostrated him.

Well, at any rate there was no nonsense of that kind with the other one! Brother John was as plain and practical as his name, a square young man with a snub nose and an untamable ring of wiry russet curls round his tonsure. He was always hungry, and his chief interest in all things that grew in gardens was whether they were eatable, and of agreeable flavour. Come autumn he would certainly find a way of working his passage into the orchards. Just now he was content to help Brother Cadfael prick out early lettuces, and wait for the soft fruits to come into season. He was a handsome, lusty, good-natured soul, who seemed to have blundered into this enclosed life by some incomprehensible error, and not yet to have realised that he had come to the wrong place. Brother Cadfael detected a lively sense of mischief the fellow to his own, but never yet given its head in a wider world, and confidently expected that some day this particular red-crested bird would certainly fly. Meantime, he got his entertainment wherever it offered, and found it sometimes in unexpected places.

'I must be in good time,' he said, unkilting his gown and dusting his hands cheerfully on his seat. 'I'm reader this week.' So he was, Cadfael recalled, and however dull the passages they chose for him in the refectory, and innocuous the saints and martyrs he would have to celebrate at chapter, John would contrive to imbue them with drama and gusto from his own sources. Give him the beheading of Saint John the Baptist, and he would shake the foundations.

'You read for the glory of God and the saints, brother,' Columbanus reminded him, with loving reproof and somewhat offensive humility, 'not for your own!' Which showed either how little he knew about it, or how false he could be, one or the other.

'The blessed thought is ever in my mind,' said Brother John with irrepressible zest, and winked at Cadfael behind his colleague's back, and set off enthusiastically along the aisles of shrubs towards the abbot's gate and the great court. They followed him more demurely, the slender, fair, agile youth and the squat, barrel-chested, bandy-legged veteran of fifty-seven. Was I ever, wondered Cadfael, rolling with his powerful seaman's gait beside the other's long, supple strides, as young and earnest as this? It cost him an effort to recall that Columbanus was actually fully twenty-five, and the sprig of a sophisticated and ambitious house. Whose fortunes, surely, were not founded wholly on piety?

This third Mass of the day was non-parochial and brief, and after it the Benedictine brothers of the abbey of Shrewsbury filed in procession from the choir into the chapter-house, and made their way to their stalls in due order, Abbot Heribert leading.

The abbot was old, of mild nature and pliant, a gentle grey ascetic very wishful of peace and harmony around him. His figure was unimpressive, though his face was beguiling in its anxious sweetness. Novices and pupils were easy in his presence, when they could reach it, which was by no means always easy, for the extremely impressive figure of Prior Robert was liable to loom between.

Prior Robert Pennant, of mixed Welsh and English blood, was more than six feet tall, attenuated and graceful, silver-grey of hair at fifty, blanched and beautiful of visage, with long, aristocratic features and lofty marble brow. There was no man in the midland shires would look more splendid in a mitre, superhuman in height and authority, and there was no man in England better aware of it, or more determined to prove it at the earliest opportunity. His very motions, sweeping across the chapter-house to his stall, understudied the pontificate.

After him came Brother Richard the sub-prior, his antithesis, large, ungainly, amiable and benevolent, of a good mind, but mentally lazy. Doubtful if he would ever become prior when Robert achieved his end, with so many ambitious and industrious younger men eyeing the prospect of advancement, and willing to go to a great deal of trouble to secure it.

After Richard came all the other brothers in their hierarchies. Brother Benedict the sacristan, Brother Anselm the precentor, Brother Matthew the cellarer, Brother Dennis the hospitaller, Brother Edmund the infirmarer, Brother Oswald the almoner, Brother Jerome, the prior's clerk, and Brother Paul, master of the novices, followed by the commonalty of the convent, and a very flourishing number they made. Among the last of them Brother Cadfael rolled to his own chosen corner, well to the rear and poorly lit, half-concealed behind one of the stone pillars. Since he held no troublesome parchment office, he was unlikely to be called upon to speak in chapter upon the various businesses of the house, and when the matter in hand was dull into the bargain it was his habit to employ the time to good account by sleeping, which from long usage he could do bolt upright and undetected in his shadowy corner. He had a sixth sense which alerted him at need, and brought him awake instantly and plausibly. He had even been known to answer a question pat, when it was certain he had been asleep when it was put to him.

On this particular May morning he remained awake long enough to enjoy Brother John's extraction of the last improbable ounce of drama from the life of some obscure saint whose day fell on the morrow, but when the cellarer began to expound a complicated matter of a legacy partly to the altar of Our Lady, partly to the infirmary, he composed himself to slumber. After all, he knew that most of the remaining time, once a couple of minor malefactors had been dealt with, would be given to Prior Robert's campaign to secure the relics and patronage of a powerful saint for the monastery. For the past few months very little else had been discussed. The prior had had it on his mind, in fact, ever since the Cluniac house of Wenlock had rediscovered, with great pride and jubilation, the tomb of their original foundress, Saint Milburga, and installed her bones triumphantly on their altar. An alien priory, only a few miles distant, with its own miracle-working saint, and the great Benedictine house of Shrewsbury as empty of relics as a plundered almsbox! It was more than Prior Robert could stomach. He had been scouring the borderlands for a spare saint now for a year or more, looking hopefully towards Wales, where it was well known that holy men and women had been common as mushrooms in autumn in the past, and as little regarded. Brother Cadfael had no wish to hear the latest of his complaints and urgings. He slept.

The heat of the sun rebounded from honed facets of pale, baked rock, scorching his face, as the floating arid dust burned his throat. From where he crouched with his fellows in cover he could see the long crest of the wall, and the steel-capped heads of the guards on the turrets glittering in the fierce light. A landscape carved out of reddish stone and fire, all deep gullies and sheer cliffs, with never a cool green leaf to temper it, and before him the object of all his journeyings, the holy city of Jerusalem, crowned with towers and domes within its white walls. The dust of battle hung in the air, dimming the clarity of battlement and gate, and the hoarse shouting and clashing of armour filled his ears. He was waiting for the trumpet to sound the final assault, and keeping well in cover while he waited, for he had learned to respect the range of the short, curly Saracen bow. He saw the banners surge forward out of hiding, streaming on the burning wind. He saw the flash of the raised trumpet, and braced himself for the blare.

The sound that brought him leaping wide-awake out of his dream was loud enough and stirring enough, but not the brazen blast of a trumpet, nor was he launched from his stillness towards the triumphant storming of Jerusalem. He was back in his stall in the dark corner of the chapter-house, and starting to his feet as alertly as the rest, and with the same consternation and alarm. And the shriek that had awakened him was just subsiding into a series of rending moans and broken cries that might have been of extreme pain or extreme ecstasy. In the open space in the centre of the chapter-house Brother Columbanus lay on his face, threshing and jerking like a landed fish, beating his forehead and his palms against the flagstones, kicking and flailing with long, pale legs bared to the knee by his contortions, and barking out of him those extraordinary sounds of shattering physical excitement, while the nearest of the brothers hovered in helpless shock, and Prior Robert with lifted hands exhorted and exclaimed.

Brother Cadfael and Brother Edmund, the infirmarer, reached the victim together, kneeled over him one on either side, and restrained him from battering his brains out against the stones of the floor, or dislocating his joints in his flailings. 'Falling sickness!' said Brother Edmund tersely, and wedged the thick cord of Columbanus' girdle between his teeth, and a fold of his habit with it, to prevent him from biting his tongue.

Brother Cadfael was less certain of the diagnosis, for these were not the grunting, helpless noises of an epileptic in an attack, but such as might be expected from a hysterical woman in a frenzy. But at least the treatment stopped half the noise, and even appeared to diminish the vigour of the convulsions, though they resumed again as soon as the restraining grip on him was loosed.

'Poor young man!' fluttered Abbot Heribert, hovering in the background. 'So sudden, so cruel an affliction! Handle him gently! Carry him to the infirmary. We must pray for his restoration.'

Chapter broke up in some disorder. With the help of Brother John, and certain others of a practical turn of mind, they got Brother Columbanus securely but comfortably swathed in a sheet, confining arms and legs so that he could do himself no injury, wedged his teeth apart with a wooden spit instead of the cloth, on which he might have gagged and choked, and carried him on a shutter to the infirmary, where they got him into bed, and secured him there with bandages round breast and thighs. He moaned and gurgled and heaved still, but with weakening force, and when they had managed to get a draught of Brother Cadfael's poppy-juice into him his moans subsided into pitiful mutterings, and the violence of his struggles against his confinement grew feebler.

'Take good care of him,' said Prior Robert, frowning anxiously over the young man's bed. 'I think someone should be constantly by to watch over him, in case the fit comes again. You have your other sick men to attend to, you cannot sit by his side day and night. Brother Jerome, I put this sufferer in your charge, and excuse you from all other duties while he needs you.'

'Willingly,' said Brother Jerome, 'and prayerfully!' He was Prior Robert's closest associate and most devoted hanger-on, and an inevitable choice whenever Robert required strict obedience and meticulous reporting, as might well be the case where a brother of the house succumbed to what might elsewhere be whispered abroad as a fit of madness.

'Stay with him in particular during the night,' said the prior, 'for in the night a man's resistance falters, and his bodily evils may rise against him. If he sleeps peacefully, you may rest also, but remain close, in case he needs you.'

'He'll sleep within the hour,' said Cadfael confidently, 'and may pass into natural sleep well before night. God willing, he may put this off before morning.'

For his part, he thought Brother Columbanus lacked sufficient work for both mind and body, and took his revenge for his deprivation in these excesses, half-wilful, half-involuntary, and both to be pitied and censured. But he retained enough caution to reserve a doubt with every conviction. He was not sure he knew any of his adopted brothers well enough to judge with certainty. Well, Brother John—yes, perhaps! But inside the conventual life or outside, cheerful, blunt, extrovert Brother Johns are few and far between.

Brother Jerome appeared at chapter next morning with an exalted countenance, and the air of one bursting with moment-ous news. At Abbot Heribert's mild reproof for leaving his patient without permission, he folded his hands meekly and bowed his head, but lost none of his rapt assurance.

'Father, I am sent here by another duty, that seemed to me even more urgent. I have left Brother Columbanus sleeping, though not peacefully, for even his sleep is tormented. But two lay-brothers are watching by him. If I have done wrong, I will abide it humbly.'

'Our brother is no better?' asked the abbot anxiously.

'He is still deeply troubled, and when he wakes he raves. But, Father, this is my errand! There is a sure hope for him! In the night I have been miraculously visited. I have come to tell you what divine mercy has instructed me. Father, in the small hours I fell into a doze beside Brother Columbanus' bed, and had a marvellously sweet dream.'

By this time he had everyone's attention, even Brother Cadfael was wide awake. 'What, another of them?' whispered Brother John wickedly into his ear. 'The plague's spreading!'

'Father, it seemed to me that the wall of the room opened, and a great light shone in, and through the light and radiating the light there came in a most beautiful young virgin, and stood beside our brother's bed, and spoke to me. She told me that her name was Winifred, and that in Wales there is a holy spring, that rose to the light where she suffered martyrdom. And she said that if Brother Columbanus bathed in the water of that well, he would

14

surely be healed, and restored at once to his senses. Then she uttered a blessing upon our house, and vanished in a great light, and I awoke.'

Through the murmur of excitement that went round the chapter-house, Prior Robert's voice rose in reverent triumph: 'Father Abbot, we are being guided! Our quest for a saint has drawn to us this sign of favour, in token that we should persevere.'

'Winifred!' said the abbot doubtfully. 'I do not recall clearly the story of this saint and martyr. There are so many of them in Wales. Certainly we ought to send Brother Columbanus to her holy spring, it would be ingratitude to neglect so clear an omen. But exactly where is it to be found?'

Prior Robert looked round for the few Welshmen among the brothers, passed somewhat hurriedly over Brother Cadfael, who had never been one of his favourites, perhaps by reason of a certain spark in his eye, as well as his notoriously worldly past, and lit gladly upon old Brother Rhys, who was virtually senile but doctrinally safe, and had the capacious if capricious memory of the very old. 'Brother, can you tell us the history of this saint, and where her well is to be found?'

The old man was slow to realise that he had become the centre of attention. He was shrunken like a bird, and toothless, and used to a tolerant oblivion. He began hesitantly, but warmed to the work as he found all eyes upon him.

'Saint Winifred, you say, Father? Everybody knows of Saint Winifred. You'll find her spring by the name they gave the place, Holywell, it's no great way in from Chester. But she's not there. You won't find her grave at Holywell.'

'Tell us about her,' coaxed Prior Robert, almost fawning in his eagerness. 'Tell us all her story.'

'Saint Winifred,' declaimed the old man, beginning to enjoy his hour of glory, 'was the only child of a knight named Tevyth, who lived in those parts when the princes were yet heathens. But this knight and all his household were converted by Saint Beuno, and made him a church there, and gave him house-room. The girl was devoted even above her parents, and pledged herself to a virgin life, hearing Mass every day. But one Sunday it happened that she was sick, and stayed at home when all the rest of the household went to church. And there came to the door the prince of those parts. Cradoc, son of the king, who had fallen in love with her at a distance. For this girl was very beautiful. *Very beautiful!*' gloated Brother Rhys, and licked his lips loudly. Prior Robert visibly recoiled, but refrained from stopping the flow by reproof. 'He pleaded that he was hot and parched from hunting,' said Brother Rhys darkly, 'and asked for a drink of water, and the girl let him in and gave him to drink. Then,' he shrilled, hunching himself in his voluminous habit and springing erect with a vigour nobody present would have credited, 'he pressed his suit upon her, and grappled her in his arms. *Thus!*' The effort was almost too much for him, and moreover, the prior was eyeing him in alarm; he subsided with dignity. 'The faithful virgin put him off with soft words, and escaping into another room, climbed from a window and fled towards the church. But finding that she had eluded him, Prince Cradoc took horse and rode after, and overtaking her just within sight of the church, and dreading that she would reveal his infamy, struck off her head with his sword.'

He paused for the murmur of horror, pity and indignation, and got it, with a flurry of prayerfully-folded hands, and a tribute of round eyes.

'Then thus piteously she came by her death and beatitude?' intoned Brother Jerome enthusiastically.

'Not a bit of it!' snapped Brother Rhys. He had never liked Brother Jerome. 'Saint Beuno and the congregation were coming out of the church, and saw what had passed. The saint drew a terrible curse upon the murderer, who at once sank to the ground, and began to melt like wax in a fire, until all his body had sunk away into the grass. Then Saint Beuno fitted the head of the virgin onto her neck, and the flesh grew together, and she stood up alive, and the holy fountain sprang up on the spot where she arose.'

They waited, spellbound, and he let them wait. He had lost interest after the death.

'And afterwards?' insinuated Prior Robert. 'What did the saint do with her restored life?'

'She went on a pilgrimage to Rome,' said Brother Rhys indifferently, 'and she attended at a great synod of saints, and was appointed to be prioress over a community of virgin sisters at Gwytherin, by Llanrwst. And there she lived many years, and did many miracles in her lifetime. If it should be called her lifetime? She was once dead already. When she died a second time, that was where it befell.' He felt nothing concerning this residue of life, he offered it with a shrug. The girl had had her chance with Prince Cradoc, and let it slip, obviously her natural bent was to be prioress of a nest of virgins, and there was nothing more to be told about her.

'And she is buried there at Gwytherin?' persisted the prior. 'And her miracles continued after death?'

'So I have heard. But it's a long time,' said the old man, 'since I've heard her name mentioned. And longer since I was in those parts.'

Prior Robert stood in the circle of sunlight that filtered between the pillars of the chapter-house, drawn to his full imposing height, and turned a radiant face and commanding eyes upon Abbot Heribert.

'Father, does it not seem to you that our reverent search for a patron of great power and sanctity is being divinely guided? This gentle saint has visited us in person, in Brother Jerome's dream, and beckoned us to bring our afflicted brother to her for healing. Shall we not hope, also, that she will again show us the next step? If she does indeed receive our prayers and restore Brother Columbanus to health of body and mind, may we not be encouraged to hope that she will come in person and dwell among us? That we may humbly beg the church's sanction to take up her blessed relics and house them fittingly here in Shrewsbury? To the great glory and lustre of our house!'

'And of Prior Robert!' whispered Brother John in Cadfael's ear.

'It certainly seems that she has shown us singular favour,' admitted Abbot Heribert.

'Then, Father, have I your leave to send Brother Columbanus with a safe escort to Holywell? This very day?'

'Do so,' said the abbot, 'with the prayers of us all, and may he return as Saint Winifred's own messenger, hale and grateful.'

The deranged man, still wandering in mind and communing with himself in incoherent ravings, was led away out of the gatehouse on the first stage of his journey immediately after the midday meal, mounted on a mule, with a high, cradling saddle to give him some security from falling, in case the violent fit took him again, and with Brother Jerome and a brawny lay-brother one on either side, to support him at need. Columbanus looked about him with wide, pathetic, childlike eyes, and seemed to know nobody, though he went submissively and trustfully where he was led.

'I could have done with a nice little trip into Wales,' said Brother John wistfully, looking after them as they rounded the corner and vanished towards the bridge over the Severn. 'But I probably shouldn't have seen the right visions. Jerome will do the job better.'

'Boy,' said Brother Cadfael tolerantly, 'you become more of an unbeliever every day.'

'Not a bit of it! I'm as willing to believe in the girl's sanctity and miracles as any man. We know the saints have power to help and bless, and I'll believe they have the goodwill, too. But when it's Prior Robert's faithful hound who has the dream, you're asking me to believe in *his* sanctity, not hers! And in any case, isn't her favour glory enough? I don't see why they should want to dig up the poor lady's dust. It seems like charnel-house business to me, not church business. And you think exactly the same,' he said firmly, and stared out his elder, eye to eye.

'When I want to hear my echo,' said Brother Cadfael, 'I will at least speak first. Come on, now, and get that bottom strip of ground dug, there are kale plants waiting to go in.'

The delegation to Holywell was gone five days, and came home towards evening in a fine shower of rain and a grand glow

18

of grace, chanting prayers as the three entered the courtyard. In the midst rode Brother Columbanus, erect and graceful and jubilant, if that word could be used for one so humble in his gladness. His face was bright and clear, his eyes full of wonder and intelligence. No man ever looked less mad, or less likely to be subject to the falling sickness. He went straight to the church and gave thanks and praise to God and Saint Winifred on his knees, and from the altar all three went dutifully to report to the abbot, prior and sub-prior, in the abbot's lodging.

'Father,' said Brother Columbanus, eager and joyous, 'I have no skill to tell what has befallen me, for I know less than these who have cared for me in my delirium. All I know is that I was taken on this journey like a man in an ill dream, and went where I was taken, not knowing how to fend for myself, or what I ought to do. And suddenly I was like a man awakened out of that nightmare to a bright morning and a world of spring, and I was standing naked in the grass beside a well, and these good brothers were pouring water over me that healed as it touched. I knew myself and them, and only marvelled where I might be, and how I came there. Which they willingly told me. And then we went, all, and many people of that place with us, to sing Mass in a little church that stands close by the well. Now I know that I owe my recovery to the intervention of Saint Winifred, and I praise and worship her from my heart, as I do God who caused her to take pity on me. The rest these brothers will tell.'

The lay-brother was large, taciturn, weary—having done all the work throughout—and by this time somewhat bored with the whole business. He made the appropriate exclamations where needed, but left the narrative in the able hands of Brother Jerome, who told all with zest. How they had brought their patient to the village of Holywell, and asked the inhabitants for directions and aid, and been shown where the saint had risen living after her martyrdom, in the silver fountain that still sprang in the same spot, furnished now with a stone basin to hold its sacred flow. There they had led the rambling Columbanus, stripped him of habit, shirt and drawers, and poured the sacred water over him, and instantly he had stood erect and lifted his hands in prayer, and given thanks for a mind restored. Afterwards he had asked them in wonder how he came there, and what had happened to him, and had been greatly chastened and exalted at his humbling and his deliverance, and most grateful to his patroness, by whose guidance he had been made whole.

'And, Father, the people there told us that the saint is indeed buried at Gwytherin, where she died after her ministry, and that the place where her body is laid has done many miracles. But they say that her tomb, after so long, is neglected and little thought of, and it may well be that she longs for a better recognition, and to be installed in some place where pilgrims may come, where she may be revered as is her due, and have room to enlarge her grace and blessing to reach more people in need.'

'You are inspired, having been present at this miracle,' said Prior Robert, tall and splendid with faith rewarded, 'and you speak out what I have felt in listening to you. Surely Saint Winifred is calling us to her rescue as she came to the rescue of Brother Columbanus. Many have need of her goodness as he had, and know nothing of her. In our hands she would be exalted as she deserves, and those who need her grace would know where to come and seek it. I pray that we may mount that expedition of faith to which she summons us. Father Abbot, give me your leave to petition the church, and bring this blessed lady home to rest here among us, and be our proudest boast. For I believe it is her will and her command.'

'In the name of God,' said Abbot Heribert devoutly, 'I approve that project, and pray the blessing of heaven upon it!'

'He had it all planned beforehand,' said Brother John over the bed of mint, between envy and scorn. 'That was all a show, all that wonder and amazement, and asking who Saint Winifred was, and where to find her. He knew it all along. He'd already picked her out from those he's discovered neglected in Wales, and decided she was the one most likely to be available, as well as the one to shed most lustre on him. But it had to come out into the open by miraculous means. There'll be another prodigy whenever he needs his way smoothed for him, until he gets the girl here safely installed in the church, to his glory. It's a great enterprise, he means to climb high on the strength of it. So he starts out with a vision, and a prodigious healing, and divine grace leading his footsteps. It's as plain as the nose on your face.'

'And are you saying,' asked Brother Cadfael mildly, 'that Brother Columbanus is in the plot as well as Brother Jerome, and that falling fit of his was a fake, too? I should have to be very sure of my reward in heaven before I volunteered to break the paving with my forehead, even to provide Prior Robert with a miracle.'

Brother John considered seriously, frowning. 'No, that I don't say. We all know our meek white lamb is liable to the horrors over a penance scamped, and ecstasies over a vigil or a fast, and pouring ice-cold water over him at Holywell would be the very treatment to jolt him back into his right wits. We could just as well have tossed him in the fish-pond here! But of course *he*'d believe what they told him, and credit it all to the saint. Catch him missing such a chance! No, I wouldn't say he was a party to it—not knowingly. But he gave them the opportunity for a splendid demonstration of grace. You notice it was Jerome who was set to take care of him overnight! It takes only one man to be favoured with a vision, but it has to be the right man.' He rolled a sprig of the young green leaves sadly between his palms, and the fragrance distilled richly on the early morning air. 'And it will be the right men who'll accompany Prior Robert into Wales,' he said with sour certainty. 'You'll see!'

No doubt about it, this young man was hankering after a glimpse of the world again, and a breath of air from outside the walls. Brother Cadfael pondered, not only with sympathy for his young assistant, but also with some pleasurable stirrings of his own. So momentous an event in the otherwise even course of monastic life ought not to be missed. Besides the undoubted possibilities of mischief!

'True!' he said thoughtfully. 'Perhaps we ought to take some steps to leaven the lump. Wales should not be left with the notion that Jerome is the best Shrewsbury can muster, that's very true.'

'You have about as much chance of being invited as I,' said

Brother John with his customary bluntness. 'Jerome is sure of his place, Prior Robert must have his right hand with him. And Columbanus, fool innocent, was the instrument of grace, and could be made to serve the same turn again. Brother Sub-Prior they have to take along, for form's sake. Surely we could think up some way of getting a foot in the door? They can't move for a few days yet, the carpenters and carvers are working hard on this splendid reliquary coffin they're going to take with them for the lady, but it will take them a while to finish it. Get your wits to work, brother! There isn't anything you couldn't do, if you've a mind! Prior or no prior!'

'Well, well, did I say you had no faith?' wondered Brother Cadfael, charmed and disarmed. 'I might worm my own way in, there could be ways, but how am I to recommend a graceless rogue like you? What are you good at, to be taken along on such an errand?'

'I'm a good hand with mules,' said Brother John hopefully, 'and you don't think Prior Robert intends to go on foot, I suppose? Or to do the grooming and feeding and watering himself? Or the mucking-out? They'll need *somebody* to do the hard work and wait on them. Why not me?'

It was, indeed, something nobody as yet seemed to have thought of. And why take a lay-brother, if there was a cloister-brother, with a sweet voice in the Mass, willing to do the sweating into the bargain? And the boy deserved his outing, since he was willing to earn it the hard way. Besides, he might be useful before the end. If not to Prior Robert, to Brother Cadfael.

'We'll see,' he said, and with that drove his mutinous protégé back to the work in hand. But after dinner, in the somnolent half-hour of sleep for the elders and play for the novices, he sought out Abbot Heribert in his study.

'Father Abbot, it is on my mind that we are undertaking this pilgrimage to Gwytherin without full consideration. First we must send to the bishop of Bangor, in whose see Gwytherin lies, for without his approval the matter cannot proceed. Now it is not essential to have a speaker fluent in Welsh there, since the bishop is obviously conversant with Latin. But not every parish priest

22

in Wales has that tongue, and it is vital to be able to speak freely with the priest at Gwytherin, should the bishop sanction our quest. But most of all, the see of Bangor is wholly within the sovereignty of the king of Gwynedd, and surely his goodwill and permission are essential as those of the church. The princes of Gwynedd speak only Welsh, though they have learned clerks. Father Prior, certainly, has a smattering of Welsh, but. . . .'

'That is very true,' said Abbot Heribert, easily dismayed. 'It is but a smattering. And the king's agreement is all-important. Brother Cadfael, Welsh is your first, best language, and has no mysteries for you. Could you. . .? The garden, I am aware. . . . But with your aid there would be no problem.

'In the garden,' said Brother Cadfael, 'everything is well forward, and can manage without me ten days or more, and take no hurt. I should be glad indeed to be the interpreter, and lend my skills also in Gwytherin.'

'Then so be it!' sighed the abbot in heartfelt relief. 'Go with Prior Robert, and be our voice to the Welsh people. I shall sanction your errand myself, and you will have my authority.'

He was old and human and gentle, full of experience, short on ambition, self-righteousness and resolution. There could have been two ways of approaching him concerning Brother John. Cadfael took the more honest and simple way.

'Father, there is a young brother concerning whose vocation I have doubts, but concerning whose goodness I have none. He is close to me, and I would that he might find his true way, for if he finds it he will not forsake it. But it may not be with us. I beg that I may take him with me, as our hewer of wood and drawer of water in this enterprise, to allow him time to consider.'

Abbot Heribert looked faintly dismayed and apprehensive, but not unsympathetic. Perhaps he remembered long-ago days when his own vocation had suffered periods of storm.

'I should be sorry,' he said, 'to refuse a choice to any man who may be better fitted to serve God elsewhere. Which of us can say he has never looked over his shoulder? You have not,' he questioned delicately, approaching the aspect that really daunted him, though with a cautiously dauntless face, 'broached this matter to Prior Robert?'

'No, Father,' said Brother Cadfael virtuously. 'I thought it wrong to charge him with so small a responsibility, when he already carries one so great.'

'Very proper!' agreed the abbot heartily. 'It would be ill-done to distract his mind from his great purpose at this stage. I should say no word to him of the reason for adding this young man to the party. Prior Robert in his own unshaken certainty is apt to take an austere view of any man who looks back, once having set his hand to the plough.'

'Yet, Father, we were not all cut out to be ploughmen. Some could be more useful labouring in other ways.'

'True!' said the abbot, and warily smiled, pondering the recurring but often forgotten riddle of Brother Cadfael himself. 'I have often wondered, I confess. . . . But never mind! Very well, tell me this young brother's name, and you shall have him.'

CHAPTER TWO

Prior Robert's fine, frosty face momentarily registered displeasure and suspicion when he heard how his delegation was to be augmented. Brother Cadfael's gnarled, guileless-eyed self-sufficiency caused him discomfort without a word amiss or a glance out of place, as though his dignity were somehow under siege. Of Brother John he knew no particular evil, but the redness of his hair, the exuberance of his health and high spirits, the very way he put live blood back into old martyrdoms with his extravagant gusto in the reading, were all offensive in themselves, and jarred on the prior's aesthetic sensibilities. However, since Abbot Heribert had innocently decreed that they should join the party, and since there was no denying that a fluent Welsh speaker might become an urgent necessity at some stage, Prior Robert accepted the fiat without demur, and made the best of it.

They set out as soon as the fine reliquary for the saint's bones was ready, polished oak ornamented with silver, to serve as a proof what honours awaited Winifred in her new shrine. In the third week of May they came to Bangor, and told their story to Bishop David, who was sympathetic, and readily gave his consent to the proposed translation, subject only to the agreement of Prince Owain, who was regent of Gwynedd owing to the illness of the old king, his father. They ran the prince to earth at Aber, and found him equally obliging, for he not only gave the desired approval, but sent his one English-speaking clerk and chaplain to show them the best and quickest way to Gwytherin, and commend them and their errand to the parish priest there. Thus episcopally and royally blessed, Prior Robert led his party on the last stage of their journey, a little too easily convinced that his progress was being divinely smoothed, and would be so to its triumphant end.

They turned aside from the Conway valley at Llanrwst, climb-
ing away from the river into forested hill country. Beyond the
watershed they crossed the Elwy where it is young and small,
and moved steadily south-eastwards through thick woods, over
another ridge of high land, to descend once again into the upland
valley of a little river, that provided some marshy water-
meadows along its banks, and a narrow band of tilled fields,
sloping and sturdy but protected by the forests, above these lush
pastures. The wooded ridge on either hand ran in oblique folds,
richly green, hiding the scattered house-steads. The fields were
already planted, and here and there orchards flowered. Below
them, where the woods drew back to leave an amphitheatre of
green, there was a small stone church, whitewashed and shim-
mering, and a little wooden house beside it.

'You see the goal of your pilgrimage,' said the chaplain Urien.
He was a compact, neat, well-shaven personage, handsomely
dressed and mounted, more of an ambassador than a clerk.

'That is Gwytherin?' asked Prior Robert.

'It is the church and priest's house of Gwytherin. The parish
stretches for several miles along the river valley, and a mile or
more from the Cledwen on either bank. We do not congregate
in villages as you English do. Land good for hunting is plentiful,
but good for tillage meagre. Every man lives where best suits him
for working his fields and conserving his game.'

'It is a very fair place,' said the sub-prior, and meant it, for
the fold on fold of well-treed hills beyond the river made a
pattern of spring beauty in a hundred different greens, and the
water-meadows were strung like a necklace of emeralds along
the fringes of a necklace of silver and lapis-lazuli.

'Good to look at, hard to work,' said Urien practically. 'See,
there's an ox-team on the far side trying to break a new strip,
now all the rest are planted. Watch the beasts strain at it, and
you'll know how the higher ground weighs.'

Across the river, some way below them and a great way off,
the snaky curve of the furrows already won patterned the slope
between cultivated fields and leaning trees, a dark brown writing
upon the hillside, and on the higher furrow, as yet uncompleted,

the oxen leaned into their yokes and heaved, and the ploughman behind them clung and dragged at the heavy share. Before the leading pair a man walked backwards, arms gently waving and beckoning, his goad only a wand, flourished for magic, not for its sting, his high, pure calls carried aloft on the air, cajoling and praising. Towards him the beasts leaned willingly, following his cries with all their might. The new-turned soil, greyish-brown and sluggish, heaved moist and fresh to light after the share.

'A harsh country,' said Urien, as one assessing, not complaining, and set his horse moving downhill towards the church. 'Come, I'll hand you over to Father Huw, and see you well-received.'

They followed him by a green path that wound out of the hills, and soon lost its view of the valley between scattered, flowering trees. A wooden house or two showed among the woods, surrounded by small garden plots, and again vanished.

'Did you see?' said Brother John in Cadfael's ear, pacing beside the sumpter mule. 'Did you see how the beasts laboured towards that fellow not to escape the goad, only to go where he willed, only to please him? And such labour! That I should like to learn!'

'It's labour for man as well as beast,' said Brother Cadfael.

'But for free goodwill! They wanted to go with him, to do what he wanted them to do. Brother, could devoted disciples do more? Do you tell me he takes no delight in what he does?'

'No man nor God who sees his faithful delight to serve him,' said Brother Cadfael patiently and carefully, 'but he knows delight. Hush, now, we're barely here, there'll be time to look round us.'

They were down in the little arena of grass and vegetable plots, clear of the trees. The stone church with its tiny turret and tinier bell visible within shone blindingly white, bluish-white against all the lush green. And out of the cabbage-patch, freshly planted, in the lee of the wooden cabin, rose a small, square man in a brown sackcloth gown hoisted to the knees, thick brown legs sturdy under him, and a thicket of curly brown hair and beard half-concealing a brown, broad, wondering face round

27

two large, dark-blue eyes. He came out hastily, scrubbing his hands on his skirts. At close quarters his eyes were larger, bluer and more astonished than ever, and as timid as the mild eyes of a doe.

'Good-day to you, Father Huw,' said Urien, reining in before him, 'I've brought you distinguished guests from England, upon important church business, and with the blessing of prince and bishop.'

When they had ridden into the clearing the priest had certainly been the only man in sight, but by the time Urien had ended his greeting a score of silent, sudden figures had appeared from nowhere, and made a wary and curious half-circle about their pastor. By the distracted look in Father Huw's eyes he was busy reckoning up in some alarm how many of these strangers his modest hut could fittingly house, and where to bestow the rest of them, and how much food there was in his larder to make a meal for so many, and where he could best commandeer whatever extra was needed. But no question of not extending a welcome. Guests were sacrosanct, and must not even be questioned on the proposed length of their stay, however ruinous.

'My poor household is at the reverend fathers' disposal,' he said, 'and whatever powers I have to serve them, also. You come fresh from Aber?'

'From Aber,' said Urien, 'from Prince Owain, and I must rejoin him there tonight. I am only the herald for these Benedictine brothers, who come on a holy errand, and when I have explained their case to you, then I leave them in your hands.' He presented them by name, Prior Robert first. 'And have no fear when I have left, for Brother Cadfael here is a man of Gwynedd himself, and speaks Welsh as well as you do.'

Huw's look of harassed apprehension was immediately eased, but in case he should be in any doubt, Cadfael favoured him with a rapid brotherly greeting in the promised language, which gratifyingly produced the identical look of slight distrust and insecurity in Prior Robert's normally assured grey eyes.

'You are welcome to this poor house you honour,' said Huw, and ran a quick eye over the horses and mules and their loads,

28

and without hesitation called a couple of names over his shoulder. A shaggy-headed elder and a sunburned boy of about ten came forward readily in answer. 'Ianto, help the good brother water the beasts, and put them in the little paddock to graze, until we see how best to stable them. Edwin, run and tell Marared we have guests, and help her bring water and wine.'

They ran to do his bidding, and several of the others who had gathered, brown, bare-legged men, slender dark women and half-naked children, drew nearer, conferred softly among themselves, and the women slipped away to their own cooking-fires and bake-ovens to bring whatever they could to contribute to Gwytherin's hospitality.

'While it's so fine and mild,' said Huw, standing aside to wave them into the little enclosure of his garden, 'it may please you best to sit in the orchard. I have benches and table there. Through the summer I live out of doors. Time enough to go within and light fires when the days draw in and the nights grow cold.'

His holding was tiny and his living poor enough, but he took good care of his fruit-trees and was a diligent gardener, Brother Cadfael noted with approval. And for one who seemed, unlike many of the parish priests of the Celtic persuasion, to be celibate, and happily so, he had the bare little house and grounds in very neat order, and could produce from his own store, or his parishioners' shared stock, clean wooden trenchers and good bread to put on them, and plain but presentable drinking-horns for his raw red wine. He performed all the ceremonies due from a host with humble dignity. The boy Edwin returned with a lively old woman, Huw's neighbour, bringing food and drink. And all the while that the visitors sat there in the sun, various of the people of Gwytherin, scattered though the parish might be, found occasion to walk past the wattle fence of the orchard and examine the party carefully, though without seeming to do so. It was not every day, or every year, indeed, that they had so momentous a visitation. Every soul in the parish would know before evening not only that monks from Shrewsbury were guests at Huw's house, but also how many they were, what they looked like, what fine horses and handsome mules they had, and most

probably what they had come for, into the bargain. But the
eyeing and the listening were done with perfect courtesy and
discretion.

'And now, since Master Urien has to return to Aber,' said
Huw, when they had eaten and were sitting at ease, 'it might be
well if he would tell me in what particular I can serve the
brothers of Shrewsbury, so that he may be assured we understand each other before he leaves us. And whatever is in my
competence I will surely do.'

Urien told the story as he had heard it, and Prior Robert elab-
orated at such length that Brother John, growing bored and rest-
less, let his eyes stray to take stock of the occasional figures that
passed along the fence, with alert ears and shy but sharp eyes.
His interest and curiosity were somewhat less discreet than
theirs. And there were some very handsome girls among them!
The one passing now, for instance, her step graceful and slow—
she knew she was watched!—and her hair a great, heavy braid
over her shoulder, the colour of polished oak, a light, silken
brown, even with silvery dashes in it like the grain of oak. . . .

'And the bishop has given his consent to your proposal?' asked
Huw, after a long minute of silence, and in a voice that suggested
wonder and doubt.

'Both bishop and prince have sanctioned it.' Prior Robert was
uneasy at the very hint of a hitch at this stage. 'The omens have
surely not misled us? Saint Winifred is here? She lived out her
restored life here, and is buried in this place?'

Huw owned that it was so, with so curious an intonation of
caution and reluctance that Cadfael decided he was trying to
recall exactly where the lady was to be found, and wondering in
what state her grave would be discovered, after all this time since
last he had so much as thought of it.

'She is here, in this cemetery?' The little whitewashed church
gleamed provocatively in the sunshine.

'No, not here.' Some relief this time, he did not have to reveal
her whereabouts immediately. 'This church is new since her time.
Her grave is in the old burial-ground of the wooden church on
the hill, a mile or more from here. It is long disused. Yes, certainly

the omens favour your plans, and beyond question the saint is here in Gwytherin. But....'

'But?' said Prior Robert with displeasure. 'Both prince and bishop have given us their blessing, and commended our cause to you. Moreover, we have heard, and they have agreed, that the saint in her stay here among you has been much neglected, and may well wish to be received where greater honour will be paid to her.'

'In my church,' said Huw humbly, 'I have never heard that the saints desired honour for themselves, but rather to honour God rightly. So I do not presume to know what Saint Winifred's will may be in this matter. That you and your house should desire to honour *her* rightly, that is another matter, and very proper. But.... This blessed virgin lived out her miraculously restored life in this place, and no other. Here she died for the second time, and here is buried, and even if my people have neglected her, being human and faulty, yet they always knew that she was here among them, and at a pinch they could rely on her, and for a Welsh saint I think that counts for much. Prince and bishop—both of whom I reverence as I ought—may not altogether understand how my flock will feel, if their holiest girl is to be dug up out of her grave and taken away into England. It may matter little to the crown and the crozier, a saint is a saint wherever her relics rest. But I tell you plainly, the people of Gwytherin are not going to like it at all!'

Brother Cadfael, stirred to an atavistic fervour of Welshness by this homely eloquence, snatched the initiative from Urien at this point, and translated with the large declamation of the bards.

In full spate, he turned his eyes away from the distracting faces, to light upon one even more distracting. The girl with the light-oak sheen on her hair was again passing the fence, and had been so charmed by what she heard, and the vehemence of its delivery, that for a moment she forgot to keep moving, and stood there at gaze, apple-blossom face radiant and rose-leaf lips laughing. And with the same fascination with which she gazed at Cadfael, Brother John gazed at her. Cadfael observed both, and was dazzled. But the next moment she caught herself up in

31

hasty alarm, and blushed beautifully, and swept away out of sight. Brother John was still gaping long after she had vanished.

'It is hardly important, surely?' said Prior Robert with ominous mildness. 'Your bishop and your prince have made their views plain. The parishioners need not be consulted.'

That, too, Cadfael interpreted, Urien choosing to remain neutral and mute.

'Impossible!' said Huw firmly, knowing himself on secure ground. 'In such a grave matter affecting the whole parish, nothing can be done without calling together the assembly of the free men, and putting the case to them fully and publicly. Doubtless the will of prince and bishop will prevail, but even so, these must be put to the people before they can say yes or no to them. I shall call such an assembly tomorrow. Your case can only be vindicated absolutely by public acceptance.'

'He says truly,' said Urien, holding the prior's austere and half affronted eyes. 'You will do well to get the goodwill of Gwytherin, however many blessings you already have. They respect their bishop, and are very content with their king and his sons, I doubt if you need grudge the delay.'

Prior Robert accepted both the warning and the reassurance, and felt the need of a period of quietude in which to review his strategy and prepare his persuasions. When Urien rose to take his leave, his errand punctiliously completed, the prior also rose, half a head taller than the tallest there, and folded his long white hands in submissive resignation.

'We have yet two hours or more to Vespers,' he said, eyeing the angle of the sun. 'I should like to withdraw into your church and spend some while in meditation, and prayer for right guidance. Brother Cadfael, you had better remain with Father Huw, and help him in any arrangements he needs to make, and you, Brother John, bestow the horses as he directs, and see them cared for. The rest will join me in intercession, that we may conduct this enterprise rightly.'

He swept away, elongated and silvery and majestic, and had to stoop his head to enter under the low round arch of the church door. Brother Richard, Brother Jerome, Brother Columbanus vanished within on his heels. Not all the time they were together there would be spent in prayer. They would be considering what arguments would be most likely to carry the day with Father Huw's free assembly, or what oblique ecclesiastical threats daunt them into submission.

Brother John looked after the lofty silver head until it stooped with accurate dignity just low enough to pass under the stone, and let out something between a sigh and an arrested gurgle of laughter, as though he had been praying for a miscalculation. What with the journey, and the exercise, and the outdoor living, he looked ruddier and healthier and more athletic than ever.

'I've been hoping all this while for a chance to get my leg over that dapple-grey,' he said. 'Richard rides him like a badly-balanced woolsack. I hope Father Huw's stabling is a mile or more away.'

Father Huw's plans for them, it seemed, involved two of the nearer and more prosperous members of his flock, but even so, in the scattered Welsh way, their houses were dispersed in valley and forest.

'I shall give up my own house to the prior and sub-prior, of course,' he said, 'and sleep in the loft above my cow. For the beasts, my grazing here is too small, and I have no stable, but Bened the smith has a good paddock above the water-meadows, and stabling with a loft, if this young brother will not mind being lodged the better part of a mile from his fellows. And for you and your two companions, Brother Cadfael, there is open house half a mile from here through the woods, with Cadwallon, who has one of the biggest holdings in these parts.'

Brother Cadfael considered the prospect of being housed with Jerome and Columbanus, and found it unattractive. 'Since I am the only one among us who has fluent Welsh,' he said diplomatically, 'I should remain close to Prior Robert's side. With your goodwill, Huw, I'll share your loft above the cow-byre, and be very comfortable there.'

'If that's your wish,' said Huw simply, 'I shall be glad of your company. And now I must set this young man on his way to the smithy.'

'And I,' said Cadfael, 'if you don't need me along with you —and yonder boy will make himself understood in whatever language, or none!—will go a piece of the way back with Urien. If I can pick up an acquaintance or so among your flock, so much the better, for I like the look of them and their valley.'

Brother John came out from the tiny paddock leading the two tall horses, the mules following on leading reins. Huw's eyes glowed almost as bright as John's, caressing the smooth lines of neck and shoulder.

'How long it is,' he said wistfully, 'since I was on a good horse!'

'Come on, then, Father,' urged Brother John, understanding the look if not the words, 'up with you! Here's a hand, if you fancy the roan. Lead the way in style!' And he cupped a palm for the priest's lifted foot, and hoisted him, dazed and enchanted, into the saddle. Up himself on the grey, he fell in alongside, ready if the older man should need a steadying hand, but the brown knees gripped happily. He had not forgotten how. 'Bravely!' said John, hugely laughing. 'We shall get on famously together, and end up in a race!'

Urien, checking his girth, watched them ride away out of the gentle bowl of the clearing. 'There go two happy men,' he said thoughtfully.

'More and more I wonder,' said Cadfael, 'how that youngster ever came to commit himself to the monastic life.'

'Or you, for instance?' said Urien, with his toe in the stirrup. 'Come, if you want to view the ground, we'll take the valley way a piece, before I leave you for the hills.'

They parted at the crest of the ridge, among the trees but where a fold of the ground showed them the ox-team still doggedly labouring at a second strip, continuing the line of the first, above the richer valley land. Two such strips in one day was prodigious work.

'Your prior will be wise,' said Urien, taking his leave, 'to take a lesson from yonder young fellow. Leading and coaxing pays better than driving in these parts. But I need not tell you—a man as Welsh as myself.'

Cadfael watched him ride away gently along the cleared track until he vanished among the trees. Then he turned back towards Gwytherin, but went steeply downhill towards the river, and at the edge of the forest stood in green shadow under an oak tree, gazing across the sunlit meadows and the silver thread of river to where the team heaved and strained along the last furrow. Here there was no great distance between them, and he could see clearly the gloss of sweat on the pelts of the oxen, and the heavy curl of the soil as it heeled back from the share. The ploughman was dark, squat and powerful, with a salting of grey in his shaggy locks, but the ox-caller was tall and slender, and the curling hair that tossed on his neck and clung to his moist brow was as fair as flax. He managed his backward walking without a glance behind, feeling his way light-footed and gracefully, as if he had eyes in the back of his heels. His voice was hoarse and tired with long use now, but still clear and merry, more effective than any goad, as he cajoled his weary beasts along the final furrow, calling and luring and praising, telling them they had done marvels, and should get their rest and their meed for it, that in moments now they would be going home, that he was proud of them and loved them, as if he had been talking to Christian souls. And the beasts heaved and leaned, throwing their weight into the yokes and keeping their eyes upon him, and plainly would do anything in their power to please him. When the plough curved to the end and halted, and the steaming oxen stood with lowered heads, the young man came and flung an arm over the neck of the near leader, and scrubbed with brisk knuckles in the curly hair on the other's brow, and Cadfael said aloud: 'Bravely! But, my friend, how did *you* stray into Wales?'

Something small, round and hard dropped rustling through the leaves above him, and hit him neatly in the middle of his weather-beaten tonsure. He clapped a hand to his crown, and said something unbecoming his habit. But it was only one of last year's oak-balls, dried out by a winter's weathering to the hardness of a pebble. He looked up into the foliage above his head, already thick and turning rich green from its early gold, and it seemed to him that the tremor of leaves where there was no wind required more explanation than the accidental fall of one small remnant of a dead year. It stilled very quickly, and even its stillness, by contrast, seemed too careful and aware. Cadfael removed himself a few yards, as if about to walk on, and doubled round again behind the next barrier of bushes to see if the bait had been taken.

A small bare foot, slightly stained with moss and bark, reached down out of the branches to a toe-hold on the trunk. Its fellow, stretched at the end of a long, slim leg, swung clear, as the boy prepared to drop. Brother Cadfael, fascinated, suddenly averted his eyes in haste, and turned his back, but he was smiling, and he did not, after all, withdraw, but circled his screen of bushes and reappeared innocently in view of the bird that had just flown down out of its nest. No boy, as he had first supposed, but a girl, and a most personable girl, too, now standing decorously in the grass with her skirts nobly disposed round her, and even the small bare feet concealed.

They stood looking at each other with candid curiosity, neither at all abashed. She might have been eighteen or nineteen years old, possibly younger, for there was a certain erect assurance about her that gave her the dignity of maturity even when newly dropped out of an oak tree. And for all her bare feet and mane of unbraided dark hair, she was no villein girl. Everything about her said clearly that she knew her worth. Her gown was of fine homespun wool, dyed a soft blue, and had embroidery at neck and sleeves. No question but she was a beauty. Her face was oval and firm of feature, the hair that fell in wild waves about her shoulders was almost black, but black with a tint of dark and brilliant red in it where the light caught, and the large, black-lashed eyes that considered Brother Cadfael with such frank interest were of almost the same colour, dark as damsons, bright as the sparkles of mica in the river pebbles.

'You are one of the monks from Shrewsbury,' she said with certainty. And to his astonishment she said it in fluent and easy English.

'I am,' said Cadfael. 'But how did you come to know all about us so soon? I think you were not among those who made it their business to walk along Huw's garden fence while we were talking. There was one very fine girl, I remember, but not a black lass like you.'

She smiled. She had an enchanting smile, sudden and radiant. 'Oh, that would be Annest. But everybody in Gwytherin knows by now all about you, and what you've come for. Father Huw is right, you know,' she warned seriously, 'we shan't like it at all. Why do you want to take Saint Winifred away? When she's been here so long, and nobody ever paid any attention to her before? It doesn't seem neighbourly or honest to me.'

It was an excellent choice of words, he thought, and marvelled how a Welsh girl came by it, for she was using English as if she had been born to it, or come to it for love.

'I question the propriety of it myself, to be truthful,' he agreed ruefully. 'When Father Huw spoke up for his parish, I confess I found myself inclining to his side of the argument.'

That made her look at him more sharply and carefully than before, frowning over some sudden doubt or suspicion in her own mind. Whoever had informed her had certainly witnessed all that went on in Father Huw's garden. She hesitated a moment, pondering, and then launched at him unexpectedly in Welsh: 'You must be the one who speaks our language, the one who translated what Father Huw said.' It seemed to trouble her more than was reasonable. 'You do know Welsh! You understand me now.'

'Why, I'm as Welsh as you, child,' he admitted mildly, 'and only a Benedictine in my middle years, and I haven't forgotten my mother-tongue yet, I hope. But I marvel how you've come to speak English as well as I do myself, here in the heart of Rhos.'

'Oh, no,' she said defensively, 'I've only learned a very little. I tried to use it for you, because I thought you *were* English. How was I to know you'd be just *that* one?' Now why should his being bilingual cause her uneasiness? he wondered. And why was she casting so many rapid, furtive glances aside towards the river, brightly glimpsed through the trees? Where, as he saw in a glance just as swift as hers, the tall, fair youngster who was no

37

Welshman, and was certainly the finest ox-caller in Gwynedd, had broken away from his placidly-drinking team, and was wading the river thigh-deep towards this particular tall oak, in a flurry of sparkling spray. The girl had been ensconced in this very tree, whence, no doubt, she had a very good view of the ploughing. And came down as soon as it was finished! 'I'm shy of my English,' she said, pleading and vulnerable. 'Don't tell anyone!'

She was wishing him away from here, and demanding his discretion at the same time. His presence, he gathered, was inconvenient.

'I've known the same trouble myself,' he said comfortably, 'when first I tried getting my tongue round English. I'll never call your efforts into question. And now I'd better be on my way back to our lodgings, or I shall be late for Vespers.'

'God go with you, then, Father,' she said, radiant and relieved.

'And with you, my child.'

He withdrew by a carefully chosen route that evaded any risk of bumping into the fair young man. And she watched him go for a long moment, before she turned eagerly to meet the ox-caller as he came splashing through the shallows and climbed the bank. Cadfael thought that she was perfectly aware how much he had observed and understood, and was pleased by his reticence. Pleased and reassured. A Welsh girl of status, with embroidery along the hems of her gown, had good need to go softly if she was meeting an outlander, a man landless and rootless here in a clan society, where to be without place in a kinship was to be without the means of living. And yet a very pleasing, comely young man, good at his work and feeling for his beasts. Cadfael looked back, when he was sure the bushes covered him, and saw the two of them draw together, still and glad, not touching, almost shy of each other. He did not look back again.

Now what I really need here, he thought as he walked back towards the church of Gwytherin, is a good, congenial acquaintance, someone who knows every man, woman and child in the parish, without having to carry the burden of their souls. A sound drinking companion with good sense is what I need.

CHAPTER THREE

He found not one of what he wanted, but three at one stroke, after Compline that evening, when he walked back with Brother John in the twilight to the smithy and croft at the edge of the valley fields. Prior Robert and Brother Richard had already withdrawn for the night into Huw's house, Jerome and Columbanus were on their way through the woods to Cadwallon's holding, and who was to question whether Brother Cadfael had also gone to his pallet in the priest's loft, or was footloose among the gossips of Gwytherin? The lodging arrangements were working out admirably. He had never felt less inclined for sleep at this soft evening hour, nor was anyone going to rouse them at midnight here for Matins. Brother John was delighted to introduce him into the smith's household, and Father Huw favoured the acquaintance for his own reasons. It was well that others besides himself should speak for the people of the parish, and Bened the smith was a highly respected man, like all of his craft, and his words would carry weight.

There were three men sitting on the bench outside Bened's door when they arrived, and the mead was going round as fast as the talk. All heads went up alertly at the sound of their steps approaching, and a momentary silence marked the solidarity of the local inhabitants. But Brother John seemed already to have made himself welcome, and Cadfael cast them a greeting in Welsh, like a fisherman casting a line, and was accepted with something warmer than the strict courtesy the English would have found. Annest with the light-brown, sunflecked hair had spread word of his Welshness far and wide. Another bench was pulled up, and the drinking-horns continued their circling in a wider ring. Over the river the light was fading gradually, the dimness green with the colours of meadow and forest, and threaded through with the string of silver water.

Bened was a thickset, muscular man of middle years, bearded and brown. Of his two companions the younger was recognisable as the ploughman who had followed the ox-team that day, and no wonder he was dry after such labour. And the third was a grey-headed elder with a long, smoothly-trimmed beard and fine, sinewy hands, in an ample homespun gown that had seen better days, perhaps on another wearer. He bore himself as one entitled to respect, and got it.

'Padrig, here, is a good poet and a fine harpist,' said Bened, 'and Gwytherin is lucky to have him staying a while among us, in Rhisiart's hall. That's away beyond Cadwallon's place, in a forest clearing, but Rhisiart has land over this way, too, both sides the river. He's the biggest landowner in these parts. There are not many here entitled to keep a harp, or maybe we'd be honoured with more visits from travelling bards like Padrig. I have a little harp myself—I have that privilege—but Rhisiart's is a fine one, and kept in use, too. I've heard his girl play on it sometimes.'

'Women cannot be bards,' said Padrig with tolerant scorn. 'But she knows how to keep it tuned, and well looked after, that I will say. And her father's a patron of the arts, and a generous, open-handed one. No bard goes away disappointed from his hall, and none ever leaves without being pressed to stay. A good household!'

'And this is Cai, Rhisiart's ploughman. No doubt you saw the team cutting new land, when you came over the ridge today.'

'I did, and admired the work,' said Cadfael heartily. 'I never saw better. A good team you had there, and a good caller, too.'

'The best,' said Cai without hesitation. 'I've worked with a good many in my time, but never known one with the way Engelard has with the beasts. They'd die for him. And as good a hand with all cattle, calving or sick or what you will. Rhisiart would be a sorry man if ever he lost him. Ay, we did a good day's work today.'

'You'll have heard from Father Huw,' said Cadfael, 'that all the free men are called to the church tomorrow after Mass, to hear what our prior is proposing. No doubt we shall see Rhisiart there.'

'See and hear him,' said Cai, and grinned. 'He speaks his mind. An open-hearted, open-natured man, with a temper soon up and soon down, and never a grudge in him, but try and move him when his mind's made up, and you're leaning on Snowdon.'

'Well, a man can but hold fast to what he believes right, and even the opponent he baulks should value him for that. And have his sons no interest in the harp, that they leave it to their sister?'

'He has no sons,' said Bened. 'His wife is dead, and he never would take another, and there's only this one girl to follow him.'

'And no male heir anywhere in his kinship? It's rare for a daughter to inherit.'

'Not a man on his side the family at all,' said Cai, 'and a pity it is. The only near kin is her mother's brother, and he has no claim, and is old into the bargain. The greatest match anywhere in this valley, is Sioned, and young men after her like bees. But God willing, she'll be a contented wife with a son on her knee long before Rhisiart goes to his fathers.'

'A grandson by a good man, and what could any lord want more,' said Padrig, and emptied the jug of mead and passed the horn along. 'Understand me, I'm not a Gwytherin man myself, and have no right to give a voice one way or the other. But if I may say a word my friends won't say for themselves—you having your duty to your prior as Cai has to his lord, or I to my art and my patrons—don't look for any easy passage, and don't take offence if your way is blocked. Nothing personal to you! But where the free men of Wales see no fair dealing, they won't call it by fair names, and they won't stand aside.'

'I should be sorry if they did,' said Cadfael. 'For my part, the ending I want is the fair ending, leaving no man with a just grievance. And what of the other lords we can expect to see there? Of Cadwallon we've heard, two of our brothers are enjoying his hospitality. And his lands are neighbour to Rhisiart's?'

'It's a fair piece beyond to Rhisiart's hall, on through the forest. But they're neighbours, boundary to boundary, yes, and friends from youth. A peaceable man, Cadwallon, he likes his

41

comfort and his hunting. His way would be to say yes to whatever bishop and prince commend, but then, his way normally
is also to say yes to Rhisiart. For that matter,' owned Bened,
tilting the last drop from the horn, 'I know no more than you
what either of them will have to say in this matter. For all I
know they'll accept your omens and bless your errand. If the free
voice goes with your prior, then Saint Winifred goes home with
you, and that's the end of it.'

It was the end of the mead, too, for that night.

'Bide the night here,' said Bened to Padrig, when the guests
rose to walk home, 'and we'll have a little music before you
leave tomorrow. My small harp needs to be played, I've kept it in
fettle for you.'

'Why, so I will, since you're so kind,' said Padrig, and weaved
his way gently into the house with his host. And Cai and Brother
Cadfael, taking their leave, set off companionably shoulder to
shoulder, to make their way back to Father Huw's house, and
thence in courtesy a measure of the way through the woods
towards Rhisiart's hall before they parted.

'I would not say more nor plainer,' said Cai confidingly,
'while Bened was present, nor in front of Padrig, for that matter,
though he's a good fellow—so are they both!—but a traveller,
not a native. This Sioned, Rhisiart's girl. . . . The truth is, Bened
would like to be a suitor for her himself, and a good, solid man
he is, and a girl might well do worse. But a widower, poor soul,
and years older than the lass, and a poor chance he has. But
you haven't seen the girl!'

Brother Cadfael was beginning to suspect that he had indeed
seen the girl, and seen more than any here had ever been allowed
to see. But he said nothing.

'A girl like a squirrel! As swift, as sudden, as black and as
red! If she had nothing, they'd still be coming from miles
around, and she will have lands any man might covet even if
she squinted! And there's poor Bened, keeping his own counsel
and feeding on his own silence, and still hoping. After all, a smith
is respected in any company. And give him his due, it isn't her
heritage he covets. It's the girl herself. If you'd seen her, you'd

42

know. In any case,' said Cai, sighing gustily for his friend, 'her father has a favourite for son-in-law already, and has had all along. Cadwallon's lad has been in and out of Rhisiart's hall, and made free with Rhisiart's servants and hawks and horses, ever since he could run, and grown up with the girl. And he's sole heir to the neighbouring holding, and what could suit either father better? They've had it made up between them for years. And the children seem ideally matched, they know each other through and through, like brother and sister.'

'I doubt if I'd say that made for an ideal match,' said Brother Cadfael honestly.

'So Sioned seems to think, too,' said Cai drily. 'So far she's resisted all pressures to accept this lad Peredur. And mind you, he's a very gay, lively, well-looking young fellow, spoiled as you please, being the only one, but show me a girl round here who wouldn't run if he lifted his finger—all but this girl! Oh, she likes him well enough, but that's all. She won't hear of marriage yet, she's still playing the heartfree child.'

'And Rhisiart bears with her?' asked Cadfael delicately.

'You don't know him, either. He dotes on her, and well he may, and she reveres him, and well *she* may, and where does that get any of us? He won't force her choice. He never misses a chance to urge how suitable Peredur is, and she never denies it. He hopes, if he bides his time, she'll come round.'

'And will she?' asked Brother Cadfael, responding to something in the ploughman's voice. His own was milder than milk.

'No accounting,' said Cai slowly, 'for what goes on in a girl's head. She may have other plans of her own. A bold, brave one she is, clever and patient at getting her own way. But what that may be, do I know? Do you? Does any man?'

'There may be one man who does,' said Brother Cadfael with guileful disinterest.

If Cai had not risen to that bait, Cadfael would have let well alone then, for it was no business of his to give away the girl's secrets, when he had stumbled upon them himself only by chance. But he was no way surprised when the ploughman drew meaningfully close against his arm, and jabbed a significant elbow into his ribs. A man who had worked closely with the young ox-caller as he had must surely have noted a few obvious things by now. This afternoon's purposeful bee-line across the meadows and through the water to a certain well-grown oak would be enough in itself for a sharp man. And as for keeping his mouth shut about it, it was pretty plain that his sympathies were with his work-mate.

'Brother Cadfael, you wouldn't be a talking man, not out of turn, and you're not tied to one side or the other in any of our little disputes here. No reason *you* shouldn't know. Between you and me, she *has* got a man in her eye, and one that wants her worse than Bened does, and has even less chance of ever getting her. You remember we were talking of my fellow on the team, Engelard? A good man with cattle, worth plenty to his lord, and Rhisiart knows it and values him fairly on it. But the lad's an *alltud*—an outlander!'

'Saxon?' asked Cadfael.

'The fair hair. Yes, you saw him today. The length and slenderness of him too. Yes, he's a Cheshire man from the borders of Maelor, on the run from the bailiffs of Earl Ranulf of Chester. Oh, not for murder or banditry or any such! But the lad was simply the most outrageous deer-poacher in the earldom. He's a master with the short bow, and always stalked them afoot and alone. And the bailiff was after his blood. Nothing for him to do, when he was cornered on the borders, but run for it into Gwynedd. And he daren't go back, not yet, and you know what it means for a foreigner to want to make a living in Wales.'

Cadfael knew indeed. In a country where every native-born man had and knew his assured place in a clan kinship, and the basis of all relationships was establishment on the land, whether as free lord or villein partner in a village community, the man from outside, owning no land here, fitting into no place, was deprived of the very basis of living. His only means of establishing himself was by getting some overlord to make compact with him, give him house-room and a stake in the land, and employ him for whatever skills he could offer. For three generations this bargain between them was revocable at any time, and the outlander might leave at the fair price of dividing his chattels equally with the lord who had given him the means of acquiring them.

'I do know. So Rhisiart took this young man into his service and set him up in a croft?'

'He did. Two years ago now, a little more. And neither of them has had any call to regret it. Rhisiart's a fair-minded master, and gives credit where it's due. But however much he respects and values him, can you see a Welsh lord ever letting his only daughter go to an *alltud*?'

'Never!' agreed Cadfael positively. 'No chance of it! It would be against all his laws and customs and conscience. His own kinship would never forgive it.'

'True as I'm breathing!' sighed Cai ruefully. 'But you try telling that to a proud, stubborn young fellow like Engelard, who has his own laws and rights from another place, where his father's lord of a good manor, and carries every bit as much weight in his feudal fashion as Rhisiart does here.'

'Do you tell me he's actually spoken for her to her father?' demanded Cadfael, astonished and admiring.

'He has, and got the answer you might expect. No malice at all, but no hope, either. Yes, and stood his ground and argued his case just the same. And comes back to the subject every chance that offers, to remind Rhisiart he hasn't given up, and never will. I tell you what, those two are two of a kind, both hot-tempered, both obstinate, but both as open and honest as you'll find anywhere, and they've a great respect for each other that somehow keeps them from bearing malice or letting this thing break them apart. But every time this comes up, the sparks fly. Rhisiart clouted Engelard once, when he pushed him too hard, and the lad came within an ace of clouting back. What would the answer to that have been? I never knew it happen with an *alltud*, but if a slave strikes a free man he stands to lose the hand that did it. But he stopped himself in time, though I don't think it was fear that stoppcd him—he knew he was in the wrong. And what did Rhisiart do, not half an hour later, but fling back and ask his pardon! Said he was an insolent, unreasonable, unWelsh rascal, but he should not have struck him. There's a battle going on all the time between those two, and neither of them can get any peace, but let any man say a word against Rhisiart in Engelard's hearing, and he'll get it back down his throat with a fist behind it. And if one of the servants ever called down Engelard, thinking to curry favour with Rhisiart, he'd soon get told that the *alltud*'s an honest man and a good worker, worth ten of the likes of his backbiters. So it goes! And I can see no good end to it.'

'And the girl?' said Cadfael. 'What does she say to all this?'

'Very little, and very softly. Maybe at first she did argue and plead, but if so it was privately with her father alone. Now she's biding her time, and keeping them from each other's throat as best she can.'

And meeting her lover at the oak tree, thought Cadfael, or any one of a dozen other private places, wherever his work takes him. So that's how she learned her English, all through those two years while the Saxon boy was busy learning Welsh from her, and that's why, though she was willing to pass the time of day in his own language with a visiting monk, she was concerned about having betrayed her accomplishment to a Welsh-speaking stranger, who might innocently blurt it abroad locally. She'd hardly want to let slip how often she's been meeting Engelard in secret, if she's biding her time, and keeping father and lover from each other's throat till she can get her own way with them. And who's to say which of the three will give way first, where all look immovable?

'It seems you've your own troubles here in Gwytherin, let alone what we've brought with us,' he said, when he parted from Cai.

'God resolves all given time,' said Cai philosophically and trudged away into the darkness. And Cadfael returned along the path with the uncomfortable feeling that God, nevertheless, required a little help from men, and what he mostly got was hindrance.

All the free men of Gwytherin came to the meeting next day, and their womenfolk and all the villein community came to the

46

Mass beforehand. Father Huw named the chief among them softly to Brother Cadfael as they made their appearance. He had seldom had such a congregation.

'Here is Rhisiart, with his daughter and his steward, and the girl's waiting-woman.'

Rhisiart was a big, bluff, hearty-looking man of about fifty, high-coloured and dark-haired, with a short, grizzled beard, and bold features that could be merry or choleric, fierce or jovial, but were far too expressive ever to be secretive or mean. His stride was long and impetuous, and his smile quick in response when he was greeted. His dress hardly distinguished him from any of the other free landholders who came thronging into the church, being plain as any, but of good homespun cloth. To judge from his bright face, he came without prejudice, willing to listen, and for all his thwarted family plans, he looked an expansively happy man, proud and fond of his daughter.

As for the girl, she followed at his heels modestly, with poised head and serene eyes. She had shoes on for this occasion, and her hair was brushed and braided into a burnished dark coil on her neck, and covered with a linen coif, but there was no mistaking her. This was the urchin of the oak tree, and the greatest heiress and most desirable prize in marriage in all this countryside.

The steward was an older man, grey-headed and balding, with a soft, good-humoured face. 'He is Rhisiart's kinsman by marriage,' whispered Huw, 'his wife's elder brother.'

'And the other girl is Sioned's tirewoman?' No need to name her, he already knew her name. Dimpled and smiling, Annest followed her friend with demure little steps into the church, and the sun stroked all the bright, silvery grain in the sheaf of her pale hair. 'She is the smith's niece,' said Father Huw helpfully. 'A good girl, she visits him often since he buried his wife, and bakes for him.'

'Bened's niece?' Brother John pricked his ears, and looked after the shapely waist and glowing hair with fascinated eyes, no doubt hoping there would be a baking day before they had to leave Gwytherin. The lodging arrangements had certainly

47

been inspired, though whether by an angel or an imp remained to be seen.

'Lower your eyes, brother,' said Jerome chidingly. 'It is not seemly to look so straightly upon women.'

'And how did he know there were women passing,' whispered Brother John rebelliously, 'if his own eyes were so dutifully lowered?'

Brother Columbanus, at least, was standing as prescribed in the presence of females, with pale hands prayerfully folded, and lofty eyelids lowered, his gaze upon the grass.

'And here comes Cadwallon now,' said Father Huw. 'These good brothers already know him, of course. And his lady. And his son Peredur.'

So this young man, loping after his parents with the long, springy gait of a yearling roebuck, was the chosen husband for Sioned, the lad she liked well enough, and had known familiarly all her life, but was in no way inclined to marry. It occurred to Cadfael that he had never asked how the groom felt about the situation, but it needed only a glimpse of Peredur's face when he caught sight of Sioned to settle the matter. Here was a tangle. The girl might have worn out in mere liking all her inclination to love, but the boy certainly had not. At sight of her his face paled, and his eyes took fire.

The parents were ordinary enough, comfortable people grown plump from placid living, and expecting things to go smoothly still as they always had. Cadwallon had a round, fleshy, smiling face, and his wife was fat, fair and querulous. The boy cast back to some more perilous ancestor. The spring of his step was a joy to watch. He was not above middle height, but so well-proportioned that he looked tall. His dark hair was cut short, and curled crisply all over his head. His chin was shaven clean, and all the bones of his face were as bold and elegant as his colouring was vivid, with russet brushings of sun on high cheekbones, and a red, audacious, self-willed mouth. Such a young person might well find it hard to bear that another, and an alien at that, should be preferred to him. He proclaimed in his every movement and glance that everything and everyone in his life had responded subserviently to his charm, until now.

At the right moment, when the church was full, Prior Robert, tall and imposing and carefully groomed, swept in through the tiny sacristy and took his place, and all the Shrewsbury brothers fell into line and followed on his heels. The Mass began.

In the deliberations of the free assembly of the parish, of course, the women had no part. Neither had the villeins, though they had their indirect influence through those of their friends who were free. So while the free men lingered after the Mass, the rest dispersed, moving away with slow dignity, and not too far, just far enough to be discreetly out of sight and earshot, but handy to detect what was passing by instinct, and confirm it as soon as the meeting broke up.

The free men gathered in the open before the church. The sun was already high, for it was little more than an hour to noon. Father Huw stood up before the assembly, and gave them the gist of the matter, as it had been presented to him. He was the father of this flock, and he owed his people truth, but he also owed his church fealty. He told them what bishop and prince had answered to the request from Shrewsbury, reverently presented, and with many proofs. Which proofs he left to Robert to deliver.

The prior had never looked holier or more surely headed for sainthood himself. He had always a sense of occasion, and beyond a doubt it had been his idea to hold the meeting here in the open, where the sun could gild and illuminate his otherworldly beauty. It was Cadfael's detached opinion that he did himself more than justice, by being less overbearing than might have been expected. Usually he overdid things, this time he got it right, or as right as something only equivocally right in itself can be got.

'They're not happy!' whispered Brother John in Cadfael's ear, himself sounding far from sad about it. There were times when even Brother John could be humanly smug. And indeed, those Welsh faces ranged round them were singularly lacking in enthusiasm for all these English miracles performed by a Welsh saint. Robert at his best was not exactly carrying his audience. They swayed and murmured, and eyed one another, and again turned as one man to eye him.

'If Owain ap Griffith wills it, and the bishop gives his blessing, too,' began Cadwallon hesitantly, 'as loyal sons of the church, and true men of Gwynedd, we can hardly. . . .'

'Both prince and bishop have blessed our errand,' said the prior loftily.

'But the girl is here, in Gwytherin,' said Rhisiart abruptly. He had the voice that might have been expected from him, large, melodious and deep, a voice that sang what it felt, and waited for thought afterwards, to find that the thought had been there already in the feeling. 'Ours, not Bishop David's! Not Owain ap Griffith's! She lived out her life here, and never said word about wanting to leave us. Am I to believe easily that she wants to leave us now, after so long? Why has she never told us? Why?'

'She has made it clear to us,' said the prior, 'by many manifestations, as I have told you.'

'But never a word to us,' cried Rhisiart, roused. 'Do you call that courtesy? Are we to believe that, of a virgin who chose to make her home here among us?'

They were with him, his assurance had fired their smouldering reluctance. They cried out from a dozen directions at once that Saint Winifred belonged to Gwytherin, and to no other place.

'Do you dare tell me,' said Prior Robert, high and clear, 'that you have visited her? That you have committed your prayers to her? That you have invoked the aid of this blessed virgin, and given her the honour that is her due? Do you know of any reason why she should desire to remain here among you? Have you not neglected even her grave?'

'And if we have,' said Rhisiart with blithe conviction, 'do you suppose the girl wonders at it? You have not lived here among us. She did. You are English, she was Welsh, she knew us, and was never so moved against us that she withdrew or complained. We know she is there, no need to exclaim or make any great outcry. If we have needs, she knows it, and never asks that we should come with prayers and tears, knocking our knees on the ground before her. If she grudged a few brambles and weeds, she would have found a means to tell us. Us, not some distant Benedictine house in England!'

Throats were opening joyfully, shouting where they had muttered. The man was a poet and a preacher, match for any Englishman. Brother Cadfael let loose his bardic blood, and rejoiced silently. Not even because it was Prior Robert recoiling into marble rage under Welsh siege. Only because it was a Welsh voice that cried battle.

'And do you deny,' thundered Robert, stretching his ascetic length to its loftiest, 'the truth of those omens and miracles I have declared to you, the beckoning that led us here?'

'No!' said Rhisiart roundly. 'I never doubted you believed and had experienced these portents. But portents can arise, miracles can be delivered, either from angels or devils. If these are from heaven, why have we not been instructed? The little saint is here, not in England. She owes us the courtesy of kinsmen. Dare you say she is turned traitor? Is there not a church in Wales, a Celtic church such as she served? What did she know of yours? I do not believe she would speak to you and not to us. You have been deceived by devils! Winifred never said word!'

A dozen voices took up the challenge, hallooing applause for their most articulate spokesman, who had put his finger on the very pulse of their resentment. Even the very system of bishoprics galled the devout adherents of the old, saintly Celtic church, that had no worldly trappings, courted no thrones, but rather withdrew from the world into the blessed solitude of thought and prayer. The murmur became a subdued rumbling, a thunder, a roar. Prior Robert, none too wisely, raised his commanding voice to shout them down.

'She said no word to you, for you had left her forgotten and unhonoured. She has turned to us for recognition, when she could get none from you.'

'That is not true,' said Rhisiart, 'though you in your ignorance may believe it. The saint is a good Welshwoman, and knows her countrymen. We are not quick in respect to rank or riches, we do not doff and bow and scrape when any man flaunts himself

51

before us. We are blunt and familiar even in praise. What we value we value in the heart, and this Welsh girl knows it. She would never leave her own unfurnished, even if we have neglected to trim her grave. It is the spirit that leans to us, and is felt by us as guardian and kin. But these bones you come hunting are also hers. Not ours, not yours! Until she tells us she wills to have them moved, here they stay. We should be damned else!'

It was the bitterest blow of Prior Robert's life to know that he had met his match and overmatch in eloquence and argument, here in a half-barbaric Welsh landholder, no great lord, but a mere squireling elevated among his inferiors to a status he barely rated, at least in Norman eyes. It was the difference between them that Robert thought in hierarchies, and Rhisiart thought in blood-ties, high and low of one mind and in one kinship, and not a man among them aware of inferiority, only of his due place in a united family.

The thunder was one voice now, demanding and assured, but it was one man who had called it into being. Prior Robert, well aware that a single adversary confronted him, subdued his angry tones, and opted for the wisdom of the dove, and the subtlety of single combat. He raised his long, elegant arms, from which the wide sleeves of his habit fell free, and smiled on the assembly, turning the smile at its most compelling and fatherly upon Rhisiart.

'Come, Brother Cadfael, say this for me to the lord Rhisiart, that it is all too easy for us, who have the same devotion at heart, to disagree about the means. It is better to speak quietly, man to man, and avoid the deformation of anger. Lord Rhisiart, I beg you to come apart with me, and let us debate this matter in quietude, and then you shall have liberty to speak out what you will. And having had my say fairly with you, I will say no word further to challenge what you have to impart to your people.'

'That is fair and generous,' said Rhisiart promptly to this offer, and stood forward with ingenuous pleasure from the crowd, which parted to let him through.

'We will not take even the shadow of dissension into the church,' said Prior Robert. 'Will you come with us into Father

Huw's house?' All those bright, sullen, roused eyes followed them in through the low doorway, and clung there to wait for them to come forth again. Not a man of the Welsh moved from his place. They trusted the voice that had spoken for them hitherto to speak for them still.

In the small, wood-scented room, dark after the brightness of the day outside, Prior Robert faced his opponent with a calm and reasonable face.

'You have spoken well,' he said, 'and I commend your faith, and the high value you set on the saint, for so do we value her highly. And at her own wish, for so we believe, we have come here, solely to serve her. Both church and state are with us, and you know better than I the duty a nobleman of Wales owes to both. But I would not willingly leave Gwytherin with a sense of grievance, for I do know that by Saint Winifred's departure Gwytherin's loss is great. That we own, and I would wish to make due reparation.'

'Reparation to Gwytherin?' repeated Rhisiart, when this was translated to him. 'I do not understand how. . . .'

'And to you,' said Robert softly and matter-of-factly, 'if you will withdraw your opposition, for then I feel sure all your fellows will do the same, and sensibly accept what bishop and prince decree.'

It occurred to Cadfael as he interpreted this, even before the prior began the slow, significant motion of one long hand into the breast of his habit, that Robert was about to make the most disastrous miscalculation of his life. But Rhisiart's face remained dubious and aloof, quite without understanding, as the prior drew from his bosom a soft leather bag drawn up with a cord at the neck, and laid it on the table, pushing it gently across until it rested against Rhisiart's right hand. Its progress over the rough boards gave out a small chinking sound. Rhisiart eyed it suspiciously, and lifted uncomprehending eyes to stare at the prior. 'I don't understand you. What is this?'

'It is yours,' said Robert, 'if you will persuade the parish to agree to give up the saint.'

Too late he felt the unbelieving coldness in the air, and sensed

53

the terrible error he had made. Hastily he did his best to recover some of the ground lost. 'To be used as you think best for Gwytherin—a great sum. . . .' It was useless. Cadfael let it lie in silence.

'Money!' said Rhisiart in the most extraordinary of tones, at once curious, derisory and revolted. He knew about money, of course, and even understood its use, but as an aberration in human relations. In the rural parts of Wales, which indeed were almost all of Wales, it was hardly used at all, and hardly needed. Provision was made in the code for all necessary exchange of goods and services, nobody was so poor as to be without the means of living, and beggars were unknown. The kinship took care of its helpless members, and every house was open as of right. The minted coins that had seeped in through the marches were a pointless eccentricity. Only after a moment of scornful wonder did it occur to Rhisiart that in this case they were also a mortal insult. He snatched away his hand from the affronting touch, and the blood surged into his face darkly red, suffusing even the whites of his eyes.

'Money? You dare offer to *buy* our saint? To buy *me*? I was in two minds about you, and about what I ought to do, but now, by God, I know what to think! You had your omens. Now I have mine!'

'You mistake me!' cried the prior, stumbling after his blunder and seeing it outdistance him at every breath. 'One cannot buy what is holy, I am only offering a gift to Gwytherin, in gratitude and compensation for their sacrifice—'

'Mine, you said it was,' Rhisiart reminded him, glowing copper bright with dignified rage. 'Mine, if I *persuaded* . . . ! Not a gift! A bribe! This foolish stuff you hoard about you more dearly far than your reputations, don't think you can use it to buy *my* conscience. I know now that I was right to doubt you. You have said your say, now I will say mine to those people without, as you promised me I should, without hindrance.'

'No, wait!' The prior was in such agitation that he actually reached out a hand and caught his opponent by the sleeve. 'Do nothing in haste! You have mistaken my meaning indeed, and

54

if I was wrong even to offer an alms to Gwytherin, I am sorry for it. But do not call it—'

Rhisiart withdrew himself angrily from the detaining clasp, and cut off the protest curtly, wheeling on Cadfael. 'Tell him he need not be afraid. I should be ashamed to tell my people that a prior of Shrewsbury tried to corrupt me with a bribe. I don't deal in that kind of warfare. But where I stand—that they shall know, and you, too.' And he strode out from them, and Father Huw put out a warning hand to prevent any of them from attempting to impede or follow him.

'Not now! He is hot now. Tomorrow something may be done to approach him, but not now. You must let him say what he will.'

'Then at least let's put in an appearance,' said the prior, magnificently picking up what pieces he could of the ruin he had created; and he swept out into the sunlight and took his stand close to the door of the church, with all his fellow-monks dutifully following on his heels, and stood with erect head and calmly folded hands, in full view, while Rhisiart thundered his declaration to the assembled people of Gwytherin.

'I have listened to what these men from Shrewsbury have had to say to me, and I have made my judgment accordingly, and now I deliver it to you. I say that so far from changing my views, I am confirmed a thousand times that I was right to oppose the sacrilege they desire. I say that Saint Winifred's place is here among us, where she has always belonged, and that it would be mortal sin to let her be taken away to a strange place, where not even the prayers would be in a tongue she knows, where foreigners not worthy to draw near her would be her only company. I pledge my opposition to the death, against any attempt to move her bones, and I urge upon you the same duty. And now this conference is ended.'

So he said, and so it was. There could be no possible way of prolonging it. The prior was forced to stand with marble face and quiet hands while Rhisiart strode away towards the forest path, and all the assembly, in awed and purposeful silence, melted away mysteriously in all directions after his departure, so that within minutes all that green, trodden arena was empty.

CHAPTER FOUR

'You should have told me what you intended,' said Father Huw,
timidly reproachful. 'I could have told you it was folly, the worst
possible. What attraction do you think money has for a man
like Rhisiart? Even if he was for sale, and he is not, you would
have had to find other means to purchase him. I thought you
had taken his measure, and were proposing to plead to him the
sorry plight of English pilgrims, who have no powerful saints of
their own, and are sadly in need of such a protectress. He would
have listened to something that entreated of his generosity.'

'I am come with the blessing of church and sovereign,' said
the prior fiercely, though the repetition was beginning to pall
even on him. 'I cannot be repudiated at the will of a local squire.
Has my order no rights here in Wales?'

'Very few,' said Cadfael bluntly. 'My people have a natural
reverence, but it leans towards the hermitage, not the cloister.'

The heated conference went on until Vespers, and poisoned
even Vespers with its bitterness, for there Prior Robert preached
a fearful sermon detailing all the omens that Winifred desired
above all things to remove to the sanctity of Shrewsbury, and
issuing her prophetic denunciation against all who stood in the
way of her translation. Terrible would be her wrath visited on
those who dared resist her will. Thus Prior Robert approached
the necessary reconciliation with Rhisiart. And though Cadfael
in translating toned down the threat as much as he dared, there
were some among the congregation who understood enough
English to get the full drift of it. He knew by their closed, mute
faces. Now they would go away to spread the word to those
who had not been present, until everyone in Gwytherin knew
that the prior had bidden them remember what befell Prince
Cradoc, whose very flesh watered away into the ground like

rain, so that he vanished utterly, as to the body expunged out of the world, as to the soul, the fearful imagination dared not guess. So also it might happen to those who dared offend against Winifred now.

Father Huw, harried and anxious, cast about him as honestly as he could for a way of pleasing everybody. It took him most of the evening to get the prior to listen, but from sheer exhaustion a calm had to set in at last.

'Rhisiart is not an impious man—'

'Not impious!' fluted Brother Jerome, appealing to heaven with uplifted eyes. 'Men have been excommunicated for less!'

'Then men have been excommunicated for no evil at all,' said Huw sturdily, 'and truly I think they sometimes have. No, I say he is a decent, devout man, open-handed and fair, and had a right to resent it when he was misunderstood and affronted. If he is ever to withdraw his opposition, it must be you, Father Prior, who make the first approach to him, and upon a different footing. Not in person first, I would not ask or advise it. But if I were to go to him, perhaps with Brother Cadfael here, who is known to be a good Welshman himself, and ask him to forget all that has been said and done, and come with an open mind to begin the discussion over again, I think he would not refuse. Moreover, the very act of seeking him out would disarm him, for he has a generous heart. I don't say he would necessarily change his mind—it would depend on how he is handled this time—but I do say he would listen.'

'Far be it from me,' said Prior Robert loftily, 'to pass over any means of saving a soul from perdition. I wish the man no ill, if he tempers his offences. It is not a humiliation to stoop to deliver a sinner.'

'O wondrous clemency!' intoned Brother Jerome. 'Saintly generosity towards the ill-doer!'

Brother John flashed a narrow, glittering glance, and shifted one foot uneasily, as if restraining an impulse to kick. Father Huw, desperate to preserve his stock of goodwill with prince, bishop, prior and people alike, cast him a warning look, and resumed hurriedly: 'I will go to Rhisiart tonight, and ask him to dine here at my house tomorrow. Then if we can come to terms between us, another assembly can be called, so that all may know there is peace.'

'Very well!' said the prior, after consideration. In that way he need never actually admit any guilt on his part, or apologise for any act of his, nor need he enquire too closely what Huw might have to say on his behalf. 'Very well, do so, and I hope you may succeed.'

'It would be a mark of your status, and the importance of this gesture,' suggested Cadfael with an earnest face, 'if your messengers went mounted. It's not yet dark, and the horses would be the better for exercise.'

'True,' said the prior, mildly gratified. 'It would be in keeping with our dignity and lend weight to our errand. Very well, let Brother John bring the horses.'

'Now that's what I call a friend!' said Brother John heartily, when they were all three in the saddle, and safely away into the early dusk under the trees, Father Huw and John on the two tall horses, Brother Cadfael on the best of the mules. 'Ten more minutes, and I should have earned myself a penance that would have lasted a month or more, and now here we are in the best company around, on a decent errand, and enjoying the quiet of the evening.'

'Did I ever say word of your coming with us?' said Cadfael slyly. 'I said the horses would add lustre to the embassage, I never went so far as to say *you* would add any.'

'I go with the horses. Did you ever hear of an ambassador riding without a groom? I'll keep well out of the way while you confer, and play the dutiful servant. And by the by, Bened will be doing his drinking up there at the hall tonight. They go the rounds, and it's Cai's turn.'

'And how did you learn so much,' wondered Cadfael, 'without a word of Welsh?'

'Oh, they knock their meaning into me somehow, and I into them. Besides, I have several words of Welsh already, and if we're held up here for a while I shall soon learn a great many more, if I can get my tongue round them. I could learn the smith's art, too. I lent him a hand at the forge this morning.'

'You're honoured. In Wales not everyone can be a smith.'

Huw indicated the fence that had begun to run alongside them on the right. 'Cadwallon's holding. We have a mile of forest to go yet to Rhisiart's hall.'

It was still no more than dusk when they emerged into a large clearing, with ploughed and planted strips surrounding a long stockade fence. The smell of wood-smoke drifted on the air, and glimmer of torches lit the open doorway of the hall. Stables and barns and folds clung to the inner side of the fence, and men and women moved briskly about the evening business of a considerable household.

'Well, well!' said the voice of Cai the ploughman, from a bench under the eaves of one of the byres. 'So you've found your way by nose to where the mead is tonight, Brother Cadfael.' And he moved up obligingly to make room, shoulder to shoulder with Bened. 'Padrig's making music within, and from all I hear it may well be war music, but he'll be with us presently. Sit yourself down, and welcome. Nobody looks on you as the enemy.'

There was a third with them already, a long man seated in deeper shadow, his legs stretched well out before him at ease, and his hair showing as a primrose pallor even in the dimness. The young outlander, Engelard, willingly gathered up his long limbs and also moved to share the bench. He had a quick, open smile vivid with white teeth.

'We've come expressly to halt the war,' said Brother Cadfael as they dismounted, and a groom of the household came running to take their bridles. 'Father Huw has the peace in hand, I'm only an assessor to see fair play. And, sadly, we'll be expected back with an answer as soon as we've spoken with your lord. But if you'll take charge of Brother John while we deal, he'll be grateful. He can speak English with Engelard, a man should practise his own tongue when he can.'

But Brother John, it appeared, had at that moment completely lost the use of his tongue in any language, for he stood at gaze, and let the reins be taken from his hands like a man in a dream. Nor was he looking at Engelard, but towards the open doorway of the hall, from which a girl's figure had issued, and was crossing gaily towards the drinkers under the eaves, a large jug carried in both hands. The lively brown eyes flickered over the visitors, took in Cadfael and the priest with easy friendliness, and opened wide upon Brother John, standing like a very lifelike statue, all thorny russet hair, weather-burned cheeks and wild, admiring eyes. Cadfael looked where Annest's eyes were looking, and approved a very upstanding, ruggedly-built, ingenuous, comely yo'ng fellow, maybe two or three years older than the girl. The Benedictine habit, kilted to the knee for riding and forgotten now, looked as much like a working Welsh tunic as made no matter, and the tonsure, however well a man (or a girl!) knew it was there, was invisible behind the burning bush of curls.

'Thirsty people you are, then!' said Annest, still with one eye upon Brother John, and set down her pitcher on the bench beside Cai, and with a flick of her skirts and a wave of her light-brown mane, sat down beside it, and accepted the horn Bened offered her. Brother John stood mute and enchanted.

'Come on, then, lad,' said Bened, and made a place for him between himself and Cai, only one remove from where the girl sat delicately sipping. And Brother John, like a man walking in his sleep, though perhaps with rather more zestful purpose, strode forward towards the seat reserved for him.

'Well, well!' said Cadfael silently to himself, and left the insoluble to the solver of all problems, and with Father Huw moved on into the hall.

'I will come,' said Rhisiart, shut into a small chamber apart with his visitors. 'Of course I will come. No man should refuse another his say. No man can be sure he will not belie himself and do himself less than justice, and God forbid I should refuse anyone his second chance. I've often spoken in haste myself, and been sorry after, and said so, as your prior has said so now.' He had not, of course, nor had Huw claimed, in so many words, that he had. Rather he had expressed his own shame and regret, but if Rhisiart attributed these to Prior Robert, Huw was desperate enough to let him continue in the delusion. 'But I tell you this, I expect little from this meeting. The gap between us is too wide. To you I can say what I have not said to any who were not there, because I am ashamed. The man offered me money. He says now he offered it to Gwytherin, but how is that possible? Am I Gwytherin? I am a man like other men, I fill my place as best I can, but remain one only. No, he offered the purse to me, to take back my voice against him. To persuade my own people to go along with his wishes. I accept his desire to talk to me again, to bring me to see this matter as he sees it. But I cannot forget that he saw it as something he could buy with money. If he wishes to change me, that must change, and be shown to be changed. As for his threats, for threats they are, and I approve you for reporting them faithfully, they move me not at all. My reverence for our little saint is the equal of his or any man's. Do you think she does not know it?'

'I am sure she does,' said Father Huw.

'And if all they want is to honour and adore her rightly, why can they not do so here, where she lies? Even dress her grave, if that is what disturbs them, that we've let it run wild?'

'A good question,' said Brother Cadfael. 'I have asked it myself. The sleep of saints should be more sacred and immune even than the sleep of ordinary men.'

Rhisiart looked him over with those fine, challenging eyes, a shade or two lighter than his daughter's, and smiled. 'Howbeit, I will come, and my thanks for all your trouble. At the hour of noon, or a little after, I will come to your dinner, and I will listen faithfully to whatever may be said to me.'

There was a good laughter echoing from end to end of the bench under the eaves, and it was tempting to join the drinkers, at least for one quick cup, as Cai demanded. Bened had got up to replenish his horn from the pitcher, and Brother John, silent and flushed but glowingly happy, sat with no barrier between him and the girl, their sleeves all but touching when she leaned

61

curiously closer, her hair dropping a stray lock against his shoulder.

'Well, how have you sped?' asked Cai, pouring mead for them. 'Will he come and talk terms with your prior?'

'He'll come,' said Cadfael. 'Whether he'll talk terms I doubt. He was greatly affronted. But he'll come to dine, and that's something.'

'The whole parish will know it before ever you get back to the parsonage,' said Cai. 'News runs faster than the wind in these parts, and after this morning they're all building on Rhisiart. I tell you, if he changed his tune and said amen, so would they. Not for want of their own doubts and waverings, but because they trust him. He took a stand, and they know he won't leave it but for good reason. Sweeten him, and you'll get your way.'

'Not my way,' said Cadfael. 'I never could see why a man can't reverence his favourite saint without wanting to fondle her bones, but there's great rivalry for such relics among the abbeys these days. A good mead, this, Cai.'

'Our Annest here brewed it,' said Bened, with tolerant pride in his niece, and clapped a hand fondly on her shoulder. 'And only one of her skills! She'll be a treasure for some man when she weds, but a sad loss to me.'

'I might bring you a good smith to work with you,' said the girl, dimpling. 'Where's the loss then?'

It was deep dusk, and with all the longing they felt to linger, they had to be away. Huw was fidgety, thinking of Prior Robert's rising impatience, his tall figure pacing the garden and looking out for the first glimpse of his messengers returning. 'We should be off. We shall be looked for. Come, brother, make your farewells.'

Brother John rose reluctantly but dutifully. The groom was leading the horses forward, an arm under each arching neck. With composed face but glowing eyes Brother John said his general goodnight and blessing. In careful but resounding Welsh! The echo swept the riders away towards the gate on a wave of laughter and goodwill, in which the girl's light voice soared gaily, and Engelard's hearty English 'God go with you!'

balanced the tongues.

'And who taught you that between evening and dark?' asked Brother Cadfael with interest, as they entered the deep green twilight under the trees. 'Bened or Cai?'

'Neither,' said Brother John, contentedly pondering a deep private satisfaction.

Small use asking how she had managed it, she having no English and he no Welsh, to determine what the phrase was she was drumming into him. There was a kind of language at work here that made short shrift of interpreters.

'Well, you can fairly claim the day hasn't been wasted,' owned Cadfael generously, 'if something's been learned. And have you made any other discoveries to add to that?'

'Yes,' said Brother John, placidly glowing. 'The day after to-morrow is baking-day at Bened's.'

'You may rest and sleep, Father Prior,' said Huw, fronting the tall, pale forehead gallantly with his low, brown one. 'Rhisiart has said he will come, and he will listen. He was gracious and reasonable. Tomorrow at noon or soon after he will be here.'

Prior Robert certainly loosed a cautious, suppressed sigh of relief. But he required more before they could all go away and sleep. Richard loomed at his shoulder, large, benign and anxious.

'And is he sensible of the wrong-mindedness of his resistance? Will he withdraw his opposition?'

In the dimness where the candle-light barely reached, Brothers Jerome and Columbanus trembled and hoped, for while doubt remained they had not been permitted to remove to their rest at Cadwallon's house. Anxious eyes appealed, reflecting the light.

Father Huw hedged, wanting his own sleep. 'He offers friendly interest and faithful consideration. I asked no more.'

Brother Cadfael said bluntly : 'You will need to be persuasive, and sincere. *He* is sincere. I am no way convinced that he can be lightly persuaded.' He was tired of nursing wounded vanities, he spoke out what was in his mind. 'Father Prior, you made your mistake with him this morning. You will need a change of heart, *his or yours*, to undo that damage.

*

Prior Robert made his dispositions as soon as Mass was over next morning, and with some care.

'Only Brother Sub-Prior and I, with Father Huw, and Brother Cadfael as interpreter, will sit at table together. You, Brother John, will make yourself useful to the cooks, and do whatever is needed, and you may also see to Father Huw's cattle and chickens. And you two, Brother Jerome, Brother Columbanus, I have a special mission for you. Since we are about Saint Winifred's business, I would have you go and spend the hours while we deliberate in vigil and prayer, imploring her aid to bring the obdurate to reason, and our errand to a successful conclusion. Not in the church here, but in her own chapel in the old graveyard where she is buried. Take your food and your measure of wine with you, and go there now. The boy Edwin will show you the way. If we prevail upon Rhisiart, as with her aid I trust we may, I will send to release you. But continue your intercessions until I do send word.'

They scattered dutifully, John, cheerfully enough, to tend the fire for Marared, and fetch and carry as she directed. The old woman, long widowed and her own sons grown, preened herself at having a strapping young fellow to keep her company, and Cadfael reflected that John might well be favoured with the best bits before the meal ever came to table. As for Jerome and Columbanus, he saw them set out with the boy, bread and meat wrapped in napkins in the breasts of their habits, and Columbanus carrying the flask with their ration of wine, and a small bottle of spring water for himself.

'It is very little to offer,' he said meekly, 'but I will touch nothing but water until our couse has prevailed.'

'More fool he,' said Brother John blithely, 'for he may well be swearing off wine for life!'

It was a fine spring morning, but capricious as May can be. Prior Robert and his attendants sat in the orchard until they were driven indoors by a sharp and sparkling shower that lasted al-

64

most half an hour. It was then approaching noon, the time when Rhisiart should join them. He would have a wet walk by the short path through the forest. Or perhaps he had waited for the sun's return at Cadwallon's house, which was on his way. Making allowances for that, they thought little of it when another half-hour passed, and he did not put in an appearance. But when he was an hour late for the meeting, and still no sign of him, Prior Robert's face grew both grim and cautiously triumphant.

'He has heard the warning I issued against his sin, and he fears to come and face me,' he said.

'He had heard the warning, indeed,' said Father Huw heavily, 'but I saw no signs of fear in him. He spoke very firmly and calmly. And he is a man of his word. I don't understand this, it is not like him.'

'We will eat, but frugally,' said the prior, 'and give him every chance of keeping his promise, if something has happened to delay him. So it may, to any man. We will wait until it is time to prepare for Vespers.'

'I'll walk as far as Cadwallon's house,' offered Brother Richard, 'for the way is all one to that point, and see if I can meet with him, or get word if he's on his way.'

He was gone more than an hour and a half, and came back alone. 'I went beyond, some way along the ride, but saw no sign of him. On my way back I asked at Cadwallon's gate, but no one had seen him pass. I feared he might have walked by the short path while I was taking the other road.'

'We'll wait for him until Vespers, and no longer,' said the prior, and by then his voice was growing grimly confident, for now he did not expect the guest to come, and the enemy would have put himself in the wrong, to Prior Robert's great gain. Until Vespers, therefore, they waited, five hours after the appointed time. The people of Gwytherin could hardly say Rhisiart had been written off too hastily.

'So it ends,' said the prior, rising and shaking out his skirts like one shaking off a doubt or an incubus. 'He has turned tail, and his opposition will carry no weight now with any man. Let us go!'

65

The sunlight was still bright but slanting over the green bowl where the church stood, and a number of people were gathering for the service. And out of the deeper green shadow where the forest path began, came, not Rhisiart, but his daughter, sailing gallantly out into the sunlight in a green gown, with her wild hair tamed and braided, and a linen coif over it, Sioned in her church-going person, with Peredur on her heels, his hand possessively cupping her elbow, though she paid little heed to that attention. She saw them issuing in a silent procession from Huw's gate, and her eyes went from person to person, lingering on Cadfael who came last, and again looking back with a small frown, as though one face was missing from the expected company.

'Where is my father?' she asked, her wide eyes surprised but not yet troubled. 'Is he not still here with you? Have I missed him? I rode as far as Cadwallon's house, and he was on foot, so if he has left more than an hour ago he may well be home by now. I came to bear him company to church and go back with him afterwards.'

Prior Robert looked down at her in some wonder, the first flickering uneasiness twitching his nostrils. 'What is she saying? Do you tell me that the lord Rhisiart set out to come to our meeting?'

'Of course!' said Sioned, amazed. 'He had said he would.'

'But he did not come,' said Robert. 'We've waited for him since noon, and we've seen no sign of him. Brother Sub-Prior went a part of the way to see if he could meet with him, but in vain. He has not been here.'

She caught the meaning of that without Cadfael's services. Her eyes flashed from face to face, distrustful and ready for anger. 'Are you telling me truth? Or have you hidden him away under lock and key until you can get Winifred out of her grave and away to Shrewsbury? He was all that stood in your way. And you have threatened him!'

Peredur closed his fingers anxiously on her arm, and drew her against his side. 'Hush, you must not say such things. These brothers would not lie to you.'

'At what hour,' asked Cadfael, 'did your father set out this morning?'

She looked at him, and was a little reassured. The ring of silent onlookers drew nearer, listening attentively, ready to take her part if she needed an army.

'A good hour before noon. He was going first to the fields in the clearing, so he would be coming here by the shortest way, cutting through a quarter of a mile of forest to the usual path. He had plenty of time to be here before noon. As far as the clearing Engelard would be with him, he was going beyond, to the byres over the hill. There are two cows there ready to drop their calves.'

'We are telling you truly, child,' said Father Huw, his voice as grave and anxious as her own, 'we waited for him, and he never came.'

'What can have happened to him? Where can he be?'

'He will have crossed with us and gone home,' urged Peredur, hovering unhappily at her shoulder. 'We'll ride back, we shall surely find him there before us.'

'No! Why should he turn back, and never come to the dinner? And if he did, why so late? He would have been home long before I dressed my hair and set out to meet him, if he had changed his mind. And besides, he never would.'

'I think,' said Father Huw, 'that my whole parish has some interest in this matter, and we had better put off everything else, even the services of the church, until we have found Rhisiart and assured ourselves that all's well with him. Truly this may be no more than a tangle of mistiming and misunderstanding, but let's resolve it first, and wonder about it afterwards. There are enough of us here. Let's send out in parties along all the roads he may have taken, and Sioned shall show us where she thinks his short cut from the upland fields would bring him to the path. He could not well meet with any dangerous beasts in these woods, but he may have had a fall, an injury that has halted or slowed him. Father Prior, will you join with us?'

'With all my heart,' said Prior Robert, 'and so will we all.'

The less active among them were sent along the open ride,

with orders to scatter on either side and comb the surroundings as they went, while the more athletic took the narrow footpath beyond Cadwallon's stockade. The woods here were not yet close-set, there was thick, springy grass under the trees, and no dense undergrowth. They spread out into a half-circle, moving along within a few paces of one another, Sioned pressing purposefully forward up the path with set lips and fixed eyes, Peredur with every evidence of desperate affection following close and murmuring agitated urgings into her unheeding ears. Whether he believed in his own reassurances or not, out of all question he was a young man fathoms deep in love, and ready to do anything to serve and protect Sioned, while she saw in him nothing but the boy from the next holding, and tiresome at that.

They were perhaps half a mile beyond Cadwallon's enclosure when Father Huw suddenly plucked at Brother Cadfael's sleeve.

'We have forgotten Brother Jerome and Brother Columbanus! The hill of the chapel is off to the right here, no great way. Ask Prior Robert, should we not send and call them to join us?'

'I had indeed forgotten,' admitted the prior. 'Yes, by all means send someone. Best one of your parishioners, they'll all know the way.'

One of the young men swerved aside obediently between the trees, and ran. The slow-moving scythe swept on into deeper forest.

'About here,' said Sioned, halting, 'he would have come down from the clearing. If we go obliquely to the right here, and spread out as before, we shall be covering his likely way.'

The ground rose, the trees grew closer, the undergrowth thicker. They began to thread the encroaching bushes, having to part company by a few yards, losing sight momentarily of their neighbours. They had gone thus only a short way when Bened the smith, crashing through bushes at Brother Cadfael's left hand, uttered a great shout of discovery and dismay, and everyone in the wavering line halted and shook to the sound.

Cadfael turned towards the cry, thrusting through thorn-branches, and came out in a narrow oval of grass surrounded every way with thick bushes, through which a used track no wider than a man's shoulders clove, the long way of the oval. Just where he must have brushed through into the clear space, Rhisiart lay on his back, his right hip hollowing the grass under him, shoulders flattened to the ground and arms spread wide. His legs were drawn up under him with bent knees, the left leg crossed over the right. His short, defiant beard pointed at the sky. So, and at the very same slanting angle, did the feathered flight of the arrow that jutted out from under the cage of his ribs.

CHAPTER FIVE

From both sides they gathered, drawn to the smith's call, breaking through bushes like the running of a startled herd of deer, and halting appalled round the oval where the body lay. Cadfael went on his knees, and looked for any sign of breath within the drawn-back lips, any pulse in the stretched throat or rise and fall of the pierced breast, but there was none. And for that first moment he was the only one who moved within the open space of grass, and what he did was done in strange, too-intense silence, as though everyone round him held his breath.

Then everything broke out at once in noise and motion. Sioned clawed through the screening circle and saw her father's body, and uttered a great shriek that was more of fury even than of grief, and flung herself forward. Peredur caught her by the wrist and pulled her round into his arms, one hand cupped behind her head to press her face into his shoulder, but she shrieked again, and struck out at him with all her strength, and breaking loose, hurled herself to her knees facing Cadfael, and reached out to embrace her father's body. Cadfael leaned across to ward her off, his hand braced into the grass under Rhisiart's right armpit.

'No! Touch nothing! Not yet! Let him alone, he has things to tell us!'

By some intuitive quickness of mind that had not deserted her even at this moment, she obeyed the tone first, and awakened to the words immediately after. Her eyes questioned him, widening, and slowly she sat back in the grass, and drew her hands together in her lap. Her lips shaped the words after him silently: '—things to tell us!' She looked from his face into the face of the dead man. She knew he was dead. She also knew that the dead speak, often in thunder. And she came of proud Welsh stock to which the blood-feud is sacred, a duty transcending even grief.

When those following gathered closer, and one reached to touch, it was she who spread her arm protectively over the body, and said with authority: 'No! Let him be!'

Cadfael had drawn back his arm, and for a moment wondered what troubled him about the palm he had lifted from the grass beside Rhisiart's breast. Then he knew. Where he knelt the grass was perceptibly damp from the morning's sharp shower, he could feel the cling of the habit when he shifted his knee. Yet under the outflung right arm the grass was dry, his hand rose from it with no hint of moisture, no scent of rain. He touched again, ran his fingers up and down alongside Rhisiart's right flank. He was down to the knee before he felt the dampness and stirred the green fragrance. He felt outwards, the width of the body, to find the same signs. Strange! Very strange! His mind recorded and forbore to wonder then, because there were other things to be observed, and all manner of dangers were falling in upon all manner of people.

The tall shape looming at his back, motionless and chill, could be none other than Prior Robert, and Prior Robert in a curious state of exalted shock, nearer to Brother Columbanus' ecstatic fit than he had ever been before or would ever be again. The high, strained voice asked, over the shuddering quietness of Sioned's tearless sobs: 'He is dead?'

'Dead,' said Cadfael flatly, and looked into Sioned's wide, dry eyes and held them, promising something as yet undefined. Whatever it was, she understood it and was appeased, for he was Welsh, too, he knew about the blood-feud. And she was the only heir, the only close kin, of a murdered man. She had a task far above sorrow.

The prior's voice soared suddenly, awed and exalted. 'Behold the saint's vengeance! Did I not say her wrath would be wreaked upon all those who stood in the way of her desire? Tell them what I am saying! Tell them to look well at the fulfilment of my prophecy, and let all other obdurate hearts take warning. Saint Winifred has shown her power and her displeasure.'

There was hardly any need for translation, they had the sense of it already. A dozen of those standing close shrank warily away, a dozen voices muttered hurried submission. Not for worlds would they stand in the saint's way.

'The impious man reaps what he sows,' declaimed Robert. 'Rhisiart had his warning, and did not heed it.'

The most timorous were on their knees by then, cowed and horrified. It was not as if Saint Winifred had meant very much to them, until someone else wanted her, and Rhisiart stated a prior claim on behalf of the parish. And Rhisiart was dead by violence, struck down improbably in his own forests.

Sioned's eyes held Cadfael's, above her father's pierced heart. She was a gallant girl, she said never a word, though she had words building up in her ripe for saying, spitting, rather, into Prior Robert's pallid, aristocratic, alabaster face. It was not she who suddenly spoke out. It was Peredur.

'I don't believe it!' He had a fine, clear, vehement voice that rang under the branches. 'What, a gentle virgin saint, to take such vengeance on a good man? Yes, a good man, however mistaken! If she had been so pitiless as to want to slay—and I do not believe it of her!—what need would she have of arrows and bows? Fire from heaven would have done her will just as well, and shown her power better. You are looking at a murdered man, Father Prior. A man's hand fitted that arrow, a man's hand drew the bow, and for a man's reason. There must have been others who had a grudge against Rhisiart, others whose plans he was obstructing, besides Saint Winifred. Why blame this killing on her?'

This forthright Welsh sense Cadfael translated into English for Robert's benefit, who had caught the dissenting tone of it, but not the content. 'And the young man's right. This arrow never was shot from heaven. Look at the angle of it, up from under his ribs into the heart. Out of the earth, rather! A man with a short bow, on his knee among the bushes? True, the ground slopes, he may even have been lower than Rhisiart, but even so. . . .'

'Avenging saints may make use of earthly instruments,' said Robert overbearingly.

'The instrument would still be a murderer,' said Cadfael.

72

'There is law in Wales, too. We shall need to send word to the prince's bailiff.'

Bened had stood all this time darkly gazing, at the body, at the very slight ooze of blood round the wound, at the jutting shaft with its trimmed feathers. Slowly he said: 'I know this arrow. I know its owner, or at least the man whose mark it bears. Where young men are living close together in a household, they mark their own with a distinctive sign, so that there can be no argument. See the tip of the feathering on one side, dyed blue.' It was as he said, and at the mention of it several there drew breath hard, knowing the mark as well as he knew it.

'It's Engelard's,' said Bened outright, and three or four hushed voices bore him out.

Sioned raised her stricken face, shocked into a false, frozen calm that suddenly melted and crumbled into dread and anger. Rhisiart was dead, there was nothing she could do now for him but mourn and wait, but Engelard was alive and vulnerable, and an outlander, with no kinship to speak for him. She rose abruptly, slender and straight, turning her fierce eyes from face to face all round the circle.

'Engelard is the most trustworthy of all my father's men, and would cut off his own drawing hand rather than loose against my father's life. Who dares say this is his work?'

'I don't say so,' said Bened reasonably. 'I do say this is marked as his arrow. He is the best shot with the short bow in all this countryside.'

'And everybody in Gwytherin knows,' spoke up a voice from among the Welshmen, not accusing, only pointing out facts, 'that he has quarrelled often and fiercely with Rhisiart, over a certain matter at issue between them.'

'Over me,' said Sioned harshly. 'Say what you mean! I, of all people, know the truth best. Better than you all! Yes, they have had high words many times, on this one matter, and only this, and would have had more, but for all that, these two have understood each other, and neither one of them would ever have done the other harm. Do you think the prize fought over does not get to know the risks to herself and both the combatants? Fight they did, but they thought more highly of each other than either did of any of you, and with good reason.'

'Yet who can say,' said Peredur in a low voice, 'how far a man may step aside even from his own nature, for love?'

She turned and looked at him with measuring scorn. 'I thought you were his friend!'

'So I am his friend,' said Peredur, paling but steadfast. 'I said what I believe of myself, no less than of him.'

'What is this matter of one Engelard?' demanded Prior Robert, left behind in this exchange. 'Tell me what they are saying.' And when Cadfael had done so, as tersely as possible: 'It would seem that at least this young man must be asked to account for his movements this day,' decreed Robert, appropriating an authority to which he had no direct right here. 'It may be that others have been with him, and can vouch for him. But if not. . . .'

'He set out this morning with your father,' said Huw, distressfully eyeing the girl's fixed and defiant face. 'You told us so. They went together as far as the cleared fields. Then your father turned to make his way down to us, and Engelard was to go a mile beyond, to the byres where the cows were in calf. We must send out and ask if any man has seen your father since he parted from Engelard. Is there any who can speak to that?'

There was a silence. The numbers gathered about them were growing steadily. Some of the slower searchers from the open ride had made their way up here without news of their own, to find the matter thus terribly resolved. Others, hearing rumours of the missing man, had followed from the village. Father Huw's messenger came up behind with Brother Columbanus and Brother Jerome from the chapel. But no one spoke up to say he had seen Rhisiart that day. Nor did any volunteer word of having encountered Engelard.

'He must be questioned,' said Prior Robert, 'and if his answers are not satisfactory, he must be held and handed over to the bailiff. For it's clear from what has been said that this man certainly had a motive for wishing to remove Rhisiart from his path.'

'Motive?' blazed Sioned, burning up abruptly as a dark and

quiet fire suddenly spurts flame. Instinctively she recoiled into Welsh, though she had already revealed how well she could follow what was said around her in English, and the chief reason for her reticence concerning her knowledge had been cruelly removed. 'Not so strong a motive as *you* had, Father Prior! Every soul in this parish knows what store you set upon getting Saint Winifred away from us, what glory it will be to your abbey, and above all, to you. And who stood in your way but my father? *Yours*, not the saint's! Show me a better reason for wanting him dead! Did any ever wish to lift hand against him, all these years! Until *you* came here with your quest for Winifred's relics? Engelard's disagreement with my father was constant and understood, yours was new and urgent. Our need could wait, we're young. Yours could not wait. And who knew better than you at what hour my father would be coming through the forest to Gwytherin? Or that he would not change his mind?'

Father Huw spread a horrified hand to hush her long before this, but she would not be hushed. 'Child, child, you must not make such dreadful accusations against the reverend prior, it is mortal sin.'

'I state facts, and let them speak,' snapped Sioned. 'Where's the offence in that? Prior Robert may point out the facts that suit him, I show you the others, those that do not suit him. My father was the sole obstacle in his path, and my father has been removed.'

'Child, I tell you every soul in this valley knew that your father was coming to my house, and the hour of his coming, and many would know all the possible ways, far better than any of these good brethren from Shrewsbury. The occasion might well suit another grudge. And you must know that Prior Robert has been with me, and with Brother Richard and Brother Cadfael here, ever since morning Mass.' And Father Huw turned in agitated supplication to Robert, wringing his hands. 'Father Prior, I beg you, do not hold it against the girl that she speaks so wildly. She is in great grief—a father lost. . . . You cannot wonder if she turns on us all.'

'I say no word of blame,' said the prior, though coldly. 'I gather she is casting doubts upon myself and my companions, but doubtless you have answered her. Tell the young woman, in my name, that both you and others here can witness for my own person, for all this day I have been within your sight.'

Grateful for at least one certainty, Huw turned to repeat as much to Sioned yet again, but she blazed back with biting promptness and force, forgetting all restraints in the need to confront Robert face to face, without the tedious intervention of interpreters. 'So you may have been, Father Prior,' she flashed in plain English. 'In any case I don't see *you* as likely to make a good bowman. But a man who would try to buy my father's compliance would be willing and able to buy some more pliable person to do even this work for him. You still had your purse! Rhisiart spurned it!'

'Take care!' thundered Robert, galled beyond the limits of his arduous patience. 'You put your soul in peril! I have borne with you thus far, making allowances for your grief, but go no further along this road!'

They were staring upon each other like adversaries in the lists before the baton falls, he very tall and rigid and chill as ice, she slight and ferocious and very handsome, her coif long ago lost among the bushes, and her sheaves of black hair loose on her shoulders. And at that moment, before she could spit further fire, or he threaten more imminent damnation, they all heard voices approaching from higher up among the woods, a man's voice and a girl's in quick, concerned exchanges, and coming rapidly nearer with a light threshing of branches, as though they had caught the raised tones and threatening sounds of many people gathered here improbably deep in the forest, and were hurrying to discover what was happening.

The two antagonists heard them, and their concentration on each other was shaken and disrupted. Sioned knew them, and a fleeting shadow of fear and desperation passed over her face. She glanced round wildly, but there was no help. A girl's arm parted the bushes above the oval where they stood, and Annest stepped through, and stood in astonishment, gazing round at the inexplicable gathering before her.

It was the narrowness of the track—no more than the shadow of a deer-path in the grass—and the abruptness with which she had halted that gave Sioned her one chance. She took it valiantly. 'Go back home, Annest,' she said loudly. 'I am coming with company. Go and prepare for guests, quickly, you'll have little time.' Her voice was high and urgent. Annest had not yet lowered her eyes to the ground, and grass and shadows veiled Rhisiart's body.

The effort was wasted. Another hand, large and gentle, was laid on Annest's shoulder while she hesitated, and moved her aside. 'The company sounds somewhat loud and angry,' said a man's voice, high and clear, 'so, with your leave, Sioned, we'll all go together.'

Engelard put the girl aside between his hands, as familiarly and serenely as a brother might have done, and stepped past her into the clearing.

He had eyes for no one but Sioned, he walked towards her with the straight gait of a proprietor, and as he came he took in her stiff erectness, and fixed face of fire and ice and despair, and his own face mirrored everything he saw in her. His brows drew together, his smile, taut and formidable to begin with, vanished utterly, his eyes burned bluer than cornflowers. He passed by Prior Robert as though he had not even been there, or not alive, a stock, a dead tree by the path. He put out his hands, and Sioned laid her hands in them, and for an instant closed her eyes. There was no frowning him away now, he was here in the midst, quite without defences. The circle, not all inimical but all hampering, was closing round him.

He had her by the hands when he saw Rhisiart's body.

The shock went into him as abruptly as the arrow must have gone into Rhisiart, stopping him instantly. Cadfael had him well in view, and saw his lips part and whisper soundlessly: 'Christ aid!' What followed was most eloquent. The Saxon youth moved with loving slowness, shutting both Sioned's hands into one of his, and with his freed right hand stroked softly over her hair, down temple and cheek and chin and throat, all with such mastered passion that she was soothed, as he meant, while he had barely stopped shaking from the shock.

He folded an arm about her, holding her close against his side, and slowly looked all round the circle of watching faces, and slowly down at the body of his lord. His face was bleakly angry.

'Who did this?'

He looked round, seeking the one who by rights should be spokesman, hesitating between Prior Robert, who arrogated to himself authority wherever he came, and Father Huw, who was known and trusted here. He repeated his demand in English, but neither of them answered him, and for a long moment neither did anyone else. Then Sioned said, with clear, deliberate warning: 'There are some here are saying that *you* did.'

'I?' he cried, astonished and scornful rather than alarmed, and turned sharply to search her face, which was intent and urgent.

Her lips shaped silently: 'Run! They're blaming you!'

It was all she could do, and he understood, for they had such a link between them that meanings could be exchanged in silence, in a look. He measured with a quick glance the number of his possible enemies, and the spaces between them, but he did not move. 'Who accuses me?' he said. 'And on what ground? It seems to me I might rather question all of you, whom I find standing here about my lord's dead body, while I have been all day out with the cows, beyond Bryn. When I got home Annest was anxious because Sioned had not returned, and the sheep boy told her there was no service at Vespers at the church. We came out to look for you, and found you by the noise you were making among you. And I ask again, and I will know before ever I give up: *Who did this?*'

'We are all asking that,' said Father Huw. 'Son, there's no man here has accused you. But there are things that give us the right to question you, and a man with nothing on his conscience won't be ashamed or afraid to answer. Have you yet looked carefully at the arrow that struck Rhisiart down? Then look at it now!'

Frowning, Engelard drew a step nearer, and looked indeed, earnestly and bitterly at the dead man, only afterwards at the arrow. He saw the flutter of deep blue, and gasped.

'This is one of mine!' He looked up with wild suspicion at them all. 'Either that, or someone has copied my mark. But no, this is mine, I know the trim, I fletched it new only a week or so ago.'

'He owns it his?' demanded Robert, following as best he could. 'He admits it?'

'Admit?' flashed Engelard in English. 'What is there to admit? I *say* it! How it was brought here, who loosed it, I know no more than you do, but I know the shaft for mine. God's teeth!' he cried furiously, 'do you think if I had any hand in this villainy should leave my mark flaunting in the wound? Am I fool as well as outlander? And do you think I would do anything to harm Rhisiart? The man who stood my friend and gave me the means of living here when I'd poached myself out of Cheshire?'

'He refused to consider you as a suitor for his daughter,' Bened said almost reluctantly, 'whatever good he did for you otherwise.'

'So he did, and according to his lights, rightly so. And I know it, knowing as much as I've learned of Wales, and even if I did smart under it, I knew he had reason and custom on his side. Never has he done anything I could complain of as unfair to me. He stood much arrogance and impatience from me, come to that. There isn't a man in Gwynedd I like and respect more. I'd as soon have cut my own throat as injured Rhisiart.'

'He knew and knows it,' said Sioned, 'and so do I.'

'Yet the arrow is yours,' said Huw unhappily. 'And as for reclaiming or disguising it, it may well have been that speedy flight after such an act would be more important.'

'If I had planned such an act,' said Engelard, 'though God forbid I should ever have to imagine a thing so vile, I could as easily have done what some devil has done now to me, and used another man's shaft.'

'But, son, it would be more in keeping with your nature,' the priest pursued sadly, 'to commit such a deed without planning, having with you only your own bow and arrows. Another approach, another quarrel, a sudden wild rage! No one supposes this was plotted beforehand.'

'I had no bow with me all this day. I was busy with the cattle, what should I want with a bow?'

'It will be for the royal bailiff to enquire into all possible matters concerning this case,' said Prior Robert, resolutely reclaiming the dominance among them. 'What should be asked at once of this young man is where he has been all this day, what doing, and in whose company.'

'In no man's company. The byres behind Bryn are in a lonely place, good pasture but apart from the used roads. Two cows dropped their calves today, one around noon, the second not before late afternoon, and that was a hard birth, and gave me trouble. But the young things are there alive and on their legs now, to testify to what I've been doing.'

'You left Rhisiart at his fields along the way?'

'I did, and went straight on to my own work. And have not seen him again until now.'

'And did you speak with any man, there at the byres? Can anyone testify as to where you were, at any time during the day?' No one was likely to try and wrest the initiative from Robert now. Engelard looked round him quickly, measuring chances. Annest came forward silently, and took her stand beside Sioned. Brother John's roused, anxious eyes followed her progress, and approved the loyalty which had no other way of expressing itself.

'Engelard did not come home until half an hour ago,' she said stoutly.

'Child,' said Father Huw wretchedly, 'where he was not does not in any way confirm where he says he was. Two calves may be delivered far more quickly than he claims, how can we know, who were not there? He had time to slip back here and do this thing, and be back with his cattle and never noticed. Unless we can find someone who testifies to having seen him elsewhere, at whatever time this deed may have been done, then I fear we should hold Engelard in safe-keeping until the prince's bailiff can take over the charge for us.'

The men of Gwytherin hovered, murmuring, some convinced, many angry, for Rhisiart had been very well liked, some hesitant, but granting that the outlander ought to be held until his innocence was established or his guilt proved. They shifted and closed, and their murmur became one of consent.

'It is fair,' said Bened, and the growl of assent answered him.

'One lone Englishman with his back to the wall,' whispered Brother John indignantly in Cadfael's ear, 'and what chance will he have, with nobody to bear out what he says? And plain truth, for certain! Does he act or speak like a murderer?'

Peredur had stood like a stock all this while, hardly taking his eyes from Engelard's face but to gaze earnestly and unhappily at Sioned. As Prior Robert levelled an imperious arm at Engelard, and the whole assembly closed in slowly in obedience, braced to lay hands on him, Peredur drew a little further back at the edge of the trees, and Cadfael saw him catch Sioned's eye, flash her a wild, wide-eyed look, and jerk his head as though beckoning. Out of her exhaustion and misery she roused a brief, answering blaze, and leaned to whisper rapidly in Engelard's ear.

'Do your duty, all of you,' commanded Robert, 'to your laws and your prince and your church, and lay hold of this man!'

There was one instant of stillness, and then they closed in all together, the only gap in their ranks where Peredur still hung back. Engelard made a long leap from Sioned's side, as though he would break for the thickest screen of bushes, and then, instead, caught up a dead, fallen bough that lay in the grass, and whirled it about him in a flailing circle, laying two unwary elders flat, and sending others reeling back out of range. Before they could reassemble, he had changed direction, leaped over one of the fallen, and was clean through the midst of them, arming off the only one who almost got a grip on him, and made straight for the gap Peredur had left in their ranks. Father Huw's voice, uplifted in vexed agitation, called on Peredur to halt him, and Peredur sprang to intercept his flight. How it happened was never quite clear, though Brother Cadfael had a rough idea, but at the very moment when his outstretched hand almost brushed Engelard's sleeve, Peredur stepped upon a rotten branch in the turf, that snapped under his foot and rolled, tossing him flat on his face, half-blinded among the bushes. And winded, possibly, for certainly he made no move to pick himself up until Engelard was past him and away.

Even then it was not quite over, for the nearest pursuers on either side, seeing how the hunt had turned, had also begun to run like hares, on courses converging with the fugitive's at the very edge of the clearing. From the left came a long-legged villein of Cadwallon's, with a stride like a greyhound, and from the right Brother John, his habit flying, his sandalled feet pounding the earth mightily. It was perhaps the first time Brother John had ever enjoyed Prior Robert's whole-hearted approval. It was certainly the last.

There was no one left in the race but these three, and fleet though Engelard was, it seemed that the long-legged fellow would collide with him before he could finally vanish. All three were hurtling together for a shattering collision, or so it seemed. The villein stretched out arms as formidably long as his legs. So, on the other side, did Brother John. A great hand closed on a thin fold of Engelard's tunic from one side. Brother John bounded exuberantly in from the other. The prior sighed relief, expecting the prisoner to be enfolded in a double embrace. And Brother John, diving, caught Cadwallon's villein round the knees and brought him crashing to the ground, and Engelard, plucking his tunic out of the enemy's grasp, leaped into the bushes and vanished in a receding susurration of branches, until silence and stillness closed over the path of his withdrawal.

Half the hunt, out of excitement rather than any real enmity, streamed away into the forest after the quarry, but half-heartedly now. They had little chance of capturing him. Probably they had no great desire to do anything of the kind, though once put to it, hounds must follow a scent. The real drama remained behind in the clearing. There, at least, justice had one clear culprit to enjoy.

Brother John unwound his arms from his victim's knees, sat up in the grass, fended off placidly a feeble blow the villein aimed at him, and said in robust but incomprehensible English: 'Ah, let well alone, lad! What did he ever do to you? But faith, I'm sorry I had to fetch you down so heavily. If you think you're hard-done-to, take comfort! I'm likely to pay dearer than you.'

He looked round him complacently enough as he clambered to his feet and dusted off the debris of leaves and twigs that clung to his habit. There stood Prior Robert, not yet unfrozen from the shock of incredulous disillusionment, tall and stiff and grey, a Norman lordling debating terrible penalties for treason. But there, also, stood Sioned, tired, distraught, worn out with passion, but with a small, reviving glow in her eyes, and there was Annest at her elbow, an arm protectively round her waist, but her flower-face turned towards John. Not much use Robert thundering and lightning, while she so smiled and blossomed, beaming her gratitude and admiration.

Brother Richard and Brother Jerome loomed like messengers of doom, one at either elbow. 'Brother John, you are summoned. You are in gross offence.'

He went with them resignedly. For all the threatening thunder-bolts he had never felt freer in his life. And having now nothing to lose but his own self-respect, he was sturdily determined not to sacrifice that.

'Unfaithful and unworthy brother,' hissed Prior Robert, towering in terrible indignation, 'what have you done? Do not deny what we have all witnessed. You have not merely connived at the escape of a felon, you have frustrated the attempt of a loyal servant to arrest him. You felled that good man deliberately, to let Engelard go free. Traitor against church and law, you have put yourself beyond the pale. If there is anything you can say in your defence, say it now.'

'I thought the lad was being harried beyond reason, on very suspect suspicion,' said Brother John boldly. 'I've talked with Engelard, I've got my own view of him, a decent, open soul who'd never do violence to any man by stealth, let alone Rhisiart, whom he liked and valued high. I don't believe he has any part in this death, and what's more, I think he'll not go far until he knows who had, and God help the murderer then! So I gave him his chance, and good luck to him!'

The two girls, their heads close together in women's solidarity, interpreted the tone for themselves, if they lacked the words, and glowed in silent applause. Prior Robert was helpless, though he did not know it. Brother Cadfael knew it very well.

'Shameless!' thundered Robert, bristling until even his suave purity showed knife-edged with affront. 'You are condemned out of your own mouth, and a disgrace to our order. I have no jurisdiction here as regards Welsh law. The prince's bailiff must resolve this crime that cries for vengeance here. But where my own subordinates are concerned, and where they have infringed the law of this land where we are guests, there two disciplines threaten you, Brother John. As to the sovereignty of Gwynedd, I cannot speak. As to my own discipline, I can and do. You are set far beyond mere ecclesiastical penance. I consign you to close imprisonment until I can confer with the secular authority here, and I refuse to you, meanwhile, all the comforts and consolations of the church.' He looked about him and took thought, brooding. Father Huw hovered miserably, lost in this ocean of complaints and accusations. 'Brother Cadfael, ask Father Huw where there is a safe prison, where he can be held.'

This was more than Brother John had bargained for, and though he repented of nothing, like a practical man he did begin to look round to weigh up the chances of evading the consequences. He eyed the gaps in the ring as Engelard had done, braced his sturdy feet well apart, and flexed his shoulders experimentally, as though he had thoughts of elbowing Brother Richard smartly in the belly, kicking the legs from under Jerome, and making a dash for freedom. He stopped himself just in time when he heard Cadfael report sedately: 'Father Huw suggests there is only one place secure enough. If Sioned is willing to allow her holding to be used, a prisoner could be safe enough there.'

At this point Brother John unaccountably lost interest in immediate escape.

'My house is at Prior Robert's disposal,' said Sioned in Welsh, with appropriate coldness, but very promptly. She had herself well in hand, she made no more lapses into English. 'There are storehouses and stables, if you wish to use them. I promise I shall not go near the prisoner, or hold the key to his prison myself. Father Prior may choose his guard from among my people as he sees fit. My household shall provide him his living, but even that charge I shall give to someone else. If I undertook it myself I fear my impartiality might be doubted, after what has happened.'

A good girl, Cadfael thought, translating this for Robert's benefit rather less than for John's. Clever enough to step resolutely round any actual lies even when she was thus wrung by one disaster after another, and generous enough to think for the wants and wishes of others. The someone else who would be charged with seeing Brother John decently housed and fed was standing cheek to cheek with her mistress as she spoke, fair head against dark head. A formidable pair! But they might not have found this unexpected and promising path open to them but for the innocence of celibate parish priests.

'That may be the best plan,' said Prior Robert, chilly but courteous, 'and I thank you for your dutiful offer, daughter. Keep him straitly, see he has what he needs for life, but no more. He is in great peril of his soul, his body may somewhat atone. If you permit, we will go before and bestow him securely, and let your uncle know what has happened, so that he may send down to you and bring you home. I will not intrude longer on a house of mourning.'

'I will show you the way,' said Annest, stepping demurely from Sioned's side.

'Hold him fast!' warned the prior, as they massed to follow her uphill through the woods. Though he might have seen for himself, had he looked closely, that the culprit's resignation had mellowed into something very like complacency, and he stepped out as briskly as his guards, a good deal more intent on keeping Annest's slender waist and lithe shoulders in sight than on any opportunity for escape.

Well, thought Cadfael, letting them go without him, and

turning to meet Sioned's steady gaze, God sort all! As doubtless he is doing, now as ever!

The men of Gwytherin cut young branches and made a green litter to carry Rhisiart's body home. Under the corpse, when they lifted it, there was much more blood than about the frontal wound, though the point of the arrow barely broke through skin and clothing. Cadfael would have liked to examine tunic and wound more closely, but forbore because Sioned was there beside him, stiffly erect in her stony grief, and nothing, no word or act that was not hieratic and ceremonial, was permissible then in her presence. Moreover, soon all the servants of Rhisiart's household came down in force to bring their lord home, while the steward waited at the gate with bards and mourning women to welcome him back for the last time, and this was no longer an enquiry into guilt, but the first celebration of a great funeral rite, in which probing would have been indecent. No hope of enquiring further tonight. Even Prior Robert had acknowledged that he must remove himself and his fellows reverently from a mourning community in which they had no rights.

When it was time to raise the litter and its burden, now stretched out decently with his twisted legs drawn out straight and his hands laid quietly at his sides, Sioned looked round for one more to whom she meant to confide a share in this honourable load. She did not find him.

'Where is Peredur? What became of him?'

No one had seen him go, but he was gone. No one had had attention to spare for him after Brother John had completed what Peredur had begun. He had slipped away without a word, as though he had done something to be ashamed of, something for which he might expect blame rather than thanks. Sioned was a little hurt, even in her greater hurt, at his desertion.

'I thought he would have wanted to help me bring my father home. He was a favourite with him, and fond of him. From a little boy he was in and out of our house like his own.'

'He maybe doubted his welcome,' said Cadfael, 'after saying a word that displeased you concerning Engelard.'

'And doing a thing afterwards that more than wiped that out?' she said, but for his ears only. No need to say outright before everyone what she knew very well, that Peredur had contrived a way out for her lover. 'No, I don't understand why he should slink away without a word, like this.' But she said no more then, only begged him with a look to walk with her as she fell in behind the litter. They went some distance in silence. Then she asked, without looking aside at him: 'Did my father yet tell you those things he had to tell?'

'Some,' said Cadfael. 'Not all.'

'Is there anything I should do, or not do? I need to know. We must make him seemly tonight.' By the morrow he would be stiff, and she knew it. 'If you need anything from me, tell me now.'

'Keep me the clothes he's wearing, when you take them off him, and take note for me where they're damp from this morning's rain, and where they're dry. If you notice anything strange, remember it. Tomorrow, as soon as I can, I'll come to you.'

'I must know the truth,' she said. 'You know why.'

'Yes, I know. But tonight sing him and drink to him, and never doubt but he'll hear the singing.'

'Yes,' she said, and loosed a great, renewing sigh. 'You are a good man. I'm glad you're here. You do not believe it was Engelard.'

'I'm as good as certain it was not. First and best, it isn't in him. Lads like Engelard hit out in a passion, but with their fists, not with weapons. Second, if it had been in his scope, he'd have made a better job of it. You saw the angle of the arrow. Engelard, I judge, is the breadth of three fingers taller than your father. How could he shoot an arrow under a man's rib-cage who is shorter than he, even from lower ground? Even if he kneeled or crouched in the undergrowth in ambush, I doubt if it could be done. And why should it ever be tried? No, this is folly. And to say that the best shot in all these parts could not put his shaft clean through his man, at any distance there where he could see him? Not more than fifty yards clear in any direction. Worse folly still, why should a good bowman choose such a blind tangled place? They have not looked at the ground, or they could not put forward such foolishness. But first and last and best, that young man of yours is too open and honest to kill by stealth, even a man he hated. And he did not hate Rhisiart. You need not tell me, I know it.'

Much of what he had said might well have been hurtful to her, but none of it was. She went with him every step of that way, and flushed and warmed into her proper, vulnerable girlhood at hearing her lover thus accepted.

'You've said no word in wonder,' she said, 'that I have not been more troubled over what has become of Engelard, and where he is gone to earth now.'

'No,' said Cadfael, and smiled. 'You know where he is, and how to get in touch with him whenever you need. I think you two have two or three places better for secrecy than your oak tree, and in one of them Engelard is resting now, or soon will be. You seem to think he'll be safe enough. Tell me nothing, unless you need a messenger, or help.'

'You can be my messenger, if you will, to another,' she said. They were emerging from the forest at the edge of Rhisiart's home fields, and Prior Robert stood tall and grim and noncommittal aside from their path, his companions discreetly disposed behind him, his hands, features, and the angle of his gently bowed head all disposed to convey respect for death and compassion for the bereaved without actually owning to forgiveness of the dead. His prisoner was safely lodged, he was waiting only to collect the last stray from his flock, and make an appropriately impressive exit. 'Tell Peredur I missed him from among those my father would have liked to carry him home. Tell him what he did was generous, and I am grateful. I am sorry he should ever have doubted it.'

They were approaching the gate, and Uncle Meurice, the steward, came out to meet them with his kindly, soft-lined face quaking and shapeless with shock and distress.

'And come tomorrow,' said Sioned on an almost soundless breath, and walked away from him alone, and entered the gateway after her father's body.

CHAPTER SIX

Sioned's message might not have been delivered so soon, for it would not have been any easy matter to turn aside at Cadwallon's house, without a word of request or excuse to Prior Robert; but in the dimness of the woods, a little above the holding, Cadfael caught a glimpse of a figure withdrawing from them, with evident intent, some fifty yards into cover, and knew it for Peredur. He had not expected to be followed, for he went only far enough to be secure from actual encounter on the path, and there sat down moodily on a fallen trunk, his back against a young tree that leaned with him, and kicked one foot in the litter of last year's leaves. Cadfael asked no permission, but went after him.

Peredur looked up at the sound of other feet rustling the beech-mast, and rose as if he would have removed further to avoid speech, but then gave up the thought, and stood mute and unwelcoming, but resigned.

'I have a word to you,' said Brother Cadfael mildly, 'from Sioned. She bade me tell you that she missed you when she would gladly have asked you to lend a shoulder for her father's bier. She sends you word that what you did was generous, and she is grateful.'

Peredur stirred his feet uneasily, and drew a little back into deeper shadow.

'There were plenty of her own people there,' he said, after a pause that seemed awkward rather than sullen. 'She had no need of me.'

'Oh, there were hands enough, and shoulders enough,' agreed Cadfael, 'nevertheless, she missed you. It seems to me that she looks upon you as one having a forward place among her own people. You have been like a brother to her from children, and she could well do with a brother now.'

The stiffness of Peredur's young body was palpable even in the green dusk, a constraint that crippled even his tongue. He got out, with a bitter spurt of laughter: 'It was not her brother I wanted to be.'

'No, that I understand. Yet you behaved like one, towards her and towards Engelard, when it came to the testing.'

What was meant to comfort and compliment appeared, instead, to hurt. Peredur shrank still deeper into his morose stillness. 'So she feels she has a debt to me, and wants to pay it but not for my sake. She does not want *me*.'

'Well,' said Cadfael equably, 'I have delivered her message, and if you'll go to her she'll convince you, as I cannot. There was another would have wanted you there, if he could have spoken.'

'Oh, hush!' said Peredur, and jerked his head aside with a motion of sudden pain. 'Don't say more....'

'No, pardon me, I know this is a grief to you, as well as to her. She said so. "He was a favourite with him," she said, "and fond of him—"'

The boy gave a sharp gasp, and turning with blundering haste, walked away rapidly through the trees, deeper into the wood, and left Brother Cadfael to return very thoughtfully to his companions, with the feel of that unbearably tender spot still wincing under his probing finger.

'You and I,' said Bened, when Cadfael walked down to the smithy after Compline, 'must do our drinking alone tonight, my friend. Huw has not yet come down from Rhisiart's hall, and Padrig will be busy singing the dead man till the small hours. Well that he was there at this time. A man's all the better for being sung to his grave by a fine poet and harpist, and it's a great thing for his children to remember. And Cai—Cai we shan't be seeing down here much for a while, not until the bailiff comes to take his prisoner off his hands.'

'You mean Brother John has *Cai* for his gaoler?' asked Cadfael, enlightened.

'He volunteered for the job. I fancy that girl of mine ran and prompted him, but he wouldn't need much prodding. Between them, Brother John will be lying snug enough for a day or two. You need not worry about him.'

'Nothing was further from my mind,' said Cadfael. 'And it's Cai who keeps the key on him?'

'You may be sure. And what with Prince Owain being away in the south, as I hear he is, I doubt if sheriff or bailiff will have much time to spare for a small matter of insubordination in Gwytherin.' Bened sighed heavily over his horn, filled this time with coarse red wine. 'It grieves me now that ever I spoke up and called attention to the blue on the feathers, at least in front of the lass. But someone would have said it. And it's truth that now, with only her Uncle Meurice as guardian, she could have got her own way. She twists him round her finger, he wouldn't have stood in her road. But now I misdoubt me, no man would be such a fool as to leave his private mark on a dead man for all to see. Not unless he was disturbed and had to take to his heels. All it needed was the corner clipping, how long does that take if you've a knife on you? No, it's hard to understand. And yet it could be so!'

By his deep gloom there was more on Bened's mind than that. Somewhere within, he was in abysmal doubt whether he had not spoken up in the hope of having a better chance with Sioned himself if his most favoured rival was removed. He shook his head sadly. 'I was glad when he broke clear as he did, but I'll be satisfied if he makes his way back to Cheshire after this alarm. And yet it's hard to think of him as a murderer.'

'We might give our minds to that, if you're willing,' said Cadfael, 'for you know the people of these parts better than I do. Let's own it, the girl's suspicion, that she spoke out to Prior Robert's face, will be what many a one here is thinking, whether he says it or not. Here are we come into the place and starting a great contention, chiefly with this one lord—no need to argue who's in the right—and there he stands as the one obstacle to what we've come for, and suddenly he's dead, murdered. What's more natural than to point the finger at us, all of us?'

'It's blasphemy even to consider such a charge against such reverend brothers,' said Bened, shocked.

'Kings and abbots are also men, and can fall to temptation. So how do we all stand in regard to this day's doings? All six of us were together or close within sight of one another until after Mass. Then Prior Robert, Brother Richard and I were with Father Huw, first in the orchard, and when it rained, half an hour before noon, in the house. None of the four of us could have gone into the forest. Brother John, too, was about the house and holding, Marared can vouch for him as well as we. The only one who left, before we all came forth for Vespers and set off to search for Rhisiart, was Brother Richard, who offered to go and see if he could meet with him or get word of him, and was gone perhaps an hour and a half, and came back empty-handed. From an hour after noon he was gone, and into the forest, too, for what it's worth, and makes no claim to have spoken with anyone until he enquired at Cadwallon's gate on his way back, which would be nearing half past two. I must speak with the gate-keeper, and see if he bears that out. Two of us are left, but not unaccounted for. Brother Jerome and Brother Columbanus were sent off to keep a vigil together at Saint Winifred's chapel, to pray for a peaceful agreement. We all saw them set off together, and they'd be in the chapel and on their knees long before ever Rhisiart came down towards the path. And there they stayed until Father Huw's messenger went to fetch them to join us. Each of them is warranty for the other.'

'I said so,' said Bened, reassured. 'Holy men do not do murder.'

'Man,' said Cadfael earnestly, 'there are as holy persons outside orders as ever there are in, and not to trifle with truth, as good men out of the Christian church as most I've met within it. In the Holy Land I've known Saracens I'd trust before the common run of the crusaders, men honourable, generous and courteous, who would have scorned to haggle and jostle for place and trade as some of our allies did. Meet every man as you find him, for we're all made the same under habit or robe or rags. Some better made than others, and some better cared for, but on the same pattern all. But there it is. As far as I can see, only one of us, Brother Richard, had any chance at all to be in the neighbourhood when Rhisiart was killed, and of all of us he makes the least likely murderer. So we're forced to look if the ground is not wide open for others, and Saint Winifred only an opportunity and an excuse. Had Rhisiart any enemies around Gwytherin? Some who might never have moved against him if we had not blown up this storm and put the temptation in their way?'

Bened considered gravely, nursing his wine. 'I wouldn't say there's a man anywhere who has not someone to wish him ill, but it's a far cry from that to murder. Time was when Father Huw himself came up against Rhisiart over a patch of land both claimed, and tempers ran high, but they settled it the proper way, by witness from the neighbours, and there's been no malice after. And there have been lawsuits—did you ever hear of a Welsh landholder without one or two lawsuits in hand? One with Rhys ap Cynan over a disputed boundary, one over some beasts that strayed. Nothing to make lasting bad blood. We thrive on suits at law. One thing's true, with the interest you've roused here, every soul for miles around knew that Rhisiart was due at Father Huw's parsonage at noon. No limit at all, there, on who might have decided to waylay him on the road.'

That was as far as they could get. The field was wide, wide enough still to include Engelard, however persuaded Cadfael might be that he was incapable of such an act. Wide enough to enfold even neighbours like Cadwallon, villeins from the village, servants of the household.

But not, surely, thought Brother Cadfael, making his way back to Huw's loft in the green and fragrant dark, not that strange young man who had been a favourite of Rhisiart, and fond of him, and in and out of his house like a son from childhood? The young man who had said of Engelard, and of himself, that a man might step far aside even from his own nature, for love, and then, presumably for love, had opened a way for Engelard to escape, as Cadfael had seen for himself. And who was now avoiding Sioned's gratitude and affection, either because it was not love, and love was the only thing he wanted from her, or for some darker reason. When he flung away in silence into the forest he had had the look of one pursued by a demon. But surely not *that* demon? So far from furthering his chances, Rhisiart's death robbed him of his most staunch ally, who had waited patiently and urged constantly, to bring his daughter to the desired match in the end. No, whichever way a man looked at him, Peredur remained mysterious and disturbing.

Father Huw did not come back from Rhisiart's house that night. Brother Cadfael lay alone in the loft, and mindful that Brother John was locked up somewhere in Sioned's barns, and there was no one to prepare food, got up in good time and went to do it himself, and then set off to Bened's paddock to see to the horses, who were also left without a groom. It suited him better to be out and working in the fresh morning than cooped up with Prior Robert, but he was obliged to return in time for chapter, which the prior had decreed should be held daily as at home, however brief the business they had to transact here.

They met in the orchard, the five of them, Prior Robert presiding in as solemn dignity as ever. Brother Richard read out the saints to be celebrated that day and the following day. Brother Jerome composed his wiry person into his usual shape of sycophantic reverence, and made all the appropriate responses. But it seemed to Cadfael that Brother Columbanus looked unusually withdrawn and troubled, his full blue eyes veiled. The contrast between his athletic build and fine, autocratic head, and his meek and anxious devoutness of feature and bearing, was always confusing to the observer, but that morning his extreme preoccupation with some inward crisis of real or imagined sin made it painful to look at him. Brother Cadfael sighed, expecting another falling fit like the one that had launched them all on this quest. Who knew what this badly-balanced half-saint, half-idiot would do next?

'Here we have but one business in hand,' said Prior Robert firmly, 'and we shall pursue it as in duty bound. I mean to press more resolutely than ever for our right to take up the relics of the saint, and remove them to Shrewsbury. But we must admit, at this moment, that we have not so far been successful in carrying the people with us. I had great hopes yesterday that all would be resolved. We made every reverent preparation to deserve success. . . .'

At this point he was interrupted by an audible sob from Brother Columbanus, that drew all eyes to that young man. Trembling and meek, he rose from his place and stood with lowered eyes and folded hands before Robert.

'Father Prior, alas, *mea culpa!* I am to blame! I have been unfaithful, and I desire to make confession. I came to chapter determined to cleanse my bosom and ask penance, for my backsliding is the cause of our continued distresses. May I speak?'

I knew there was something brewing, thought Brother Cadfael, resigned and disgusted. But at least without rolling on the ground and biting the grass, this time!

'Speak out,' said the prior, not unkindly. 'You have never sought to make light of your failings, I do not think you need fear our too harsh condemnation. You have been commonly your own sternest judge.' So he had, but that, well handled, can be one way of evading and forestalling the judgments of others.'

Brother Columbanus sank to his knees in the orchard turf. And very comely and aristocratic he looked, Cadfael admitted, again admiring with surprise the compact grace and strength of his body, and the supple flow of his movements.

'Father, you sent me with Brother Jerome, yesterday, to keep vigil in the chapel, and pray earnestly for a good outcome, in amity and peace. Father, we came there in good time, before eleven, as I judge, and having eaten our meal, we went in and took our places, for there are prayer-desks within, and the altar is kept clean and well-tended. Oh, Father, my will to keep vigil was good, but the flesh was weak. I had not been half an hour kneeling in prayer, when I fell asleep on my arms on the desk, to my endless shame. It is no excuse that I have slept badly and thought much since we came here. Prayer should fix and purify the mind. I slept, and our cause was weakened. I must have slept all the afternoon, for the next thing I remember is

Brother Jerome shaking me by the shoulder and telling me there was a messenger calling us to go with him.'

He caught his breath, and a frantic tear rolled down his cheek, circling the bold, rounded Norman bone. 'Oh, do not look askance at Brother Jerome, for he surely never knew I had been sleeping, and there is no blame at all to him for not observing and reporting my sin. I awoke as he touched me, and arose and went with him. He thought me as earnest in prayer as he, and knew no wrong.'

Nobody, probably, had thought of looking askance at Brother Jerome until then, but Cadfael was probably the quickest and most alert, and the only one who caught the curious expression of apprehension, fading rapidly into complacency, that passed over Brother Jerome's normally controlled countenance. Jerome had not been pursuing the same studies as Cadfael, or he would have been far from complacent. For Brother Columbanus in his self-absorbed innocence had just removed all certainty that Jerome had spent the previous noon and afternoon motionless in Saint Winifred's chapel, praying for a happy solution. His only guarantor had been fast asleep throughout. He could have sauntered out and gone anywhere he chose.

'Son,' said Prior Robert, in an indulgent voice he would certainly never have used to Brother John, 'your fault is human, and frailty is in our nature. And you redeem your own error, in defending your brother. Why did you not tell us of this yesterday?'

'Father, how could I? There was no opportunity, before we learned of Rhisiart's death. Thus burdened, how could I burden you further at that time? I kept it for this chapter, the right place for erring brothers to receive their penance, and make their abasement. As I do abase myself, as all unworthy the vocation I chose. Speak out sentence on me, for I desire penance.'

The prior was opening his lips to give judgment, patiently enough, for such devout submission and awareness of guilt disarmed him, when they were distracted by the clap of the wooden bar of the garden gate, and there was Father Huw himself advancing across the grass towards them, hair and beard even more disordered than usual, and his eyes heavy and tired with sleep-lessness, but his face resolved and calm.

'Father Prior,' he said, halting before them, 'I have just come from holding council with Cadwallon, and Rhys, and Meurice, and all the men of substance in my parish. It was the best oppor-tunity, though I'm sad indeed about the cause. They all came to the mourning for Rhisiart. Every man there knew how he had been struck down, and how such a fate was prophesied. . . .'

'God forbid,' said Prior Robert hastily, 'that I should threaten any man's death. I said that Saint Winifred would be revenged in her own time on the man who stood in the way and did her offence, I never said word of killing.'

'But when he was dead you did claim that this was the saint's vengeance. Every man there heard it, and most believed. I took this chance of conferring with them again in the matter. They do not wish to do anything that is against the will of heaven, nor to give offence to the Benedictine order and the abbey of Shrews-bury. They do not think it right or wise, after what has hap-pened, even to put any man, woman or child of Gwytherin in peril. I am commissioned, Father Prior, to tell you that they withdraw all opposition to your plans. The relics of Saint Winifred are yours to take away with you.'

Prior Robert drew a great breath of triumph and joy, and whatever will he might have had to deal even the lightest punish-ment left him in an instant. It was everything he had hoped for. Brother Columbanus, still kneeling, cast up his eyes radiantly towards heaven and clasped his hands in gratitude, and somehow contrived to look as though he had brought about this desired consummation himself, the deprivation caused by his unfaith-fulness compensated in full by this reward of his penitence. Brother Jerome, just as determined to impress prior and priest with his devotion, threw up his hands and uttered a reverent Latin invocation of praise to God and the saints.

'I am certain,' said Prior Robert magnanimously, 'that the people of Gwytherin never wished to offend, and that they have done wisely and rightly now. I am glad, for them as for my abbey, that we may complete our work here and take our leave in amity with you all. And for your part in bringing about this good ending, Father Huw, we are all grateful. You have done well for your parish and your people.'

'I am bound to tell you,' said Huw honestly, 'that they are not at all happy at losing the saint. But none of them will hinder what you wish. If you so will, we will take you to the burial place today.'

'We will go in procession after the next Mass,' said the prior, unwonted animation lighting up his severe countenance now that he had his own way, 'and not touch food until we have knelt at Saint Winifred's altar and given thanks.' His eyes lit upon Brother Columbanus, patiently kneeling and gazing upon him with doglike eyes, still insistent upon having his sin recognised. Robert looked faintly surprised for a moment, as if he had forgotten the young man's existence. 'Rise, brother, and take heart, for you see that there is forgiveness in the air. You shall not be deprived of your share in the delight of visiting the virgin saint and paying honour to her.'

'And my penance?' insisted the incorrigible penitent. There was a good deal of iron in Brother Columbanus' meekness.

'For penance you shall undertake the menial duties that fell to Brother John, and serve your fellows and their beasts until we return home. But your part in the glory of this day you shall have, and help to bear the reliquary in which the saint's bones are to rest. We'll carry it with us, and set it up before the altar. Every move we make I would have the virgin approve plainly, in all men's sight.'

'And will you break the ground today?' asked Father Huw wearily. No doubt he would be glad to have the whole episode over and forgotten, and be rid of them all, so that Gwytherin could settle again to its age-old business, though short of one good man.

'No,' said Prior Robert after due thought. 'I wish to show forth at every stage our willingness to be guided, and the truth of what we have claimed, that our mission was inspired by Saint Winifred herself. I decree that there shall be three nights of vigil and prayer before the chapel altar, before ever we break the sod, to confirm to all that what we are doing is indeed right and blessed. We are six here, if you will join us, Father Huw. Two by two we will watch nightlong in the chapel, and pray to be guided rightly.'

They took up the silver-inlaid coffin made in implicit faith in Shrewsbury, and carried it in procession up through the woods, past Cadwallon's house, taking the right-hand path that led them obliquely away from the scene of Rhisiart's death, until they came to a small clearing on a hillside, ringed round on three sides by tall, thick clumps of hawthorn, then in snowy bloom. The chapel was of wood, dark with age, small and shadowy within, a tiny bell-turret without a bell leaning over the doorway. Round it the old graveyard lay spread like billowing green skirts, thick with herbs and brambles and tall grasses. By the time they reached this place they had a silent and ever-growing company of local inhabitants following them, curious, submissive, wary. There was no way of telling whether they still felt resentment. Their eyes were steady, observant and opaque, determined to miss nothing and give nothing away.

At the sagging wooden gate that still hung where the path entered, Prior Robert halted, and made the sign of the cross with large, grave gestures. 'Wait here!' he said, when Huw would have led him forward. 'Let us see if prayer can guide my feet, for I have prayed. You shall not show me the saint's grave. I will show it to you, if she will be my aid.'

Obediently they stood and watched his tall figure advance with measured steps, as if he felt his way, the skirts of his habit sweeping through the tangles of grass and flowers. Without hesitation and without haste he made his way to a little, over-grown mound aligned with the east end of the chapel, and sank to his knees at its head.

'Saint Winifred lies here,' he said.

Cadfael thought about it every step of the way, as he went up through the woods that afternoon to Rhisiart's hall. A man could count on Prior Robert to be impressive, but that little miracle had been a master-stroke. The breathless hush, the rippling outbreak of comment and wonder and awe among the men of Gwytherin were with him still. No question but the remotest villein hut and the poorest free holding in the parish would be buzzing with the news by now. The monks of Shrewsbury were vindicated. The saint had taken their prior by the hand and led him to her grave. No, the man had never before been to that place, nor had the grave been marked in any way, by a belated attempt to cut the brambles from it, for instance. It was as it had always been, and yet he had known it from all the rest.

No use at all pointing out, to a crowd swayed by emotion, that if Prior Robert had not previously been to the chapel, Brothers Jerome and Columbanus, his most faithful adherents, had, only the previous day, and with the boy Edwin to guide them, and what more probable than that one of them should have asked the child the whereabouts of the lady they had come all this way to find?

And now, with this triumph already establishing his claim, Robert had given himself three whole days and nights of delay, in which other, similar prodigies might well confirm his ascendancy. A very bold step, but then, Robert was a bold and resourceful man, quite capable of gambling his chances of providing further miracles against any risk of contrary chance refuting him. He meant to leave Gwytherin with what he had come for, but to leave it, if not fully reconciled, then permanently cowed. No scuttling away in haste with his prize of bones, as though still in terror of being thwarted.

But he could not have killed Rhisiart, thought Cadfael with certainty. That I know. Could he have gone so far as to procure . . . ? He considered the possibility honestly, and discarded it. Robert he endured, disliked, and in a fashion admired. At Brother John's age he would have detested him, but Cadfael was old, experienced and grown tolerant.

He came to the gatehouse of Rhisiart's holding, a wattle hut shored into a corner of the palisade fence. The man knew him again from yesterday, and let him in freely. Cai came across the enclosed court to meet him, grinning. All grins here were somewhat soured and chastened now, but a spark of inward mischief survived.

'Have you come to rescue your mate?' asked Cai. 'I doubt he wouldn't thank you, he's lying snug, and feeding like a fighting cock, and no threats of the bailiff yet. *She's* said never a word, you may be sure, and Father Huw would be in no hurry. I reckon we've a couple of days yet, unless your prior makes it his business, where it's none. And if he does, we have boys out will give us plenty of notice before any horseman reaches the gate. Brother John's in good hands.'

It was Engelard's fellow-worker speaking, the man who knew him as well as any in this place. Clearly Brother John had established himself with his gaoler, and Cai's mission was rather to keep the threatening world from him, than to keep him from sallying forth into the world. When the key was needed for the right purpose, it would be provided.

'Take care for your own head,' said Cadfael, though without much anxiety. They knew what they were doing. 'Your prince may have a lawyer's mind, and want to keep in with the Benedictines along the border.'

'Ah, never fret! An escaped felon can be nobody's fault. And everybody's quarry and nobody's prize! Have you never hunted zealously in all the wrong places for something you desired not to find?'

'Say no more,' said Cadfael, 'or I shall have to stop my ears. And tell the lad I never even asked after him, for I know there's no need.'

'Would you be wishing to have a gossip with him?' offered Cai generously. 'He's lodged over yonder in a nice little stable that's clean and empty, and he gets his meals princely, I tell you!'

'Tell me nothing, for I might be asked,' said Cadfael. 'A blind eye and a deaf ear can be useful sometimes. I'll be glad to spend a while with you presently, but now I'm bound to *her*. We have business together.'

Sioned was not in the hall, but in the small chamber curtained off at its end, Rhisiart's private room. And Rhisiart was private there with his daughter, stretched out straight and still on draped furs, on a trestle table, with a white linen sheet covering him. The girl sat beside him, waiting, very formally attired, very grave, her hair austerely braided about her head. She looked older, and taller, now that she was the lady-lord of this holding. But she rose to meet Brother Cadfael with the bright, sad, eager smile of a child sure now of counsel and guidance.

'I looked for you earlier. No matter, I'm glad you're here. I have his clothes for you. I did not fold them; if I had, the damp would have spread evenly through, and now, though they may have dried off, I think you'll still feel a difference.' She brought them, chausses, tunic and shirt, and he took them from her one by one and felt at the cloth testingly. 'I see,' she said, 'that you already know where to feel.'

Rhisiart's hose, though partly covered by the tunic he had worn, were still damp at the back of the thighs and legs, but in front dry, though the damp had spread round through the threads to narrow the dry part to a few inches. His tunic was moist all down the back to the hem, the full width of his shoulders still shaped in a dark patch like spread wings, but all the breast of it, round the dark-rimmed slit the arrow had made, was quite dry. The shirt, though less definitely, showed the same pattern. The fronts of the sleeves were dry, the backs damp. Where the exit wound pierced his back, shirt and tunic were soaked in blood now drying and encrusted.

'You remember,' said Cadfael, 'just how he lay when we found him?'

'I shall remember it my life long,' said Sioned. 'From the hips up flat on his back, but his right hip turned into the grass, and his legs twisted, the left over the right, like. . . .' She hesitated, frowning, feeling for her own half-glimpsed meaning, and found it. 'Like a man who has been lying on his face, and heaves himself over in his sleep on to his back, and sleeps again at once.'

'Or,' said Cadfael, 'like a man who has been taken by the left shoulder, as he lay on his face, and heaved over on to his back. After he was well asleep!'

She gazed at him steadily, with eyes hollow and dark like

wounds. 'Tell me all your thoughts. I need to know. I must know.'

'First, then,' said Brother Cadfael, 'I call attention to the place where this thing happened. A close-set, thicketed place, with plenty of bushes for cover, but not more than fifty paces clear view in any direction. Is that an archer's ground? I think not. Even if he wished the body to be left in woodlands where it might lie undiscovered for hours, he could have found a hundred places more favourable to him. An expert bowman does not need to get close to his quarry, he needs room to draw on a target he can hold in view long enough for a steady aim.'

'Yes,' said Sioned. 'Even if it could be believed of him that he would kill, that rules out Engelard.'

'Not only Engelard, any good bowman, and if someone so incompetent as to need so close a shot tried it, I doubt if he could succeed. I do not like this arrow, it has no place here, and yet here it is. It has one clear purpose, to cast the guilt on Engelard. But I cannot get it out of my head that it has some other purpose, too.'

'To kill!' said Sioned, burning darkly.

'Even that I question, mad though it may seem. See the angle at which it enters and leaves. And then see how the blood is all at the back, and not where the shaft entered. And remember all we have said and noted about his clothes, how they were wet behind, though he lay on his back. And how you yourself said it was the attitude of a man who had heaved himself over from lying on his face. And one more thing I found out yesterday, as I kneeled beside him. Under him the thick grass was wet. But all down by his right side, shoulder to hip and body-wide, it was bone-dry. There was a brisk shower yesterday morning, half an hour of rain. When that rain began, your father was lying on his face, already dead. How else could that patch of grass have remained dry, but sheltered by his body?'

'And then,' said Sioned low but clearly, 'as you say, he was taken by his left shoulder and heaved over on to his back. When he was well asleep. Deep asleep!'

'So it looks to me!'

'But the arrow entered his breast,' she said. 'How, then, could he fall on his face?'

'That we have to find out. Also why he bled behind, and not in front. But lie on his face he did, and that from before the rain began until after it ceased, or the grass beneath him could not have been dry. From half an hour before noon, when the first drops fell, until some minutes past noon, when the sun came out again. Sioned, may I, with all reverence, look closely again now at his body?'

'I know no greater reverence anyone can pay to a murdered man,' she said fiercely, 'than to seek out by all possible means and avenge him on his murder. Yes, handle him if you must. I'll help you. No one else! At least,' she said with a pale and bitter smile, 'you and I are not afraid to touch him, in case he bleeds in accusation against us.'

Cadfael was sharply arrested in the act of drawing down the sheet that covered Rhisiart's body, as though what she had said had put a new and promising idea into his head. 'True! There are not many who do not believe in that trial. Would you say everyone here holds by it?'

'Don't your people believe it? Don't you?' She was astonished. Her eyes rounded like a child's

'My cloister-brothers. . . . Yes, I dare say all or most believe in it. I? Child, I've seen too many slaughtered men handled over and over after a battle by those who finish them off, and never known one of them gush fresh blood, once the life was out of him. But what I believe or don't believe is not to the point. What the murderer believes well may be. No, you have endured enough. Leave him now to me.'

Nevertheless, she did not turn her eyes away, as Cadfael drew off the covering sheet. She must have anticipated the need to examine the body further, for as yet she had left him naked, unshrouded. Washed clean of blood, Rhisiart lay composed and at rest, a thick, powerful trunk brown to the waist, whiter below. The wound under his ribs, an erect slit, now showed ugly and torn, with frayed, bluish lips, though they had done their best to smooth the lacerated flesh together.

'I must turn him,' said Cadfael. 'I need to see the other wound.'

She did not hesitate, but with the tenderness of a mother rather than a daughter she slipped an arm under her father's shoulders, and with her free hand flattened under him from the other side, raised the stiffened corpse until he lay on his right side, his face cradled in the hollow of her arm. Cadfael steadied the stretched-out legs, and leaned to peer closely at the wound high on the left side of the back.

'You would have trouble pulling out the shaft. You had to withdraw it frontally.'

'Yes.' She shook for a moment, for that had been the worst of the ordeal. 'The tip barely broke the skin behind, we had no chance to cut it off. Shame to mangle him so, but what could we do? And yet all that blood!'

The steel point had indeed done little more than puncture the skin, leaving a small, blackened spot, dried blood with a bluish bruise round it. But there was a further mark there, thin and clear and faint. From the black spot the brown line of another upright slit extended, a little longer above the arrow-mark than below, its length in all about as great as the width of Cadfael's thumb-joint, and a faint stain of bruising extending it slightly at either end, beyond where the skin was broken. All that blood—though in fact it was not so very much, though it took Rhisiart's life away with it—had drained out of this thin slit, and not from the wound in his breast, though that now glared, and this lay closed and secret.

'I have done,' said Cadfael gently, and helped her to lay her father at peace again. When they had smoothed even the thick mane of his hair, they covered him again reverently. Then Cadfael told her exactly what he had seen. She watched him with great eyes, and thought for some moments in silence. Then she said: 'I did see this mark you speak of. I could not account for it. If you can, tell me.'

'It was there his life-blood came out,' said Cadfael. 'And not by the puncture the arrow certainly made, but by a prior wound. A wound made, as I judge, by a long dagger, and a very thin and sharp one, no common working knife. Once it was withdrawn, the wound was nearly closed. Yet the blade passed clean through him. For it was possible, afterwards, to trace and turn that same thrust backwards upon itself, and very accurately, too. What we took for the exit wound is no exit wound at all, but an entry wound. The arrow was driven in from the front after he was dead, to hide the fact that he was stabbed in the back. That was why the ambush took place in thick undergrowth, in a tangled place. That was why he fell on his face, and why, afterwards, he was turned on his back. And why the upward course of the arrow is so improbable. It never was shot from any bow. To *thrust* in an arrow is hard work, it was made to get its power from flight. I think the way was opened first with a dagger.'

'The same that struck him down from behind,' she said, white and translucent as flame.

'It would seem so. Then the arrow was inserted after. Even so he could not make it penetrate further. I mistrusted that shot from the first. Engelard could have put a shaft through a couple of oak boards and clean away at that distance. So could any archer worth his pay. But to thrust it in with your hands—no, it was a strong, lusty arm that made even this crude job of it. And at least he got the line right. A good eye, a sensitive hand.'

'A devil's heart,' said Sioned, 'and Engelard's arrow! Someone who knew where to find them, and knew Engelard would not be there to prevent.' But for all her intolerable burdens, she was still thinking clearly. 'I have a question yet. Why did this murderer leave it so long between killing and disguising his kill? My father was dead before ever the rain came. You have shown it clearly. But he was not turned on his back to receive Engelard's arrow until after the rain had stopped. More than half an hour. Why? Was his murderer startled away by someone passing close? Did he wait in the bushes to be sure Rhisiart was dead before he dared touch him? Or did he only think of this devilish trick later, and have to go and fetch the shaft for his purpose? Why so long?'

'That,' said Cadfael honestly, 'I do not know.'

'What do we know? That whoever it was wished to pin this thing upon Engelard. Was that the whole cause? Was my father

just a disposable thing, to get rid of Engelard? Bait to trap another man? Or did someone want my father disposed of, and
only afterwards realise how easy, how convenient, to dispose of
Engelard, too?'

'I know no more than you,' said Cadfael, himself shaken. And
he thought, and wished he had not, of that young man fretting
his feet tormentedly among the leaves, and flinching from
Sioned's trust as from a death-wound. 'Perhaps whoever it was
did the deed, and slipped away, and then paused to think, and
saw how easy it might be to point the act away from himself,
and went back to do it. All we are sure of is this, and, child,
thank God for it. Engelard has been set up as a sacrificial victim,
and is clear of all taint. Keep that at heart, and wait.'

'And whether we discover the real murderer or not, if ever it
should be needful you will speak out for Engelard?'

'That I will, with all my heart. But for now, say nothing of
this to anyone, for *we* are still here, the troublers of Gwytherin's
peace, and never think that I have set us apart as immaculate.
Until we know the guilty, we do not know the innocent.'

'I take back nothing,' said Sioned firmly, 'of what I said concerning your prior.'

'Nevertheless, he could not have done it. He was not out of
my sight.'

'No, that I accept. But he buys men, and he is utterly set upon
getting his saint, and now, as I understand, he has his will. It
is a cause. And never forget, Welshman, as well as Englishmen,
may be for sale. I pray not many. But a few.'

'I don't forget,' said Cadfael.

'Who is he? *Who?* He knows my father's movements. He
knows where to lay hands on Engelard's arrows. He wants God
knows what from my father's death, but certainly he wants to
pin murder on Engelard. Brother Cadfael, who can this man be?'

'That, God willing,' he said, 'you and I between us will find
out. But as at this moment, I cannot judge nor guess, I am utterly
astray. What was done I see, but why, or by whom, I know no
more than you. But you have reminded me how the dead are
known to rebel against the touch of those who struck them

down, and as Rhisiart has told us much, so he may yet tell us all.

He told her, then, of the three nights of prayer and vigil Prior Robert had decreed, and how all the monks and Father Huw, by turns, would share the duty. But he did not tell her how Columbanus, in his single-minded innocence and his concern for his own conscience, had added one more to those who had had the opportunity to lie in wait for her father in the forest. Nor did he admit to her, and hardly to himself, that what they had discovered here lent a sinister meaning to Columbanus' revelation. Jerome out hunting his man with bow and arrow was a most unlikely conception, but Jerome creeping up behind a man's back in thick cover, with a sharp dagger in hand. . . .

Cadfael put the thought behind him, but it did not go far. There was a certain credibility about it that he did not like at all.

'Tonight and for two nights following, two of us will be keeping watch in the chapel from after Compline in the evening until Prime in the morning. All six of us can be drawn into the same trial, and not one can feel himself singled out. After that, we'll see. Now this,' said Brother Cadfael, 'is what you must do. . . .'

CHAPTER SEVEN

After Compline, in the soft evening light, with the slanting sunset filtering through young viridian leaves, they went up, all six together, to the wooden chapel and the solitary graveyard, to bring their first pair of pilgrims to the vigil. And there, advancing to meet them in the clearing before the gate, came another procession, eight of Rhisiart's household officers and servants, winding down out of the woods with their lord's bier upon their shoulders, and their lord's daughter, now herself their lord, walking erect and dignified before them, dressed in a dark gown and draped with a grey veil, under which her long hair lay loose in mourning. Her face was calm and fixed, her eyes looked far. She could have daunted any man, even an abbot. Prior Robert baulked at sight of her. Cadfael was proud of her.

So far from checking at sight of Robert, she gave a slight spring of hope and purpose to her step, and came on without pause. Face to face with him at three paces distance, she halted and stood so still and quiet that he might have mistaken this for submission, if he had been fool enough. But he was not a fool, and he gazed and measured silently, seeing a woman, a mere girl, who had come to match him, though not yet recognising her as his match.

'Brother Cadfael,' she said, without taking her eyes from Robert's face, 'stand by me now and make my words plain to the reverend prior, for I have a prayer to him for my father's sake.'

Rhisiart was there at her back, not coffined, only swathed and shrouded in white linen, every line of body and face standing clear under the tight wrappings, in a cradle of leafy branches, carried on a wooden bier. All those dark, secret Welsh eyes of the men who bore him glowed like little lamps about a catafalque, betraying nothing, seeing everything. And the girl was so young, and so solitary. Prior Robert, even in his assured situation, was uneasy. He may even have been moved.

'Make your prayer, daughter,' he said.

'I have heard that you intend to watch three nights in reverence to Saint Winifred, before you take her hence with you. I ask that for the ease of my father's soul, if he has offended against her, which was never his intent, he may be allowed to lie those three nights before her altar, in the care of those who keep watch. I ask that they will spare one prayer for forgiveness and rest to his soul, one only, in a long night of prayer. Is that too much to ask?'

'It is a fair asking,' said Robert, 'from a loyal daughter.' And after all, he came of a noble family, and knew how to value the ties of blood and birth, and he was not all falsity.

'I hope for a sign of grace,' said Sioned, 'all the more if you approve me.'

There was no way that such a request could do anything but add lustre and glory to his reputation. His opponent's heiress and only child came asking his countenance and patronage. He was more than gratified, he was charmed. He gave his consent graciously, aware of more pairs of Gwytherin eyes watching him than belonged to Rhisiart's bearers. Scattered though the households were, apart from the villein community that farmed as one family, the woods were full of eyes now wherever the strangers went. A pity they had not kept as close a watch on Rhisiart when he was man alive!

They installed his green bier on the trestles before the altar, beside the reliquary that awaited Saint Winifred's bones. The altar was small and plain, the bier almost dwarfed it, and the light that came in through the narrow east window barely illuminated the scene even by morning sunlight. Prior Robert had brought altar-cloths in the chest, and with these the trestles were draped. There the party from Rhisiart's hall left their lord lying in state, and quietly withdrew on the way home.

'In the morning,' said Sioned, before she went with them, 'I shall come to say my thanks to those who have asked grace for my father during the night. And so I shall do each morning, before we bury him.'

She made the reverence due to Prior Robert, and went away without another word, without so much as a glance at Brother Cadfael, drawing the veil close round her face.

So far, so good! Robert's vanity and self-interest, if not his compunction, had assured her of her chance, it remained to be seen what would come of it. The order of their watches had been decreed by Robert himself, in consultation with no one but Father Huw, who wished to be the first to spend the night opening his heart to the saint's influence, if she pleased to make her presence known. His partner was Brother Jerome, of whose obsequious attendance the prior occasionally grew weary, and Cadfael was thankful for the accidental choice that suited him best. That first morning, at least, no one would know what to expect. After that the rest would have due warning, but surely no way of evading the issue.

In the morning, when they went to the chapel, it was to find a fair number of the inhabitants of Gwytherin already gathered there, though unobtrusively, lurking in the edges of the woods and under the fragrant shadow of the hawthorn hedges. Only when the prior and his companions entered the chapel did the villagers emerge silently from cover and gather close, and the first of them to draw near was Sioned, with Annest at her elbow. Way was opened for the two girls, and the people of Gwytherin closed in after them, filling the doorway of the chapel and blocking off the early light, so that only the candles on the altar cast a pale glow over the bier where the dead man lay.

Father Huw got up from his knees somewhat creakily, leaning on the solid wood of the desk till he could get his old legs straightened and working again. From the other desk beside him Jerome rose briskly and supply. Cadfael thought suspiciously of devout watchkeepers who fell asleep as comfortably as possible on their folded arms, but at the moment that was of no importance. He would hardly have expected heaven to open and rain down roses of forgiveness at Jerome's request, in any case.

'A quiet watch,' said Huw, 'and all most calm. I was not

visited by any great experience, but such hardly fall to humble parish priests. We have prayed, child, and I trust we have been heard.'

'I am grateful,' said Sioned. 'And before you go, will you do one more kindness for me and mine? As you have all been sufferers in this trouble and dissension, will you show your own will to mercy? You have prayed for him, now I ask you to lay your hand, each of you, upon my father's heart, in token of reassurance and forgiveness.'

The people of Gwytherin, still as trees in the doorway, but live as trees, too, and all eyes as a tree is all leaves, made never a sound, and missed never a move.

'Gladly!' said Father Huw, and stepped to the bier and laid his rough hand gently on the stilled heart, and by the wagging of his beard his lips were again moving in silent intercession. All eyes turned upon Brother Jerome, for Brother Jerome was hesitating.

He did not look greatly disturbed, but he did look evasive. The face he turned upon Sioned was benevolent and sweet, and having bestowed on her the obligatory glance of compassion, he modestly lowered his eyes before her as was prescribed, and turned to look trustfully at Prior Robert.

'Father Huw holds the cure of this parish, and is subject to one discipline, but I to another. The lord Rhisiart surely carried out his religious duties faithfully, and I feel with him. But he died by violence, unconfessed and unshriven, and such a death leaves the health of his soul in doubt. I am not fit to pronounce in this case. I have prayed, but blessing is not for me to dispense without authority. If Prior Robert feels it is justified, and gives me leave, I will gladly do as I am asked.'

Along this devious path Cadfael followed him with some amazement and considerable doubt. If the prior had himself authorised the death, and sent his creature out to accomplish it, Jerome could not have turned the threat back on his superior more neatly. On the other hand, knowing Jerome, this could as well be his way of flattering and courting, at this opportunity as at every other. And if Robert graciously gave his leave, did he suppose that would protect him, as having plainly handed on the guilt and the threat where they truly belonged, and leave him free to touch his victim with impunity? It would have mattered less if Cadfael had firmly believed that the murdered bleed when the murderer touches, but what he believed was very different, simply that the belief was general among most people, and could drive the guilty, when cornered, to terror and confession. That very terror and stress might even produce some small effusion of blood, though he doubted it. He was beginning to think that Jerome doubted it, too.

The watching eyes had changed their quarry, and hung heavily upon the prior. He frowned, and considered gravely for some moments, before he gave judgment. 'You may do what she wishes, with a good conscience. She is asking only for forgiveness, which is every man's to give, not for absolution.'

And Brother Jerome, gratefully acknowledging the instruction, stepped readily to the bier, and laid his hand upon the swathed heart without a tremor. No spurt of red showed through the shroud to accuse him. Complacently he followed Prior Robert out of the chapel, the others falling in behind, and the silent, staring people fell back from the doorway and let them pass.

And where, thought Cadfael, following, does that leave us? Is he quite hardy about the ordeal, not believing in it at all, or does he feel he has passed the guilt to the guilty, whatever his own part in it, and is therefore out of danger? Or had he no part in it at all, and was all this to no purpose? He is quite narrow enough to refuse the girl a kindness, unless he could turn it to his own credit and advantage.

Well, we shall see tomorrow, reasoned Cadfael, what Robert will do when he's asked for his own forgiveness, instead of being generous with another man's.

However, things did not turn out quite as he had expected. Prior Robert had certainly elected to take that night's watch himself, along with Brother Richard. But as the two were on their way to the chapel, and passing by Cadwallon's holding, the prior was hailed by the gateman, and Cadwallon himself came hastening out to intercept him, with a burly, handsomely-dressed Welshman in a short riding tunic at his heels.

The first Cadfael knew of it was when the prior came striding back into Huw's garden with the stranger beside him, just at the hour when he should have been sinking to his knees in the sombre chapel with its tiny lights, to keep nightlong company with his dead man, in a confrontation which might yet produce fruitful evidence. But here he was, just in time to prevent Cadfael from slipping away to Bened's smithy to exchange the news of the day, and share a cup of wine. And plainly not seriously displeased at having his night's vigil disrupted, either.

'Brother Cadfael, we have a visitor, and I shall require your services. This is Griffith ap Rhys, Prince Owain's bailiff in Rhos. Cadwallon sent to him concerning the death of the lord Rhisiart, and I must make my own statement to him, and discuss what is to be done. He will be enquiring of all those who may have witness to deliver, but now he requires that I shall render my account first. I have had to send Brother Richard on to the chapel without me.'

Jerome and Columbanus had been about to set out for their own beds in Cadwallon's house, but they lingered dutifully at hearing this. 'I will go in your place, Father Prior,' offered Jerome devotedly, certain he would be refused.

'No, you have had one sleepless night.' (Had he? In that dim interior there was no being sure, even if Father Huw had been a suspicious man. And Jerome was not the kind to wear himself out needlessly.) 'You must get your rest.'

'I would gladly take your place, Father Prior,' offered Columbanus just as ardently.

'You have your turn tomorrow. Beware, brother, of taking too much to yourself, of arrogance in the guise of humility. No, Brother Richard will keep the vigil alone tonight. You may wait, both, until you have given your witness as to what you did and saw the day before yesterday, and then leave us, and get your proper sleep.'

That was a long and tedious session, and greatly fretted Brother Cadfael, who was obliged to fall back on his own conception of truth, not, indeed, by translating falsely, but by adding his own view of those things that had happened in the forest by Rhisiart's body. He did not suppress anything Robert said, but he severed plain fact from supposition, the thing observed from the conclusion leaped to, on his own authority. Who was there with Welsh enough to challenge him, except Griffith ap Rhys himself? And that experienced and sceptical officer soon proved himself not only a quick and agile listener, but a very shrewd dissector of feelings and motives, too. He was, after all, Welsh to the bone, and Welsh bones were at the heart of this tangle. By the time he had dealt with Columbanus and Jerome, those two faithful watchers of whom one had turned out to be a treasonous sleeper-on-duty (though neither they nor Prior Robert saw fit to mention that lapse!), Cadfael was beginning to feel he could rely on the good sense of the prince's bailiff, and need not have gone to so much trouble to suppress most of what he himself knew and was about. Better so, though, he decided finally, for what he most needed now was time, and a day or two saved by sending Griffith all round the parish after evidence might see the satisfactory conclusion of his own enquiries. Official justice does not dig deep, but regards what comes readily to the surface, and draws conclusions accordingly. A nagging doubt now and then is the price it pays for speedy order and a quiet land. But Cadfael was not prepared to let the nagging doubt occur in the person of either Engelard or Brother John. No, better go his own way to the end, and have a finished case to present to bailiff and prince.

So there was nothing at all for Sioned to do, when she came the next morning, but to ask Brother Richard, that large, lazy, kindly man who willed peace and harmony all round him, for his personal pity towards her father, and his benediction in the laying on of hands. Which he gave willingly and guilelessly, and departed still in ignorance of what he had done, and what he had been absolved from doing.

'I missed you,' said Bened, briefly visited between Mass and dinner. 'Padrig came down for a while, we were talking over the old days, when Rhisiart was younger. Padrig's been coming here a good many years now. He knows us all. He asked after you.'

'Tell him we'll share a cup one of these days, here or there. And say I'm about Rhisiart's business, if that's any comfort.'

'We're getting used to you,' said Bened, stooping to his fire, where a sinewy boy was bending into the bellows. 'You should stay, there'd be a place for you.'

'I've got my place.' said Cadfael. 'Never fret about me. I chose the cowl with both eyes open. I knew what I did.'

'There are some I can't reconcile with you,' said Bened, with the iron in hand for the shoe that waited.

'Ah, priors and brothers come and go, as mixed as the rest of men, but the cloister remains. Now, there are some who did lose their way, I grant you,' said Cadfael, 'mostly young things who mistook a girl's "no" for the end of the world. Some of them might make very useful craftsmen, if ever they broke free. Always supposing they were free men, and could get entry to, say, the smith's mystery. . . .'

'He has a good arm and wrist on him, that one,' said Bened reflectively, 'and knows how to jump and do as he's bid when the man bidding knows his business. That's half the craft. If he hasn't let Rhisiart's killer loose on the world, then there isn't an outlander would be more welcome here. But that I don't yet know, though the poor girl up yonder may think she does. How if she's wrong? Do *you* know?'

'Not yet,' owned Cadfael. 'But give us time, and we shall know.'

On this third day of Brother John's nominal captivity he found himself more closely confined. The word had gone round that the bailiff was in the parish and asking questions everywhere concerning the circumstances of Rhisiart's death, and it was known that he had had a lengthy session with the prior at Father Huw's parsonage, and must certainly have been urged and admonished as to his duty to take action also in the matter of Brother John's crime. Not that John had any complaints as to his lodging, his food or his company; he had seldom been so completely content. But for two days, with brief intervals when caution had seemed advisable, he had been out from dawn to dusk about the holding, lending a hand with the cattle, replenishing the wood-pile, fetching and carrying, planting out in the vegetable garden, and had had neither time nor inclination to worry about his situation. Now that he was hustled out of sight, and sat idle in the stable, the realities fretted even John, and the want of Welsh, or of Brother Cadfael to supply the want, was a frustration no longer so easy to bear. He did not know what Cadfael and Sioned were up to, he did not know what was happening to Saint Winifred, or to Prior Robert and his fellows, and above all he did not know where Engelard was, or how he was to be extricated from the tangle of suspicion roused against him. Since his instinctive gesture of solidarity, John took a proprietorial interest in Engelard, and wanted him safe, vindicated, and happy with his Sioned.

But Sioned, true to her word, did not come near him, and there was no one else in the holding who could talk to him freely. Simple things could be conveyed, but there was no way of communicating to him everything he wanted and needed to know. There was he, willing but useless, wondering and fretting how his friends were faring, and quite unable to do anything to aid them.

Annest brought his dinner, and sat by him while he ate, and the same want of words troubled her. It was all very well teaching him simple words and phrases in Welsh by touching the thing she meant, but how to set about pouring out to him, as she would have liked, all that was happening at the chapel, and what the village was saying and thinking? The helplessness of talking at all made their meetings almost silent, but sometimes they did speak aloud, he in English, she in Welsh, saying things because they could not be contained, things that would be understood by the other only in some future day, though the tone might convey at least the sense of friendship, like a kind of restrained caress. Thus they conducted two little monologues which yet were an exchange and a comfort.

Sometimes, though they did not know it, they were even answering each other's questions.

'I wonder who she was,' said Annest, soft and hesitant, 'that one who drove you to take the cowl? Sioned and I, we can't help wondering how a lad like you ever came to do it.' Now if he had known Welsh, she could never have said that to him.

'How did I ever come to think that Margery such a beauty!' marvelled John. 'And take it so hard when she turned me down? But I'd never really seen beauty then—I'd never seen *you*!'

'She did us all a bad turn,' said Annest, sighing, 'whoever she was, driving you into that habit for life!'

'Dear God,' said John, 'to think I might have married her! At least she did me that much of a favour, with her "no". There's only the matter of a cowl between you and me, not a wife.' And that was the first moment when he had entertained the dazzling idea that escape from his vows might be possible at all. The thought caused him to turn his head and look with even closer and more ardent attention at the fair face so close to his. She had smooth, rounded, apple-blossom cheeks, and delicate, sun-glossed bones, and eyes like brook-water in the sun over bright pebbles, glittering, polished, crystal-clear.

'Do you still fret after her?' wondered Annest in a whisper. 'A conceited ninny who hadn't the wit to know a good man when she saw one?' For he was indeed a very well-grown, handy, handsome, good-humoured young fellow, with his long, sturdy legs and his big, deft hands, and his bush of russet curls, and the girl who thought herself too good for him must have been the world's fool. 'I hate her!' said Annest, leaning unwarily towards him.

The lips that tantalised him with soft utterances he could not understand were only a little way from his own. He resorted in desperation to a kind of sign-language that needed no interpreter. He hadn't kissed a girl since Margery, the draper's daughter, threw him over when her father became bailiff of Shrewsbury, but it seemed he hadn't forgotten how. And Annest melted into his arms, where she fitted a great deal better than his too-hasty vows had ever fitted him.

'Oh, Annest!' gasped Brother John, who had never in his life felt less like a brother, 'I think I love you!'

Brother Cadfael and Brother Columbanus walked up through the woodland together, to keep the third night of prayer. The evening was mild and still but overcast, and under the trees the light grew dusky green. Until the last moment it had remained a possibility that Prior Robert, having missed his chosen night of duty, might elect to be present on this last occasion, but he had said no word, and to tell the truth, Cadfael was beginning to wonder if that long session with the bailiff had really been necessary at all, or whether the prior had welcomed it as an alternative to keeping the night-watch and facing Sioned with her request in the morning. Not necessarily a proof of any guilt on his part, beyond the guilt of still wishing to refuse grace to Rhisiart, without actually having to do so face to face with his daughter. For whatever virtues might be found in Prior Robert, humility was not one, nor magnanimity. He was invariably sure of his own rightness, and where it was challenged he was not a forgiving man.

'In this quest and this vigil, brother,' said Columbanus, his long young steps keeping easy pace with Cadfael's seaman's roll, 'we are greatly privileged. The history of our abbey will record our names, and brothers in the generations to come will envy us.'

'I have already heard,' said Cadfael drily, 'that Prior Robert is proposing to write a life of Saint Winifred, and complete it with the story of this translation to Shrewsbury. You think he'll record the names of *all* his companions?' Yours, however, he thought, he well might mention, as the afflicted brother who first fell sick and was sent to Holywell to be cured. And Jerome's, who had the dream that took you there. But mine, I feel sure, will remain a silence, and so much the better!

'I have a fault to atone for,' recalled Columbanus devoutly, 'having betrayed my trust once in this same chapel, I, who most of all should have been faithful.' They were at the decrepit gate, the tangle of the graveyard before them, threaded by a narrow path just discernible through the long grass. 'I feel a holy air reaching out to me,' said the young man, quivering, his face uplifted and pale. 'I am drawn into a light. I believe we are approaching a wonder, a miracle of grace. Such mercy to me, who fell asleep in betrayal of her service!' And he led the way to the open door, his stride lengthening in eagerness, his hands extended as if to clasp a mistress rather than make obeisance before a saint. Cadfael followed morosely but resignedly, used to these uncomfortable ardours, but not looking forward to being confined in so small a chapel with them overnight. He had thinking as well as praying to do, and Columbanus was not conducive to either activity.

Inside the chapel the air was heavy with the scent of old wood, and the spices and incense of the draperies on which the reliquary lay, and the faint, aromatic aura of years of dust and partial disuse. A small oil-lamp burned with a dark yellow flame on the altar, and Cadfael went forward and lit the two altar candles from it, and set them one on either side. Through the narrow east window the fragrance of the falling may-blossom breathed freshness on a very light breeze, causing the flames to flicker for a few minutes. Their faint, dancing radiance glanced from every near surface, but did not reach the corners of the roof, or fix the walls in place. They were in a narrow cavern of brown, wood-scented darkness, with a dim focus of light before them, that shone on an empty coffin and an un-coffined body, and just showed them the rough outlines of the two prayer-desks drawn up side by side at a little distance from the catafalque. Rhisiart lay nearer to them, the black and silver bulk of the reliquary like a low wall shading him from the altar lights.

Brother Columbanus bowed humbly low to the altar, and took his place at the desk on the right. Brother Cadfael settled solidly at the one on the left, and with practised movements sought and found the best place for his knees. Stillness came down on them gently. He composed himself for a long watch, and said his prayer for Rhisiart, not the first he had said for him. Great darkness and constant, feeble light, the slow flowing of time from far beyond his conception to far beyond his power to follow, the solitude about him and the troubled and peopled world within, all these settled into their perpetual pattern, a steady rhythm as perfect as sleep. He thought no more of Columbanus, he forgot that Columbanus existed. He prayed as he breathed, forming no words and making no specific requests, only holding in his heart, like broken birds in cupped hands, all those people who were in stress or in grief because of this little saint, for if he suffered like this for their sake, how much more must she feel for them?

The candles would last the night, and by instinct he traced time by the rate at which they dwindled, and knew when it was near to midnight.

He was thinking of Sioned, to whom he had nothing but himself to offer in the morning, this pietistic innocent being essentially nothing, and Cadfael himself by no means enough, when he heard the faintest and strangest of sounds issuing from the prie-dieu on his right, where Columbanus leaned in total absorption. Not now with face hidden on his linked hands, but uplifted and strained upwards into what light could reach him, and faint though it was, it conjured his sharp profile into prim- rose pallor. His eyes were wide open and staring beyond the chapel wall, and his lips open and curved in ecstasy, and singing, a mere thread of Latin chant in praise of virginity. It was barely audible, yet clear as in a dream. And before Cadfael was fully aware of what he heard, he saw the young man thrust himself upwards, holding by the desk, and stand upright before the altar. The chant ceased. Suddenly he reared himself erect to his tallest, drawing back his head as though he would see through the roof into a spring night full of stars, and spreading out his arms on either side like a man stretched on a cross. He gave a great, wordless cry, seemingly both of pain and triumph, and fell for- ward full-length on the earthen floor, crashing to the ground stiffly, arms still outspread, body stretched to the very toes, and lay still, his forehead against the trailing fringe of the altar-cloth that spilled from beneath Rhisiart's body.

Cadfael got up in a hurry and went to him, torn between anxiety and alarm on one hand, and disgusted resignation on the other. Exactly what was to be expected of the idiot, he thought with exasperation, even as he was on his knees feeling at the prone brow, and adjusting a fold of the altar drapery under it to ease the position of nose and mouth, turning the young man's head to one side so that he could breathe freely. I should have recognised the signs! Never an opportunity but he can produce a devotional fit or a mystic ecstasy to order. One of these days he'll be drawn into that light of his, and never come back. Yet I've noticed he can fall flat on his face without hurting himself, and go into pious convulsions over his visions or his sins without ever hurling himself against anything sharp or hard, or even biting his tongue. The same sort of providence that takes care of drunken men looks out for Columbanus in his throes. And he reflected at the back of his mind, and tartly, that there ought somewhere to be a moral in that, lumping all excesses together.

No convulsions this time, at any rate. He had simply seen whatever he had seen, or thought he had seen, and fallen down before it in this destroying rapture. Cadfael shook him by the shoulder gently, and then more sharply, but he was rigid and unresponsive. His forehead was cool and smooth, his features, very dimly seen, yet looked serene, composed, if anything, in a gentle and joyful peace. But for the rigidity of body and limbs, and that unnatural attitude as though he lay stretched on a cross, he might have been asleep. All Cadfael had been able to do by way of easing him was to turn his head so that he lay on his right cheek, pillowed on the draperies. When he tried to bend the right arm and turn the young man more comfortably on his side, the joints resisted him, so he let well alone.

And now, he thought, what am I supposed to do? Abandon my watch and go down and fetch the prior with help for him? What could they do for him that I cannot do here? If I can't rouse him, then neither could they. He'll come out of it when the right time comes, and not before. He's done himself no injury, his breathing is steady and deep. His heart beats strongly and regularly, he has no fever. Why interfere with a man's peculiar pleasures, if they're doing him no harm? It isn't cold here, and he can have one of these altar-cloths for blanket, a fancy that ought to please him. No, we came to watch out the night together, and so we will, I here on my knees as is due, and he wherever he may be at this moment in his dreams.

He covered Columbanus, adjusted the cloths to cushion his head, and went back to his own prie-dieu. But whatever this visitation had done for Columbanus, it had shattered all possibility of thought or concentration for Cadfael. The more he tried to focus his mind, whether upon his duty of prayer and meditation, or the urgent need to consider where Sioned stood now, and what more could be done, the more was he drawn to look again at the prone body, and listen again to make sure it still breathed as evenly as ever. What should have been a profitable night hung heavy upon him, wasted as worship, useless as thought, as long and dreary and tedious a night as he had ever passed.

The first dove-grey softening of the darkness came as a blessing, bringing release at least within sight. The narrow space of sky seen through the altar window changed from grey to pale, clear green, from green to saffron, from saffron to gold, a cloudless morning, the first sunray piercing through the slit and falling on the altar, the reliquary, the shrouded body, and then striking like a golden sword across the chapel, leaving Columbanus in darkness. Still he lay rigid, yet breathing deeply and softly, and no touch or word could reach him.

He was in the same condition when Prior Robert came with his fellows, and Sioned with Annest in attendance, and all the people from the village and the nearby holdings, silent and watchful as before, to see the end of this three-night vigil.

Sioned was the first to enter, and the dimness within, after the brightness without, made her blind for a moment, so that she halted in the doorway until her eyes should grow accustomed to the change. Prior Robert was close behind her when she saw the soles of Brother Columbanus' sandals upturned before her, just touched by the sunray from the window, while the rest of him lay still in shadow. Her eyes widened in wonder and horror, and before Cadfael could rise and turn to reassure her she had uttered a sharp cry: 'What is it? Is he dead?'

The prior put her aside quickly, and strode past her, and was brought up short with his foot on the hem of Columbanus' habit.

'What happened here? Columbanus! Brother!' He stooped and laid his hand upon a rigid shoulder. Columbanus slept and dreamed on, unmoved and unmoving. 'Brother Cadfael, what does this mean? What has befallen him?'

'He is not dead,' said Cadfael, putting first things first, 'nor do I think he is in any danger. He breathes like a man peacefully sleeping. His colour is good, he is cool to the touch, and has no injury. Simply, at midnight he suddenly stood up before the altar, and spread out his arms and fell forward thus in trance. He has lain all night like this, but without distress or agitation.'

'You should have called us to his aid,' said the prior, shaken and dismayed.

'I had also a duty,' said Cadfael shortly, 'to remain here and keep the vigil I was sent to keep. And what could have been done for him more than I have done, in giving him a pillow for his head and a cover against the chill of the night? Nor, I think, would he have been grateful if we had carried him away before the appointed time. Now he has kept his own watch faithfully, and if we cannot rouse him we may bear him away to his bed, without doing violence to his sense of duty.'

'There is something in that,' said Brother Richard earnestly, 'for you know that Brother Columbanus has several times been visited and favoured by visions, and it might have been a great wrong to take him away from the very place where such blessings befell him. An offence, perhaps, against the saint herself, if she was pleased to reveal herself to him. And if that is so, then he will awake when the time is right that he should, and it might do him great harm to try and hasten the hour.'

'It is true,' said the prior, a little reassured, 'that he seems at peace, and has a good colour, and no sign of trouble or pain. This is most strange. Is it possible that this young brother will be the occasion of another such prodigy as when his affliction first drew us to Saint Winifred?'

'He was the instrument of grace once,' said Richard, 'and may be so again. We had better carry him down to his bed at Cadwallon's house, and keep him quiet and warm, and wait. Or had we not better take him to Father Huw's parsonage, so that he may be close to the church? It may be that his first need will be to give thanks.'

With a heavy altar-cloth and their girdles they made a sling in which to carry Columbanus, lifting him from the floor, stiff as a branch, even his extended arms still rigid. They laid him on his back in their improvised litter, and he suffered whatever they did to him, and made no sound or sign. A few of the watching natives, moved and awed by the spectacle, came forward to lend a hand in carrying him down through the forest to Huw's house. Cadfael let them go. He turned to look at Sioned, as she was looking at him, with dubious and speculative eyes.

'Well, I, at least,' he said, 'am in my right senses, and can and will do what you have not asked of me.' And he stepped to Rhisiart's side, and laid his hand upon the dead man's heart, and signed his forehead with a cross.

She walked beside him as they followed the slow procession down towards the village.

'What more can we do? If you know of anything, only tell me. We have not been favoured so far. And today is to be his burial.'

'I know it,' said Cadfael, and brooded. 'As for this affair in the night, I'm torn two ways. I should think it possible it was all planned, to reinforce our cause with another miracle, but for two things. To me Prior Robert's amazement and concern, however I look at them, seem to be true and not false. And Columbanus has shown these strange properties before, and the way they overtake him is violent and perilous, and it's hard to believe he is feigning. A tumbler at a fair, making his living by playing the devil with his own body, could not outdo Columbanus when the fit comes on him. I am not able to judge. I think there are some who live on a knife-edge in the soul, and at times are driven to hurl themselves into the air, at the mercy of heaven or hell which way to fall.'

'All I know,' said Sioned, burning darkly red like a slow torch, 'is that my father whom I loved is murdered, and I want justice on the murderer, and I do not want a blood price. There is no price I will accept for Rhisiart's blood.'

'I know, I know!' said Cadfael. 'I am as Welsh as you. But keep a door open to pity, as who knows when you or I may need it! And have you spoken with Engelard? And is all well with him?'

She quivered and flushed and softened beside him, like a frost-blighted flower miraculously revived by a southern wind. But she did not answer. There was no need.

'Ah, you'll live!' said Brother Cadfael, satisfied. 'As he'd want you to. Even if he did set his face against, like a proper Welsh lord. You'd have got your way in the end, you were right about that. And listen, I have thought of two things you should yet do. We must try whatever we can. Don't go home now. Let Annest take you to Bened's smithy to rest, and the both of you come to Mass. Who knows what we may learn once our half-fledged saint regains his senses? And then, also, when you bury your father, make certain Peredur comes with *his* father. He might try to avoid else, if he's eluded you this far, but if you ask him, he cannot refuse. I am still in more minds than one, and none of them very clear, concerning Master Peredur.'

CHAPTER EIGHT

It was the little brazen bell ringing for Mass that penetrated Brother Columbanus' enchanted sleep at last. It could not be said that it awoke him, rather it caused him to open his closed eyes, quiver through all his frozen members, flex his stiff arms, and press his re-quickened hands together over his breast. Otherwise his face did not change, nor did he seem to be aware of those who were gathered anxiously about the bed on which he lay. They might not have been there at all. All Brother Columbanus responded to was the bell, the first call to worship. He stirred and sat up. He rose from the bed, and stood firmly on his feet. He looked radiant, but still private and apart.

'He is preparing to take his usual place with us,' said the prior, moved and awed. 'Let us go, and make no attempt yet to rouse him. When he has given thanks he'll come back to us, and speak out what he has experienced.'

And he led the way to the church, and as he had supposed, Columbanus fell into his usual place as the youngest in the attendant brotherhood now that John was disgraced, and followed modestly, and modestly took part in the service, still like a man in a dream.

The church was full as it would hold, and there were more people clustered outside the doorway. The word had gone round already that something strange and wonderful had happened at Saint Winifred's chapel, and revelations might very well follow at Mass.

Not until the end did any further change occur in the condition of Brother Columbanus. But when the prior, slowly and expectantly, as one turning a key and almost confident of entry, took the first step towards the doorway, suddenly Columbanus gave a great start, and uttered a soft cry, staring wonderingly about him at all these known faces. His own visage came to life, smiling. He put out a hand as if to arrest the prior's departure, and said in a high voice: 'Oh, Father, I have been so blessed, I have known such bliss! How did I come here, when I know I was elsewhere, and translated out of night's darkness into so glorious a light? And surely this is again the world I left! A fair world enough, but I have been in a fairer, far beyond any deserts of mine. Oh, if I could but tell you!'

Every eye was upon him, and every ear stretched to catch his least word. Not a soul left the church, rather those without crowded in closer.

'Son,' said Prior Robert, with unwontedly respectful kindness, 'you are here among your brothers, engaged in the worship of God, and there is nothing to fear and nothing to regret, for the visitation granted you was surely meant to inspire and arm you to go fearless through an imperfect world, in the hope of a perfect world hereafter. You were keeping night watch with Brother Cadfael at Saint Winifred's chapel—do you remember that? In the night something befell you that drew your spirit for a time away from us, out of the body, but left that body unharmed and at rest like a child asleep. We brought you back here still absent from us in the spirit, but now you are here with us again, and all is well. You have been greatly privileged.'

'Oh, greatly, far more than you know,' sang Columbanus, glowing like a pale lantern. 'I am the messenger of such goodness, I am the instrument of reconciliation and peace. Oh, Father. . . . Father Huw . . . brothers . . . let me speak out here before all, for what I am bidden to tell concerns all.'

Nothing, thought Cadfael, could have stopped him, so plainly did his heavenly embassage override any objection mere prior or priest might muster. And Robert was proving surprisingly compliant in accepting this transfer of authority. Either he already knew that the voice from heaven was about to say something entirely favourable to his plans and conducive to his glory, or else he was truly impressed, and inclining heart and ear to listen as devoutly as any man there present.

'Speak freely, brother,' he said, 'let us share your joy.'

'Father, at the hour of midnight as I knelt before the altar I heard a sweet voice crying my name, and I arose and went forward to obey the call. What happened to my body then I do not know, you tell me it was lying as if asleep when you came. But it seemed to me that as I stepped towards the altar there was suddenly a soft, golden light all about it, and there rose up, floating in the midst of the light, a most beautiful virgin, who moved in a miraculous shower of white petals, and distilled most sweet odours from her robe and from her long hair. And this gracious being spoke to me, and told me that her name was Winifred, and that she was come to approve our enterprise, and also to forgive all those who out of mistaken loyalty and reverence had opposed it hitherto. And then, oh, marvellous goodness! —she laid her hand on Rhisiart's breast, as his daughter has begged us to do in token of our mere personal forgiveness, but she in divine absolution, and with such perfection of grace, I cannot describe it.'

'Oh, son,' said Prior Robert in rapture, riding over the quivering murmurs that crossed the church like ripples on a pool, 'you tell a greater wonder than we dared hope. Even the lost saved!'

'It is so! And, Father, there is more! When she laid her hand on him, she bade me speak out to all men in this place, both native and stranger, and make known her merciful will. And it is this: "Where my bones shall be taken out of the earth," she said, "there will be an open grave provided. What I relinquish, I may bestow. In this grave," said Winifred, "let Rhisiart be buried, that his rest may be assured, and my power made manifest."'

'What could I do,' said Sioned, 'but thank him for his good offices, when he brought divine reassurance for my father's weal? And yet it outrages me, I would rather have stood up and said that I am not and never have been in the least doubt that my father is in blessedness this moment, for he was a good man who never did a mean wrong to anyone. And certainly it's kind of Saint Winifred to offer him the lodging she's leaving, and graciously forgive him, but—forgiveness for what? Absolution for what? She might rather have praised him while she was about it, and said outright that he was justified, not forgiven.'

'Yet a very ambassadorial message,' admitted Cadfael appreciatively, 'calculated to get us what we came for, assuage the people of Gwytherin, make peace all round—'

'And to placate me, and cause me to give up the pursuit of my father's murderer,' said Sioned, 'burying the deed along with the victim. Except that I will not rest until I know.'

'—and shed reflected glory upon Prior Robert, I was going to say. And I wish I knew which mind conceived the idea!'

They had met for a few hurried minutes at Bened's smithy, where Cadfael had gone to borrow mattock and spade for the holy work now to be undertaken. Even a few of the men of Gwytherin had come forward and asked to have a share in breaking the sacred earth, for though they were still reluctant to lose their saint, if it was her will to leave them they had no wish to cross her. Prodigious things were happening, and they intended to be in receipt of her approval and blessing rather than run the risk of encountering her arrows.

'It seems to me most of the glory is falling, rather, on Brother Columbanus of late,' said Sioned shrewdly. 'And the prior took it meekly, and never made any attempt to filch it back from him. That's the one thing that makes me believe he may be honest.'

She had said something that caused Cadfael to pause and look attentively at her, scrubbing dubiously at his nose. 'You may well be right. And certainly this story is bound to go back to Shrewsbury with us, and spread through all our sister houses, when we come home with our triumph. Yes, Columbanus will certainly have made himself a great name for holiness and divine favour in the order.'

'They say an ambitious man can make a grand career in the cloister,' she said. 'Maybe he's busy laying the foundations, a great step up towards being prior himself when Robert becomes abbot. Or even abbot, when Robert supposes *he's* about to become abbot! For it's not *his* name they'll be buzzing round the shires as the visionary the saints use to make their wants known.'

'That,' agreed Cadfael, 'may not even have dawned on Robert yet, but when the awe of the occasion passes it will. And he's the one who's pledged to write a life of the saint, and complete it with the account of this pilgrimage. Columbanus may very well end up as an anonymous brother who happened to be charged with a message to the prior from his patroness. Chroniclers can edit names out as easily as visionaries can noise them abroad. But I grant you, this lad comes of a thrusting Norman family that doesn't put even its younger sons into the Benedictine habit to spend their lives doing menial work like gardening.'

'And we're no further forward,' said Sioned bitterly.

'No. But we have not finished yet.'

'But as I see it, this is devised to be an ending, to close this whole episode in general amity, as if everything was resolved. But everything is *not* resolved! Somewhere in this land there is a man who stabbed my father in the back, and we're all being asked to draw a veil over that and lose sight of it in the great treaty of peace. But I want that man found, and Engelard vindicated, and my father avenged, and I won't rest, or let anyone else rest, until I get what I want. And now tell me what I am to do.'

'What I've already told you,' said Cadfael. 'Have all your household party and friends gathered at the chapel to watch the grave opened, and make sure that Peredur attends.'

'I've already sent Annest to beg him to come,' said Sioned. 'And then? What have I to say or do to Peredur?'

'That silver cross you wear round your neck,' said Cadfael. 'Are you willing to part with it in exchange for one step ahead towards what you want to know?'

'That and all the rest of the valuables I own. You know it.'

'Then this,' said Cadfael, 'is what you will do. . . .'

With prayers and psalms they carried their tools up to the tangled graveyard by the chapel, trimmed back the brambles and wild flowers and long grass from the little mound of Winifred's grave, and reverently broke the sod. By turns they laboured, all taking a share in the work for the merit to be acquired. And most of Gwytherin gathered round the place in the course of the day, all work left at a standstill in the fields and crofts, to watch the end of this contention. For Sioned had spoken truly. She and all her household servants were there among the rest, in mourning and massed to bring out Rhisiart's body for burial when the time came, but this funeral party had become, for the time being, no more than a side-issue, an incident in the story of Saint Winifred, and a closed incident at that.

Cadwallon was there, Uncle Meurice was there, and Bened, and all the other neighbours. And there at his father's elbow, withdrawn and brooding, stood young Peredur, by the look of him wishing himself a hundred leagues away. His thick dark brows were drawn together as though his head ached, and wherever his brown eyes wandered, it was never towards Sioned. He had crept here reluctantly at her express asking, but he could not or would not face her. The bold red mouth was chilled and pale from the tension with which it was tightened against his teeth. He watched the dark pit deepen in the grass, and breathed hard and deep, like a man containing pain. A far cry from the spoiled boy with the long, light step and the audacious smile, who so plainly had taken it for granted that the world was his for the wooing. Peredur's demons were at him within.

The ground was moist but light, not hard to work, but the grave was deep. Gradually the diggers sank to the shoulders in the pit, and by mid-afternoon Brother Cadfael, shortest of the party, had almost disappeared from view when he took his final turn in the depths. No one dared to doubt openly if they were in the right place, but some must have been wondering. Cadfael, for no good reason that he could see, had no doubts at all. The girl was here. She had lived many years as an abbess after her brief martyrdom and miraculous restoration, yet he thought of her as that devout, green girl, in romantic love with celibacy and holiness, who had fled from Prince Cradoc's advances as from the devil himself. By some perverse severance of the heart in two he could feel both for her and for the desperate lover, so roughly molten out of the flesh and presumably exterminated in the spirit. Did anyone ever pray for him? He was in greater need than Winifred. In the end, perhaps the only prayers he ever benefited by were Winifred's prayers. She was Welsh, and capable of detachment and subtlety. She might well have put in a word for him, to reassemble his liquefied person and congeal it again into the shape of a man. A chastened man, doubtless, but still the same shape as before. Even a saint may take pleasure, in retrospect, in having been once desired.

The spade grated on something in the dark, friable soil, something neither loam nor stone. Cadfael checked his stroke instantly at its suggestion of age, frailty and crumbling dryness. He let the blade lie, and stooped to scoop away with his hands the cool, odorous, gentle earth that hid the obstruction from him. Dark soil peeled away under his fingers from a slender, pale, delicate thing, the gentle dove-grey of pre-dawn, but freckled with pitted points of black. He drew out an arm-bone, scarcely more than child size, and stroked away the clinging earth. Islands of the same soft colouring showed below, grouped loosely together. He did not want to break any of them. He hoisted the spade and tossed it out of the pit.

'She is here. We have found her. Softly, now, leave her to me.'

Faces peered in upon him. Prior Robert gleamed in silvery agitation, thirsting to plunge in and dredge up the prize in person, but deterred by the clinging darkness of the soil and the whiteness of his hands. Brother Columbanus at the brink towered and glittered, his exalted visage turned, not towards the depths where this fragile virgin substance lay at rest, but rather to the heavens from which her diffused spiritual essence had addressed him. He displayed, no doubt of it, an aura of distinct proprietorship that dwarfed both prior and sub-prior, and shone with its full radiance upon all those who watched from the distance. Brother Columbanus meant to be, was, and knew that he was, memorable in this memorable hour.

Brother Cadfael kneeled. It may even have been a significant omen that at this moment he alone was kneeling. He judged that he was at the feet of the skeleton. She had been there some centuries, but the earth had dealt kindly, she might well be whole, or virtually whole. He had not wanted her disturbed at all, but now he wanted her disturbed as little as might be, and delved carefully with scooping palms and probing, stroking finger-tips to uncover the whole slender length of her without damage. She must have been a little above medium height, but willowy as a seventeen-year-old girl. Tenderly he stroked the earth away from round her. He found the skull, and leaned on stretched arms, fingering the eye-sockets clear, marvelling at the narrow elegance of the cheek-bones, and the generosity of the dome. She had beauty and fineness in her death. He leaned over her like a shield, and grieved.

'Let me down a linen sheet,' he said, 'and some bands to raise it smoothly. She shall not come out of here bone by bone, but whole woman as she went in.'

They handed a cloth down to him, and he spread it beside the slight skeleton, and with infinite care eased her free of the loose soil, and edged her by inches into the shroud of linen, laying the disturbed arm-bone in its proper place. With bands of cloth slung under her she was drawn up into the light of day, and laid tenderly in the grass at the side of her grave.

'We must wash away the soil-marks from her bones,' said Prior Robert, gazing in reverent awe upon the prize he had gone to such trouble to gain, 'and wrap them afresh.'

'They are dry and frail and brittle,' warned Cadfael impatiently. 'If she is robbed of this Welsh earth she may very well crumble to Welsh earth herself in your hands. And if you keep her here in the air and the sun too long, she may fall to dust in any case. If you are wise, Father Prior, you'll wrap her well as she lies, and get her into the reliquary and seal her from the air as tight as you can, as quickly as you can.'

That was good sense, and the prior acted on it, even if he did not much relish being told what to do so brusquely. With hasty but exultant prayers they brought the resplendent coffin out to the lady, to avoid moving her more than they must, and with repeated swathings of linen bound her little bones carefully together, and laid her in the coffin. The brothers who made it had realised the need for perfect sealing to preserve the treasure, and taken great pains to make the lid fit down close as a skin, and line the interior with lead. Before Saint Winifred was carried back into the chapel for the thanksgiving Mass the lid was closed upon her, the catches secured, and at the end of the service the prior's seals were added to make all fast. They had her imprisoned, to be carried away into the alien land that desired her patronage. All the Welsh who could crowd into the chapel or cling close enough to the doorway to catch glimpses of the proceedings kept a silence uncannily perfect, their eyes following every move, secret eyes that expressed no resentment, but by their very attention, fixed and unwavering, implied an unreconciled opposition they were afraid to speak aloud.

'Now that this sacred duty is done,' said Father Huw, at once relieved and saddened, 'it is time to attend to the other duty which the saint herself has laid upon us, and bury Rhisiart honourably, with full absolution, in the grave she has bequeathed to him. And I call to mind, in the hearing of all, how great a blessing is thus bestowed, and how notable an honour.' It was as near as he would go to speaking out his own view of Rhisiart, and in this, at least, he had the sympathy of every Welshman there present.

That burial service was brief, and after it six of Rhisiart's oldest and most trusted servants took up the bier of branches, a little wilted now but still green, and carried it out to the graveside. The same slings which had lifted Saint Winifred waited to lower Rhisiart into the same bed.

Sioned stood beside her uncle, and looked all round her at the circle of her friends and neighbours, and unclasped the silver cross from her neck. She had so placed herself that Cadwallon and Peredur were close at her right hand, and it was simple and natural to turn towards them. Peredur had hung back throughout, never looking at her but when he was sure she was looking away, and when she swung round upon him suddenly he had no way of avoiding.

'One last gift I want to give to my father. And I would like you, Peredur, to be the one to give it. You have been like a son to him. Will you lay this cross on his breast, where the murderer's arrow pierced him? I want it to be buried with him. It is my farewell to him here, let it be yours, too.'

Peredur stood dumbstruck and aghast, staring from her still

and challenging face to the little thing she held out to him, in front of so many witnesses, all of whom knew him, all of whom were known to him. She had spoken clearly, to be heard by all. Every eye was on him, and all recorded, though without understanding, the slow draining of blood from his face, and his horror-stricken stare. He could not refuse what she asked. He could not do it without touching the dead man, touching the very place where death had struck him.

His hand came out with aching reluctance, and took the cross from her. To leave her thus extending it in vain was more than he could stand. He did not look at it, but only desperately at her, and in her face the testing calm had blanched into incredulous dismay, for now she believed she knew everything, and it was worse than anything she had imagined. But as he could not escape from the trap she had laid for him, neither could she release him. It was sprung, and now he had to fight his way out of it as best he could. They were already wondering why he made no move, and whispering together in concern at his hanging back.

He made a great effort, drawing himself together with a frantic briskness that lasted only a moment. He took a few irresolute steps towards the bier and the grave, and then baulked like a frightened horse, and halted again, and that was worse, for now he stood alone in the middle of the circle of witnesses, and could go neither forward nor back. Cadfael saw sweat break in great beads on his forehead and lip.

'Come, son,' said Father Huw kindly, the last to suspect evil, 'don't keep the dead waiting, and don't grieve too much for them, for that would be sin. I know, as Sioned has said, he was like another father to you, and you share her loss. So do we all.'

Peredur stood quivering at Sioned's name, and at the word 'father', and tried to go forward, and could not move. His feet would not take him one step nearer to the swathed form that lay by the open grave. The light of the sun on him, the weight of all eyes, bore him down. He fell on his knees suddenly, the cross still clutched in one hand, the other spread to hide his face.

'He cannot!' he cried hoarsely from behind the shielding palm.

'He cannot accuse me! I am not guilty of murder! What I did was done when Rhisiart was already dead!'

A great, gasping sigh passed like a sudden wind round the clearing and over the tangled grave, and subsided into a vast silence. It was a long minute before Father Huw broke it, for this was his sheep, not Prior Robert's, a child of his flock, and hitherto a child of grace, now stricken into wild self-accusation of some terrible sin not yet explained, but to do with violent death.

'Son Peredur,' said Father Huw firmly, 'you have not been charged with any ill-doing by any other but yourself. We are waiting only for you to do what Sioned has asked of you, for her asking was a grace. Therefore do her bidding, or speak out why you will not, and speak plainly.'

Peredur heard, and ceased to tremble. A little while he kneeled and gathered his shattered composure about him doggedly, like a cloak. Then he uncovered his face, which was pale, despairing but eased, no longer in combat with truth but consenting to it. He was a young man of courage. He got to his feet and faced them squarely.

'Father, I come to confession by constraint, and not gladly, and I am as ashamed of that as of what I have to confess. But it is not murder. I did not kill Rhisiart. I found him dead.'

'At what hour?' asked Brother Cadfael, wholly without right, but nobody questioned the interruption.

'I went out after the rain stopped. You remember it rained.' They remembered. They had good reason. 'It would be a little after noon. I was going up to the pasture our side of Bryn, and I found him lying on his face in that place where afterwards we all saw him. He was dead then, I swear it! And I was grieved, but also I was tempted, for there was nothing in this world I could do for Rhisiart, but I saw a way. . . .' Peredur swallowed and sighed, bracing his forehead against his fate, and went on. 'I saw a means of ridding myself of a rival. Of the favoured rival. Rhisiart had refused his daughter to Engelard, but Sioned had not refused him, and well I knew there was no hope for me, however her father urged her, while Engelard was there between us. Men might easily believe that Engelard should kill Rhisiart, if—if there was some proof. . . .'

'But *you* did not believe it,' said Cadfael, so softly that hardly anyone noticed the interruption, it was accepted and answered without thought.

'No!' said Peredur almost scornfully. 'I knew him, he never would!'

'Yet you were willing he should be taken and accused. It was all one to you if it was death that removed him out of your way, so he was removed.'

'No!' said Peredur again, smouldering but aware that he was justly lashed. 'No, not that! I thought he would run, take himself away again into England, and leave us alone, Sioned and me. I never wished him worse than that. I thought, with him gone, in the end Sioned would do what her father had wished, and marrv me. I could wait! I would have waited years. . . .'

He did not say, but there were two there, at least, who knew, and remembered in his favour, that he had opened the way for Engelard to break out of the ring that penned him in, and deliberately let him pass, just as Brother John, with a better conscience, had frustrated the pursuit.

Brother Cadfael said sternly: 'But you went so far as to steal one of this unfortunate young man's arrows, to make sure all eyes turned on him.'

'I did not steal it, though no less discredit to me that I used it as I did. I was out with Engelard after game, not a week earlier, with Rhisiart's permission. When we retrieved our arrows, I took one of his by error among mine. I had it with me then.'

Peredur's shoulders had straightened, his head was up, his hands, the right still holding Sioned's cross, hung gently and resignedly at his sides. His face was pale but calm. He had got the worst of it off his back, after what he had borne alone these last days confession and penance were balm.

'Let me tell the whole of it, all the thing I did, that has made me a monster in my own eyes ever since. I will not make it less than it was, and it was hideous. Rhisiart was stabbed in the back, and the dagger withdrawn and gone. I turned him over on his back, and I turned that wound back to front, and I tell you, my hands burn now, but I did it. He was dead, he suffered nothing. I pierced my own flesh, not his. I could tell the line of the wound, for the dagger had gone right through him, though the breast wound was small. I took my own dagger, and opened the way for Engelard's arrow to follow, and I thrust it through and left it standing in him for witness. And I have not had one quiet moment, night or day,' said Peredur, not asking pity, rather grateful that now his silence was broken and his infamy known, and nothing more to hide, 'since I did this small, vile thing, and now I am glad it's out, whatever becomes of me. And at least grant me this, I did not make my trap in such a way as to accuse Engelard of shooting a man in the back! I knew him! I lived almost side by side with him since he came here a fugitive, we were of an age, we could match each other. I have liked him, hunted with him, fought with him, been jealous of him, even hated him because he was loved where I was not. Love makes men do terrible things,' said Peredur, not pleading, marvelling, 'even to their friends.'

He had created, all unconsciously, a tremendous hush all about him, of awe at his blasphemy, of startled pity for his desolation, of chastened wonder at their own misconceivings. The truth fell like thunder, subduing them all. Rhisiart had not been shot down with an arrow, but felled from behind at close quarters, out of thick cover, a coward's killing. Not saints, but men, deal in that kind of treachery.

Father Huw broke the silence. In his own province, where no alien dignitaries dared intrude, he grew taller and more secure in his gentle, neighbourly authority. And great violence had been done to what he knew to be right, and great requital was due from the sinner, and great compassion due to him.

'Son Peredur,' he said, 'you stand in dire sin, and cannot be excused. Such violation of the image of God, such misuse of a clean affection—for such I know you had with Rhisiart—and such malice towards an innocent man—for such you proclaimed Engelard—cannot go unpunished.'

'God forbid,' said Peredur humbly, 'that I should escape any part of what is due. I want it! I cannot live with myself if I have only this present self to live with!'

'Child, if you mean that, then give yourself into my hands, to be delivered up both to secular and religious justice. As to the law, I shall speak with the prince's bailiff. As to the penance due before God, that is for me as your confessor, and I require that you shall wait my considered judgment.'

'So I will, Father,' said Peredur. 'I want no unearned pardon. I take penance willingly.'

'Then you need not despair of grace. Go home now, and remain withindoors until I send for you.'

'I will be obedient to you in all things. But I have one prayer before I go.' He turned slowly and faced Sioned. She was standing quite still where the awful dread had fallen upon her, her hands clutched to her cheeks, her eyes fixed in fascination and pain upon the boy who had grown up as her playfellow. But the rigidity had ebbed out of her, for though he called himself a monster, he was not, after all, the monster she had briefly thought him. 'May I now do what you asked of me? I am not afraid now. He was a fair man always. He won't accuse me of more than my due.'

He was both asking her pardon and saying his farewell to any hope he had still cherished of winning her, for now that was irrevocably over. And the strange thing was that now he could approach her, even after so great an offence, without constraint, almost without jealousy. Nor did her face express any great heat or bitterness against him. It was thoughtful and intent.

'Yes,' she said, 'I still wish it.' If he had spoken the whole truth, and she was persuaded that he had, it was well that he should take his appeal to Rhisiart, in a form every man there would acknowledge. In otherworldly justice the body would clear him of the evil he had not committed, now that confession was made of what he had.

Peredur went forward steadily enough now, sank to his knees beside Rhisiart's body, and laid first his hand, and then Sioned's cross, upon the heart he had pierced, and no gush of blood sprang at his touch. And if there was one thing certain, it was that here was a man who did believe. He hesitated a moment, still kneeling, and then, feeling a need rather to give thanks for this acceptance than to make any late and unfitting display of affection, stooped and kissed the right hand that lay quiet over the left on Rhisiart's breast, their clasped shape showing through the close shroud. That done, he rose and went firmly away by the downhill path towards his father's house. The people parted to let him through in a great silence, and Cadwallon, starting out of a trance of unbelieving misery, lurched forward in haste and went trotting after his son.

CHAPTER NINE

The evening was drawing in by the time they had buried Rhisiart, and it was too late for Prior Robert and his companions to take their prize and leave at once for home, even if it had been a seemly thing to do, after all that had happened. Some ceremony was due to the community the saint was leaving, and the houses that had offered hospitality freely even to those who came to rob them.

'We will stay this night over, and sing Vespers and Compline in the church with you, and give due thanks,' said the prior. 'And after Compline one of us will again watch the night through with Saint Winifred, as is only proper. And should the prince's bailiff require that we stay longer, we will do as he asks. For there is still the matter of Brother John, who stands in contempt of the law, to our disgrace.'

'At present,' said Father Huw deprecatingly, 'the bailiff is giving his attention to the case of Rhisiart's murder. For though we have suffered many revelations in that matter, you see that we are no nearer knowing who is guilty. What we have seen today is one man who certainly is innocent of the crime, whatever his other sins may be.'

'I fear,' said Prior Robert with unwonted humility, 'that without ill intent we have caused you great grief and trouble here, and for that I am sorry. And greatly sorry for the parents of that sinful young man, who are suffering, I think, far worse than he, and without blame.'

'I am going to them now,' said Huw. 'Will you go on ahead, Father Prior, and sing Vespers for me? For I may be delayed some time. I must do what I can for this troubled household.'

The people of Gwytherin had begun to drift away silently by many paths, vanishing into the woods to spread the news of the day's happening to the far corners of the parish. In the long grass of the graveyard, trampled now by many feet, the dark, raw shape of Rhisiart's grave made a great scar, and two of his men were filling in the earth over him. It was finished. Sioned turned towards the gate, and all the rest of her people followed.

Cadfael fell in beside her as the subdued, straggling procession made its way home towards the village.

'Well,' he said resignedly, 'it was worth trying. And we can't say it got us nothing. At least we know now who committed the lesser crime, if we're very little nearer knowing who committed the greater. And we know why there were two, for they made no sense, being one and the same. And at any rate, we have shaken the devil off that boy's back. Are you quite revolted at what he did? As *he* is?'

'Strangely,' said Sioned, 'I don't believe I am. I was too sick with horror, that short time while I thought him the murderer. After that, it was simple relief that he was not. He has never gone short of anything he wanted, you see, until he wanted me.'

'It was a real wanting,' said Brother Cadfael, remembering long-past hungers of his own. 'I doubt if he'll ever quite get over it, though I'm pretty sure he'll make a sound marriage, and get handsome children like himself, and be very fairly content. He grew up today, she won't be disappointed, whoever she may be. But she'll never be Sioned.'

Her tired, woeful, discouraged face had softened and warmed, and suddenly she was smiling beside him, faintly but reassuringly. 'You are a good man. You have a way of reconciling people. But no need! Do you think I did not see how he dragged himself painfully to this afternoon's business, and has gone striding away with his head up to embrace his punishment? I might really have loved him a little, if there had been no Engelard. But only a little! He may do better than that.'

'You are a fine girl,' said Brother Cadfael heartily. 'If I had met you when I was thirty years younger, I should have made Engelard sweat for his prize. Peredur should be thankful even for such a sister. But we're no nearer knowing what we want and need to know.'

'And have we any more shafts left to loose?' she asked ruefully. 'Any more snares to set? At least we've freed the poor soul we caught in the last one.'

He was silent, glumly thinking.

'And tomorrow,' she said sadly, 'Prior Robert will take his saint and all his brothers, and you with them, and set out for home, and I shall be left with nobody to turn to here. Father Huw is as near a saint himself, in his small, confused way, as ever Winifred was, but no use to me. And Uncle Meurice is a gentle creature who knows about running a manor, but nothing about anything else, and wants no trouble and no exertion. And Engelard must go on hiding, as well you know. Peredur's plot against him is quite empty now, we all know it. But does that prove he did not kill my father, after a raging quarrel?'

'In the back?' said Cadfael, unguardedly indignant.

She smiled. 'All that proves is that you know him! Not everyone does. Some will be saying at this moment, perhaps, after all . . . that Peredur may have been right without even knowing it.'

He thought about it and was dismayed, for no question but she was right. What, indeed, did it prove if another man had wished to burden him with the guilt? Certainly not that the guilt was *not* his. Brother Cadfael confronted his own voluntarily assumed responsibility, and braced himself to cope with it.

'There is also Brother John to be considered,' said Sioned. It may well be that Annest, walking behind, had prodded her.

'I have not forgotten Brother John,' agreed Cadfael.

'But I think the bailiff well may have done. He would shut his eyes or look the other way, if Brother John left for Shrewsbury with the rest of you. He has troubles enough here, what does he want with alien trouble?'

'And if Brother John should seem to him to have left for Shrewsbury, he would be satisfied? And ask no questions about one more outlander taken up by a patron here?'

'I always knew you were quick,' said Sioned, brown and bright and animated, almost herself again. 'But would Prior Robert pursue him still, when he hears he's gone from custody? I don't see him as a forgiving man.'

'No, nor he is, but how would he set about it? The Benedictine order has no real hold in Wales. No, I think he'd let it ride, now he has what he came for. I'm more concerned for Engelard. Give me this one more night, child, and do this for me! Send your people home, and stay the night over with Annest at Bened's croft, and if God aids me with some new thought—for never forget God is far more deeply offended even than you or I by this great wrong!—I'll come to you there.'

'We'll do that,' said Sioned. 'And you'll surely come.'

They had slowed to let the cortège move well ahead of them, so that they could talk freely. They were approaching the gate-house of Cadwallon's holding, and Prior Robert and his companions were far in front and had passed by the gate, bent upon singing Vespers in good time. Father Huw, issuing forth in haste and agitation in search of help, seemed relieved rather than dismayed to find only Cadfael within call. The presence of Sioned checked him to a decent walk and a measured tone, but did nothing to subdue the effect of his erected hair and frantic mien.

'Brother Cadfael, will you spare some minutes for this afflicted household? You have some skills with medicines, you may be able to advise. . . .'

'His mother!' whispered Sioned in immediate reassurance. 'She weeps herself into a frenzy at everything that crosses her. I knew this would set her off. Poor Peredur, he has his penance already! Shall I come?'

'Better not,' he said as softly, and moved to meet Father Huw. Sioned was, after all, the innocent cause of Peredur's fall from grace, she would probably be the last person calculated to calm his mother's anguish. And Sioned understood him so, and went on, and left the matter to him, so calmly that it was clear she expected no tragic results from the present uproar. She had known Cadwallon's wife all her life, no doubt she had learned to treat her ups and downs as philosophically as Cadfael did Brother Columbanus' ecstasies and excesses. He never really hurt himself in his throes, either!

'Dame Branwen is in such a taking,' fluttered Father Huw distractedly, steering Cadfael in haste towards the open door of the hall. 'I fear for her wits. I've seen her upset before, and hard enough to pacify, but now, her only child, and such a shock. . . . Really, she may do herself an injury if we cannot quiet her.'

Dame Branwen was indeed audible before they even entered the small room where husband and son were trying to soothe her, against a tide of vociferous weeping and lamentation that all but deafened them. The lady, fat and fair and outwardly fashioned only for comfortable, shallow placidity, half-sat, half-lay on a couch, throwing her substantial person about in extravagant distress, now covering her silly, fond face, now throwing her arms abroad in sweeping gestures of desolation and despair, but never for one moment ceasing to bellow her sorrow and shame. The tears that flowed freely down her round cheeks and the shattering sobs that racked her hardly seemed to impede the flow of words that poured out of her like heavy rain.

Cadwallon on one side and Peredur on the other stroked and patted and comforted in vain. As often as the father tried to assert himself she turned on him with wild reproaches, crying that he had no faith in his own son, or he could never have believed such a terrible thing of him, that the boy was bewitched, under some spell that forced false confession out of him, that he ought to have stood up for him before everybody and prevented the tale from being accepted so lightly, for somewhere there was witch-craft in it. As often as Peredur tried to convince her he had told truth, that he was willing to make amends, and she must accept his word, she rounded on him with fresh outbursts of tears, screaming that her own son had brought dreadful disgrace upon himself and her, that she wondered he dare come near her, that she would never be able to lift up her head again, that he was a monster. . . .

As for poor Father Huw, when he tried to assert his spiritual authority and order her to submit to the force of truth and accept her son's act with humility, as Peredur himself had done in making full confession and offering full submission, she cried out that she had been a God-fearing and law-abiding woman all her life, and done everything to bring up her child in the same

146

way, and she could not now accept his guilt as reflecting upon her.

'Mother,' said Peredur, haggard and sweating worse than when he faced Rhisiart's body, 'nobody blames you, and nobody will. What I did I did, and it's I who must abide the consequence, not you. There isn't a woman in Gwytherin won't feel for you.'

At that she let out a great wail of grief, and flung her arms about him, and swore that he should not suffer any grim penalties, that he was her own boy, and she would protect him. And when he extricated himself with fading patience, she screamed that he meant to kill her, the unfeeling wretch, and went off into peals of ear-piercing, sobbing laughter.

Brother Cadfael took Peredur firmly by the sleeve, and hauled him away to the back of the room. 'Show a little sense, lad, and take yourself out of her sight, you're fuel to her fire. If nobody marked her at all she'd have stopped long ago, but now she's got herself into this state she's past doing that of her own accord. Did our two brothers stop in here, do you know, or go on with the prior?'

Peredur was shaking and tired out, but responded hopefully to this matter-of-fact treatment. 'They've not been here, or I should have seen them. They must have gone on to the church.'

Naturally, neither Columbanus nor Jerome would dream of absenting himself from Vespers on such a momentous day.

'Never mind, you can show me where they lodge. Columbanus brought some of my poppy syrup with him, in case of need, the phial should be there with his scrip, he'd hardly have it on him. And as far as I know, he's had no occasion to use it, his cantrips here in Wales have been of a quieter kind. We can find a use for it now.'

'What does it do?' asked Peredur, wide-eyed.

'It soothes the passions and kills pain—either of the body or the spirit.'

'I could use some of that myself,' said Peredur with a wry smile, and led the way out to one of the small huts that lined the stockade. The guests from Shrewsbury had been given the best lodging the house afforded, with two low brychans, and a small chest, with a rush lamp for light. Their few necessaries occupied almost no space, but each had a leather scrip to hold them, and both of these dangled from a nail in the timber wall. Brother Cadfael opened first one, and then the other, and in the second found what he was seeking.

He drew it out and held it up to the light, a small phial of greenish glass. Even before he saw the line of the liquid in it, its light weight had caused him to check and wonder. Instead of being full to the stopper with the thick, sweet syrup, the bottle was three-quarters empty.

Brother Cadfael stood stock-still for a moment with the phial in his hand, staring at it in silence. Certainly Columbanus might at some time have felt the need to forestall some threatening spiritual disturbance but Cadfael could recall no occasion when he had said any word to that effect, or shown any sign of the rosy, reassuring calm the poppies could bring. There was enough gone from the bottle to restore serenity three times over, enough to put a man to sleep for hours. And now that he came to think back, there had been at least one occasion when a man had slept away hours of the day, instead of keeping the watch he was set to keep. The day of Rhisiart's death Columbanus had failed of his duty, and confessed as much with heartfelt penitence. Columbanus, who had the syrup in his possession, and knew its use. . . .

'What must we do?' asked Peredur, uneasy in the silence. 'If it tastes unpleasant you'll have trouble getting her to drink it.'

'It tastes sweet.' But there was not very much of it left, a little reinforcement with something else soothing and pleasant might be necessary. 'Go and get a cup of strong wine, and we'll see how that goes down.'

They had taken with them a measure of wine that day, he remembered, the ration for the two of them, when they set off for the chapel. Columbanus had drawn and carried it. And a bottle of water for himself, since he had made an act of piety of renouncing wine until their mission was accomplished. Jerome had done well, getting a double ration.

Brother Cadfael stirred himself out of his furious thoughts

to deal with the immediate need. Peredur hurried to do his bidding, but brought mead instead of wine.

'She's more likely to drink it down before she thinks to be obstinate, for she likes it better. And it's stronger.'

'Good!' said Cadfael. 'It will hide the syrup better. And now, go somewhere quiet, and harden your heart and stop your ears and stay out of her sight, for it's the best thing you can do for her, and God knows the best for yourself, after such a day. And leave agonising too much over your sins, black as they are, there isn't a confessor in the land who hasn't heard worse and never turned a hair. It's a kind of arrogance to be so certain you're past redemption.'

The sweet, cloying drink swirled in the cup, the syrup unwinding into it in a long spiral that slowly melted and vanished. Peredur with shadowy eyes watched and was silent.

After a moment he said, very low: 'It's strange! I never could have done so shabbily by anyone I hated.'

'Not strange at all,' said Cadfael bluntly, stirring his potion. 'When harried, we go as far as we dare, and with those we're sure of we dare go very far, knowing where forgiveness is certain.'

Peredur bit his lip until it was biddable. '*Is* it certain?'

'As tomorrow's daylight, child! And now be off out of my way, and stop asking fool questions. Father Huw will have no time for you today, there's more important business waiting.'

Peredur went like a docile child, startled and comforted, and wherever he hid himself, he did it effectively, for Cadfael saw no more of him that evening. He was a good lad at heart, and this wild lunge of his into envy and meanness had brought him up short against an image of himself that he did not like at all. Whatever prayers Huw set him by way of penance were likely to hit heaven with the irresistible fervour of thunderbolts, and whatever hard labour he was given, the result was likely to stand solid as oak and last for ever.

Cadfael took his draught, and went back to where Dame Branwen was still heaving and quivering with uncontrollable sobs, by this time in genuine distress, exhausted by her efforts but unable to end them. He took advantage of her sheer weariness to present the cup to her as soon as he reached her side, and with abrupt authority that acted on her before she could muster the fibre of stubbornness.

'Drink this!' And automatically she drank it, half of it going down out of pure surprise, the second half because the first had taught her how dry and sore her throat was from all its exertions, and how smooth was the texture and how sweet the taste of this brew. The very act of swallowing it broke the frightening rhythm of the huge sighs that had convulsed her almost worse than the sobbing. Father Huw had time to mop his brow with a fold of his sleeve before she was able to resume her complaints. Even then, by comparison with what had gone before, they sounded half-hearted.

'We women, we mothers, we sacrifice our lives to bringing up children, and when they're grown they reward us by bringing disgrace upon us. What did I ever do to deserve this?'

'He'll do you credit yet,' said Cadfael cheerfully. 'Stand by him in his penance, but never try to excuse his sin, and he'll think the better of you for it.'

That went by her like the wind sighing at the time, though she may have remembered it later. Her voice declined gradually from its injured self-justification, dwindled into a half-dreamy monologue of grief, and took on at length a tone of warm and drowsy complacency, before it lapsed into silence. Cadwallon breathed deep and cautiously, and eyed his advisers.

'I should call her women and get her to bed,' said Cadfael. 'She'll sleep the night through, and it'll do her nothing but good.' And you more good still, he thought but did not say. 'Let your son rest, too, and never say another word about his trouble but by the way, like any other daily business, unless he speaks up first. Father Huw will take care of him faithfully.'

'I will,' said Huw. 'He's worth our efforts.'

Dame Branwen went amiably where she was led, and the house was wonderfully quiet. Cadfael and Huw went out together, pursued as far as the gate by Cadwallon's distracted gratitude. When they were well away from the holding, at the end of the stockade, the quietness of the dusk came down on them softly, a cloud descending delicately upon a cloud.

'In time for supper, if not for Vespers,' said Huw wearily. 'What should we have done without you, Brother Cadfael? I have no skill at all with women, they confuse me utterly. I marvel how you have learned to deal with them so ably, you, a cloistered brother.'

Cadfael thought of Bianca, and Arianna, and Mariam, and all the others, some known so briefly, all so well.

'Both men and women partake of the same human nature, Huw. We both bleed when we're wounded. That's a poor, silly woman, true, but we can show plenty of poor, silly men. There are women as strong as any of us, and as able.' He was thinking of Mariam—or was it of Sioned? 'You go to supper, Huw, and hold me excused, and if I can be with you before Compline, I will. I have some business first at Bened's smithy.'

The empty phial swung heavily in the pocket in his right sleeve, reminding him. His mind was still busy with the implications. Before ever he reached Bened's croft he had it clear in his mind what must be done, but was no nearer knowing how to set about it.

Cai was with Bened on the bench under the eaves, with a jug of rough wine between them. They were not talking, only waiting for him to appear, and there could be no reason for that, but that Sioned had told them positively that he would.

'A fine tangle it turns out,' said Bened, shaking his grizzled head. 'And now you'll be off and leave us holding it. No blame to you, you have to go where your duty is. But what are we to do about Rhisiart when you're gone? There's more than half this parish thinks your Benedictines have killed him, and the lesser half thinks some enemy here has taken the chance to blame you, and get clean away into cover. We were a peaceful community until you came, nobody looked for murder among us.'

'God knows we never meant to bring it,' said Cadfael. 'But there's still tonight before we go, and I haven't shot my last bolt yet. I must speak with Sioned. We've things to do, and not much time for doing them.'

'Drink one cup with us before you go in to her,' insisted Cai. 'That takes no time at all, and is a powerful aid to thought.'

They were seated all together, three simple, honest men, and the wine notably lower in the jug, when someone turned in at the gate, light feet came runing in great haste along the path, and suddenly there was Annest confronting them, skirts flying and settling about her like wings folding, her breath short and laboured, and excitement and consternation in her face. And ready to be indignant at the very sight of them sitting peacefully drinking wine.

'You'd better stir yourselves,' she said, panting and sparkling. 'I've been along to Father Huw's house to see what's going on there—Marared and Edwin between them have been keeping an eye open for us. Do you know who's there taking supper with the Benedictines? Griffith ap Rhys, the bailiff! And do you know where he's bound, afterwards? Up to our house, to take Brother John to prison!'

They were on their feet fast enough at this news, though Bened dared to question it. 'He can't be there! The last I heard of him he was at the mill.'

'And that was this morning, and I tell you now he's eating and drinking with Prior Robert and the rest. I've seen him with my own eyes, so don't tell me he can't be there. And here I find you sitting on your hams drinking, as though we had all the time in the world!'

'But *why* in such a hurry tonight?' persisted Bened. 'Did the prior send for him, because he's wanting to be away tomorrow?'

'The devil was in it! He came to Vespers just by way of compliment to Father Huw, and who should he find celebrating instead but Prior Robert, and the prior seized on it as just the chance he wanted, and has hung on to him and persuaded him Brother John must be taken in charge tonight, for he can't leave without knowing he's safely in the hands of the law. He says the bailiff should deal with him for the secular offence of hindering the arrest of a criminal, and when he's served his penalty he's to be sent back to Shrewsbury to answer for his defiance of discipline, or else the prior will send an escort to fetch him. And what could the bailiff do but fall in with it, when it was put to him like that? And here you sit—!'

'All right, girl, all right,' said Cai placatingly. 'I'm off this minute, and Brother John will be out of there and away to a safe place before ever the bailiff gets near us. I'll take one of your ponies, Bened. . . .'

'Saddle another for me,' said Annest with determination. 'I'm coming with you.'

Cai went off at a jogtrot to the paddock, and Annest, drawing breath more easily now that the worst was told, drank off the wine he had left in his cup, and heaved a huge, resolute sigh.

'We'd better be out of here fast, for that young brother who looks after the horses now will be coming down after supper to get them. The prior means to be there to see John safe bound. "There's time yet before Compline," he said. He was complaining of wanting you, too, to interpret for him, they were managing lamely with only Latin between them. Dear God, what a day it's been!'

And what a night, thought Cadfael, it's still likely to be. 'What else was going on there?' he asked. 'Did you hear anything that might give me a light? For heaven knows I need one!'

'They were debating which one of them should watch the night through at the chapel. And that same young fair one, the one who has visions, up and prayed it might be him. He said he'd been unfaithful to his watch once, and longed still to make amends. And the prior said he might. That much I understood myself. All the prior's thinking about seems to be making all the trouble he can for John,' said Annest resentfully, 'or I should think he might have sent somebody else instead. That young brother—what is it you call him?'

'Columbanus,' said Brother Cadfael.

'That's him, Columbanus! He begins to put on airs as if he *owned* Saint Winifred. I don't want her to go away at all, but at least it was the prior who first thought of it, and now if there's a halo for anybody it's shifted to this other fellow's head.'

She did not know it, but she had indeed given Cadfael a light, and with every word she said it burned more steadily. 'So he's to be the one who watches the night through before the altar—and alone, is he?'

'So I heard.' Cai was coming with the ponies, at a gay trot out of the meadow. Annest rose eagerly and kilted her gown, knotting her girdle tightly about the broad pleat she drew up over her hips. 'Brother Cadfael, you don't think it wrong of me to love John? Or of him to love me? I don't care about the rest of them, but I should be sorry if *you* thought we were doing something wicked.'

Cai had not bothered with a saddle for himself, but had provided one for her. Quite simply and naturally Brother Cadfael cupped his hands for her foot, to give her a lift on to the pony's broad back, and the fresh scent of her linen and the smooth coolness of her ankle against his wrists as she mounted made one of the best moments of that interminably long and chaotic day. 'As long as I may live, girl,' he said, 'I doubt if I shall ever know two creatures with less wickedness between them. He made a mistake, and there should be provision for everybody to make one fresh start. I don't think he's making any mistake this time.'

He watched her ride away, setting an uphill pace to which Cai adapted himself goodhumouredly. They had a fair start, it would be ten minutes or more yet before Columbanus came to fetch the horses, and even then he had to take them back to the parsonage. It might be well to put in an appearance and go with Robert dutifully to interpret his fulminations, too, in which case there was need of haste, for he had now a great deal to say to Sioned, and this night's moves must be planned thoroughly. He withdrew into the croft as soon as Annest and Cai were out of sight, and Sioned came out of the shadows eagerly to meet him.

'I expected Annest to be here before you. She went to find out what's happening at Father Huw's. I thought best to stay out of sight. If people think I'm away home, so much the better. You haven't seen Annest?'

'I have, and heard all her news,' said Cadfael, and told her what was in the wind, and where Annest was gone. 'Never fear for John, they'll be there well ahead of any pursuit. We have other business, and no time to waste, for I shall be expected to ride with the prior, and it's as well I should be there to see fair play. If we manage our business as well as I fancy Cai and Annest will manage theirs, before morning we may know what we want to know.'

'You've found out something,' she said with certainty. 'You are changed. You are sure!'

He told her briefly all that had happened at Cadwallon's house, how he had brooded upon it without enlightenment as to how it was to be used, and how Annest in innocence had shown him. Then he told her what he required of her.

'I know you can speak English, you must use it tonight. This may be a more dangerous trap than any we've laid before, but I shall be close by. And you may call in Engelard, too, if he'll promise to stay close in cover. But, child, if you have any doubts or fears, if you'd rather let be, and have me try some other way, say so now, and so be it.'

'No,' she said, 'no doubts and no fears. I can do anything. I dare do anything.'

'Then sit down with me, and learn your part well, for we haven't long. And while we plan, can I ask you to bring me some bread and a morsel of cheese? For I've missed my supper.'

Prior Robert and Brother Richard rode into Rhisiart's yard with the prince's bailiff between them, his two henchmen and Brother Cadfael close behind, at about half past seven, in a mild twilight, with all the unhurried ceremony of the law, rather as if Griffith ap Rhys held his commission from Saint Benedict, and not from Owain Gwynedd. The bailiff was, in fact, more than a little vexed at this unfortunate encounter, which had left him no alternative but to comply with Robert's demands. An offence against Welsh law was alleged, and had been reported to him, and he was obliged to investigate it, where, considering the circumstances, he would much have preferred to pack all the Benedictine delegation back to Shrewsbury, and let them sort out their own grudges there, without bothering a busy man who had plenty of more important things on his mind. Unhappily

Cadwallon's villein, the long-legged fellow who had been brought down by Brother John, had given vociferous evidence in support of the accusation, or it would have been easier to ignore it.

There was no one on duty at the gate, which was strange, and as they rode in, a number of people seemed to be running hither and thither in a distracted way, as if something unforeseen had happened, and confused and conflicting orders were being given from several authorities at once. No groom ran to attend to them, either. Prior Robert was displeased. Griffith ap Rhys was mildly and alertly interested. When someone did take notice of them, it was a very handsome young person in a green gown, who came running with her skirts gathered in her hands, and her light-brown hair slipping out of its glossy coil to her shoulders.

'Oh, sirs, you must excuse us this neglect, we've been so disturbed! The gate-keeper was called away to help, and all the grooms are hunting. . . . But I'm ashamed to let our troubles cast a shadow over our hospitality. My lady's resting, and can't be disturbed, but I'm at your service. Will it please you light down? Shall I have lodgings made ready?'

'We don't propose to stay,' said Griffith ap Rhys, already suspecting this artless goodwill, and approving the way she radiated it. 'We came to relieve you of a certain young malefactor you've had in hold here. But it seems you've suffered some further calamity, and we should be sorry to add to your troubles, or disturb your lady, after the grievous day she's endured.'

'Madam,' said Prior Robert, civilly but officiously, 'you are addressing the prince's bailiff of Rhos, and I am the prior of Shrewsbury abbey. You have a brother of that abbey in confinement here, the royal bailiff is come to relieve you of his care.'

All of which Cadfael duly and solemnly translated for Annest's benefit, his face as guileless as hers.

'Oh, sir!' She opened her eyes wide and curtseyed deeply to Griffith and cursorily to the prior, separating her own from the alien. 'It's true we had such a brother here a prisoner. . . .'

'Had?' said Robert sharply, for once detecting the change of tense.

'Had?' said Griffith thoughtfully.

'He's gone, sir! You see what confusion he's left behind. This evening, when his keeper took him his supper, this brother struck him down with a board torn loose from the manger in his prison, and dropped the bolt on him and slipped away. It was some time before we knew. He must have climbed the wall, you see it is not so high. We have men out now looking for him in the woods, and searching everywhere here within. But I fear he's clean gone!'

Cai made his entrance at the perfect time, issuing from one of the barns with shaky steps, his head wreathed in a white cloth lightly dabbled with red.

'The poor man, the villain broke his head for him! It was some time before he could drag himself to the door and hammer on it, and make himself heard. There's no knowing how far the fellow may have got by now. But the whole household is out hunting for him.'

The bailiff, as in duty bound, questioned Cai, but gently and briefly, questioned all the other servants, who ran to make themselves useful and succeeded only in being magnificently confusing. And Prior Robert, burning with vengeful zeal, would have pressed them more strenuously but for the bailiff's presence and obvious prior right, and the brevity of the time at his disposal if he was to get back for Compline. In any case, it was quite clear that Brother John was indeed over the wall and clean gone. Most willingly they showed the place where he had been confined, and the manger from which he had ripped the board, and the board itself, artistically spattered at one end with spots of Cai's gore, though it may, of course, have been pigment borrowed from the butcher.

'It seems your young man has given us all the slip,' said Griffith, with admirable serenity for a man of law who has lost a malefactor. 'There's nothing more to be done here. They could hardly expect such violence from a Benedictine brother, it's no blame to them.'

With considerable pleasure Cadfael translated that neat little stab. It kindled a spark in the speaking eyes of the young person in green, and Griffith did not miss it. But to challenge it would have been folly. The clear brown eyes would have opened wide enough and deep enough to drown a man in their innocence. 'We'd best leave them in peace to mend their broken mangers and broken heads,' said Griffith, 'and look elsewhere for our fugitive.'

'The wretch compounds his offences,' said Robert, furious. 'But I cannot allow his villainy to disrupt my mission. I must set out for home tomorrow, and leave his capture to you.'

'You may trust me to deal properly with him,' said Griffith drily, 'when he is found.' If he laid the slightest of emphasis on the 'when', no one appeared to remark it but Cadfael and Annest. By this time Annest was quite satisfied that she liked this princely official, and could trust him to behave like a reasonable man who is not looking for trouble, or trying to make it for others as harmless as himself.

'And you will restore him to our house when he has purged his offences under Welsh law?'

'When he has done so,' said Griffith, decidedly with some stress this time on the 'when', 'you shall certainly have him back.'

With that Prior Robert had to be content, though his Norman spirit burned at being deprived of its rightful victim. And on the ride back he was by no means placated by Griffith's tales of the large numbers of fugitive outlaws who had found no difficulty in living wild in these forests, and even made friends among the country people, and been accepted into families, and even into respectability at last. It galled his orderly mind to think of insubordination mellowing with time and being tolerated and condoned. He was in no very Christian mood when he swept into Father Huw's church, only just in time for Compline.

They were all there but Brother John, the remaining five brethren from Shrewsbury and a good number of the people of Gwytherin, to witness the last flowering of Brother Columbanus' devotional gift of ecstasy, now dedicated entirely to Saint Winifred, his personal patroness who had healed him of madness, favoured him with her true presence in a dream, and made known her will through him in the matter of Rhisiart's burial.

For at the end of Compline, rising to go to his self-chosen vigil, Columbanus turned to the altar, raised his arms in a sweeping gesture, and prayed aloud in a high, clear voice that the virgin martyr would deign to visit him once more in his holy solitude, in the silence of the night, and reveal to him again the inexpressible bliss from which he had returned so reluctantly to this imperfect world. And more, that this time, if she found him worthy of translation out of the body, she would take him up living into that world of light. Humbly he submitted his will to endure here below, and do his duty in the estate assigned him, but rapturously he sent his desire soaring to the timber roof, to be uplifted out of the flesh, transported through death without dying, if he was counted ready for the assumption.

Everyone present heard, and trembled at such virtue. Everyone but Brother Cadfael, who was past trembling at the arrogance of man, and whose mind, in any case, was busy and anxious with other, though related, matters.

CHAPTER TEN

Brother Columbanus entered the small, dark, wood-scented chapel, heavy with the odours of centuries, and closed the door gently behind him, without latching it. There were no candles lighted, tonight, only the small oil-lamp upon the altar, that burned with a tall, unwavering flame from its floating wick. That slender, single turret of light cast still shadows all around, and being almost on a level with the bier of Saint Winifred, braced on trestles before it, made of it a black coffin shape, only touched here and there with sparkles of reflected silver.

Beyond the capsule of soft golden light all was darkness, perfumed with age and dust. There was a second entrance, from the minute sacristy that was no more than a porch beside the altar, but no draught from that or any source caused the lamp-flame to waver even for an instant. There might have been no storms of air or spirit, no winds, no breath of living creature, to disturb the stillness.

Brother Columbanus made his obeisance to the altar, briefly and almost curtly. There was no one to see, he had come alone, and neither seen nor heard any sign of another living soul in the graveyard or the woods around. He moved the second prayer-desk aside, and set the chosen one squarely in the centre of the chapel, facing the bier. His behaviour was markedly more practical and moderate than when there were people by to see him, but did not otherwise greatly differ. He had come to watch out the night on his knees, and he was prepared to do so, but there was no need to labour his effects until morning, when his fellows would come to take Saint Winifred in reverent procession on the first stage of her journey. Columbanus padded the prie-dieu for his knees with the bunched skirts of his habit, and made himself as comfortable as possible with his gowned arms broadly folded as a pillow for his head. The umber darkness was scented and heavy with the warmth of wood, and the night outside was not cold. Once he had shut out the tiny, erect tower of light and the few bright surfaces from which it was reflected, the drowsiness he was inviting came stealing over him in long, lulling waves until it washed over his head, and he slept.

It seemed, after the fashion of sleep, no time at all before he was startled awake, but in fact it was more than three hours, and midnight was approaching, when his slumbers began to be strangely troubled with a persistent dream that someone, a woman, was calling him by name low and clearly, and over and over and over again: 'Columbanus. . . . Columbanus . . .' with inexhaustible and relentless patience. And he was visited, even in sleep, by a sensation that this woman had all the time in the world, and was willing to go on calling for ever, while for him there was no time left at all, but he must awake and be rid of her.

He started up suddenly, stiff to the ends of fingers and toes, ears stretched and eyes staring wildly, but there was the enclosing capsule of mild darkness all about him as before, and the reliquary dark, too, darker than before, or so it seemed, as if the flame of the lamp, though steady, had subsided, and was now more than half hidden behind the coffin. He had forgotten to check the oil. Yet he knew it had been fully supplied when last he left it, after Rhisiart's burial, and that was only a matter of hours ago.

It seemed that of all his senses, hearing had been the last to return to him, for now he was aware, with a cold crawling of fear along his skin, that the voice of his dream was still with him, and had been with him all along, emerging from dream into reality without a break. Very soft, very low, very deliberate, not a whisper, but the clear thread of a voice, at once distant and near, insisting unmistakably: 'Columbanus . . . Columbanus . . . Columbanus, what have you done?'

Out of the reliquary the voice came, out of the light that was dwindling even as he stared in terror and unbelief.

'Columbanus, Columbanus, my false servant, who blasphemes

against my will and murders my champions, what will you say in your defence to Winifred? Do you think you can deceive me as you deceive your prior and your brothers?'

Without haste, without heat, the voice issued forth from the darkening apse of the altar, so small, so terrible, echoing eerily out of its sacred cave.

'You who claim to be my worshipper, you have played me false like the vile Cradoc, do you think you will escape his end? I never wished to leave my resting-place here in Gwytherin. Who told you otherwise but your own devil of ambition? I laid my hand upon a good man, and sent him out to be my champion, and this day he has been buried here, a martyr for my sake. The sin is recorded in heaven, there is no hiding-place for you. Why,' demanded the voice, cold, peremptory and menacing in its stillness, 'have you killed my servant Rhisiart?'

He tried to rise from his knees, and it was as if they were nailed to the wood of the prie-dieu. He tried to find a voice, and only a dry croaking came out of his stiff throat. She could not be there, there was no one there! But the saints go where they please, and reveal themselves to whom they please, and some-times terribly. His cold fingers clutched at the desk, and felt nothing. His tongue, like an unplaned splinter of wood, tore the roof of his mouth when he fought to make it speak.

'There is no hope for you but in confession, Columbanus, murderer! Speak! Confess!'

'No!' croaked Columbanus, forcing out words in frantic haste. 'I never touched Rhisiart! I was here in your chapel, holy virgin, all that afternoon, how could I have harmed him? I sinned against you, I was faithless, I slept. . . . I own it! Don't lay a greater guilt on me. . . .'

'It was not you who slept,' breathed the voice, a tone higher, a shade more fiercely, 'liar that you are! Who carried the wine? Who poisoned the wine, causing even the innocent to sin? Brother Jerome slept, not you! *You* went out into the forest and waited for Rhisiart, and struck him down.'

'No . . . no, I swear it!' Shaking and sweating, he clawed at the desk before him, and could get no leverage with his palsied hands to prise himself to his feet and fly from her. How can you fly from beings who are everywhere and see everything? For nothing mortal could possibly know what this being knew. 'No, it's all wrong, I am misjudged! I was asleep here when Father Huw's messenger came for us. Jerome shook me awake. . . . The messenger is witness. . . .'

'The messenger never passed the doorway. Brother Jerome was already stirring out of his poisoned sleep, and went to meet him. As for you, you feigned and lied, as you feign and lie now. Who was it brought the poppy syrup? Who was it knew its use? You were pretending sleep, you lied even in confessing to sleep, and Jerome, as weak as you are wicked, was glad enough to think you could not accuse him, not even seeing that you were indeed accusing him of worse, of *your* act, of *your* slaying! He did not know you lied, and could not charge you with it. But *I* know, and I do charge you! And my vengeance loosed upon Cradoc may also be loosed upon you, if you lie to me but once more!'

'No!' he shrieked, and covered his face as though she dazzled him with lightnings, though only a thin, small, terrible sound threatened him. 'No, spare! I am not lying! Blessed virgin, I have been your true servant . . . I have tried to do your will . . . I know nothing of this! I never harmed Rhisiart! I never gave poisoned wine to Jerome!'

'Fool!' said the voice in a sudden loud cry. 'Do you think you can deceive *me*? *Then what is this?*'

There was a sudden silvery flash in the air before him, and something fell and smashed with a shivering of glass on the floor just in front of the desk, spattering his knees with sharp fragments and infinitesimal, sticky drops, and at the same instant the flame of the lamp died utterly, and black darkness fell.

Shivering and sick with fear, Columbanus groped forward along the earth floor, and slivers of glass crushed and stabbed under his palms, drawing blood. He lifted one hand to his face, whimpering, and smelled the sweet, cloying scent of the poppy syrup, and knew that he was kneeling among the fragments of the phial he had left safe in his scrip at Cadwallon's house.

It was no more than a minute before the total darkness eased, and there beyond the bier and the altar the small, oblong shape of the window formed in comparative light, a deep, clear sky, moonless but starlit. Shapes within the chapel again loomed very dimly, giving space to his sickening terror. There was a figure standing motionless between him and the bier.

It took a little while for his eyes to accustom themselves to the dimness, and assemble out of it this shadowy, erect pallor, a woman lost in obscurity from the waist down, but head and shoulders feebly illuminated by the starlight from the altar window. He had not seen her come, he had heard nothing. She had appeared while he was dragging his torn palm over the shards of glass, and moaning as if at the derisory pain. A slender, still form swathed from head to foot closely in white, Winifred in her grave clothes, long since dust, a thin veil covering her face and head, and her arm outstretched and pointing at him.

He shrank back before her, scuffling abjectly backwards along the floor, making feeble gestures with his hands to fend off the very sight of her. Frantic tears burst out of his eyes, and frantic words from his lips.

'It was for you! It was for you and for my abbey! I did it for the glory of our house! I believed I had warranty—from you and from heaven! He stood in the way of God's will! He would not let you go. I meant only rightly when I did what I did!'

'Speak plainly,' said the voice, sharp with command, 'and say out what you did.'

'I gave the syrup to Jerome—in his wine—and when he was asleep I stole out to the forest path, and waited for Rhisiart. I followed him. I struck him down. . . . Oh, sweet Saint Winifred, don't let me be damned for striking down the enemy who stood in the way of blessedness. . . .'

'Struck in the back!' said the pale figure, and a sudden cold gust of air swept over her and shuddered in her draperies, and surging across the chapel, blew upon Columbanus and chilled him to the bone. As if she had touched him! And she was surely a pace nearer, though he had not seen her move. 'Struck in the back, as mean cowards and traitors do! Own it! Say it all!'

'In the back!' babbled Columbanus, scrambling back from her like a broken animal, until his shoulders came up against the wall, and he could retreat no farther. 'I own it. I confess it all! Oh, merciful saint, you know all, and I cannot hide from you! Have pity on me! Don't destroy me! It was all for you, I did it for you!'

'You did it for yourself,' charged the voice, colder than ice and burning like ice. 'You who would be master of whatever order you enter, you with your ambitions and stratagems, you setting out wilfully to draw to yourself all the glory of possessing me, to work your way into the centre of all achievements, to show as the favourite of heaven, the paragon of piety, to elbow Brother Richard out of his succession to your prior, and if you could, the prior out of his succession to your abbot. You with your thirst to become the youngest head under a mitre in this or any land! I know you, and I know your kind. There is no way too ruthless for you, provided it leads to power.'

'No, no!' he panted, bracing himself back against the wall, for certainly she was advancing upon him, and now in bitter, quiet fury, jetting menace from her outstretched finger-tips. 'It was all for you, only for you! I believed I was doing your will!'

'My will to evil?' the voice rose into a piercing cry, sharp as a dagger. 'My will to murder?'

She had taken one step too many. Columbanus broke in frenzied fear, clawed himself upright by the wall, and struck out with both hands, beating at her blindly to fend her off from touching, and uttering thin, babbling cries as he flailed about him. His left hand caught in her draperies and dragged the veil from her face and head. Dark hair fell round her shoulders. His fingers made contact with the curve of a smooth, cool cheek, cool, but not cold, smooth with the graceful curves of firm young flesh, where in his sick horror he had expected to plunge his hand into the bony hollows of a skull.

He uttered a scream that began in frantic terror and ended in soaring triumph. The hand that had shrunk from contact turned suddenly to grasp hold, knotting strong fingers in the dark tangle of hair. He was very quick, Columbanus. It took him no more than the intake of a breath to know he had a flesh-and-blood woman at the end of his arm, and scarcely longer to know who she must be, and what she had done to him, with this intolerable trap in which she had caught him. And barely another breath to consider that she was here alone, and to all appearances had set her trap alone, and if she survived he was lost, and if she did not survive, if she vanished—there was plenty left of the night!—he was safe, and still in command of all this expedition, and inheritor of all its glory.

It was his misfortune that Sioned was almost as quick in the uptake as he. In a darkness in which vision hardly helped or hindered, she heard the great, indrawn breath that released him from the fear of hell and heaven together, and felt the wave of animal anger that came out from him like a foul scent, almost as sickening as the odour of his fear. She sprang back from it by instinct, and repeated the lunge of intent, dragging herself out of his grasp at the price of a few strands of hair. But his clawing hand, cheated, loosed the fragments and caught again at the linen sheet that draped her, and that would not tear so easily. She swung round to her left, to put as much distance as she could between her body and his right hand, but she saw him lunge into the breast of his habit, and saw the brief, sullen flash of the steel as he whipped it out and followed her swing, hacking into dimness. The same dagger, she thought, swooping beneath its first blind stab, that killed my father.

Somewhere a door had opened fully on the night, for the wind blew through the chapel suddenly, and sandalled feet thudded in with the night air, a thickset, powerful body driving the draught before it. A loud voice thundered warning. Brother Cadfael erupted into the chapel from the sacristy like a bolt from a crossbow, and drove at full speed into the struggle.

Columbanus was in the act of striking a second time, and with his left hand firmly clutching the linen sheet wound about Sioned's body. But she was whirling round away from him to unloose those same folds that held her, and the blow that was meant for her heart only grazed painfully down her left forearm. Then his grip released her, and she fell back against the wall, and Columbanus was gone, hurtling out at the door in full flight, and Brother Cadfael was embracing her with strong, sustaining arms, and upbraiding her with a furious, bracing voice, while he held her in a bear's hug, and felt at her as tenderly and fervently as a mother.

'For God's sake, fool daughter, why did you get within his reach? I *told* you, keep the bier between you and him . . . !'

'Get after him,' shouted Sioned wrathfully, 'do you want him clean away? I'm sound enough, go get *him*! He killed my father!'

They headed for the door together, but Cadfael was out of it first. The girl was strong, vigorous and vengeful, a Welshwoman to the heart, barely grazed, he knew the kind. The wind of action blew her, she felt no pain and was aware of no effusion of blood, blood she wanted, and with justification. She was close on his heels as he rolled like a thunderbolt down the narrow path through the graveyard towards the gate. The night was huge, velvet, sewn with stars, their veiled and delicate light barely casting shadows. All that quiet space received and smothered the sound of their passage, and smoothed the stillness of the night over it.

Out of the bushes beyond the graveyard wall a man's figure started, tall, slender and swift, leaping to block the gateway. Columbanus saw him, and baulked for a moment, but Cadfael was running hard behind him, and the next instant the fugitive made up his mind and rushed on, straight at the shadow that moved to intercept him. Hard on Cadfael's heels, Sioned suddenly shrieked: 'Take care, Engelard! He has a dagger!'

Engelard heard her, and swerved to the right at the very moment of collision, so that the stroke meant for his heart only ripped a fluttering ribbon of cloth from his sleeve. Columbanus would have bored his way past at speed, and run for the cover of the woods, but Engelard's long left arm swept round hard into the back of his neck, sending him off-balance for a moment, though he kept his feet, and Engelard's right fist got a tight grip on the flying cowl, and twisted. Half-strangled, Columbanus whirled again and struck out with the knife, and this time

Engelard was ready for the flash, and took the thrusting wrist neatly in his left hand. They swayed and wrestled together, feet braced in the grass, and they were very fairly matched if both had been armed. That unbalance was soon amended. Engelard twisted at the wrist he held, ignoring the clawing of Columbanus' free hand at his throat, and the numbed fingers opened at last and let the dagger fall. Both lunged for it, but Engelard scooped it up and flung it contemptuously aside into the bushes, and grappled his opponent with his bare hands. The fight was all but over. Columbanus hung panting and gasping, both arms pinned, looking wildly round for a means of escape and finding none.

'Is this the man?' demanded Engelard.

Sioned said: 'Yes. He has owned to it.'

Engelard looked beyond his prisoner then for the first time, and saw her standing in the soft starlight that was becoming to their accustomed eyes almost as clear as day. He saw her dishevelled and bruised and gazing with great, shocked eyes, her left arm gashed and bleeding freely, though the cut was shallow. He saw smears of her blood dabbling the white sheet in which she was swathed. By starlight there is little or no colour to be seen, but everything that Engelard saw at that moment was blood-red. This was the man who had murdered in coward's fashion Engelard's well-liked lord and good friend—whatever their differences!—and now he had tried to kill the daughter as he had killed the father.

'You dared, you dared touch her!' blazed Engelard in towering rage. 'You worthless cloister rat!' And he took Columbanus by the throat and hoisted him bodily from the ground, shook him like the rat he had called him, cracked him in the air like a poisonous snake, and when he had done with him, flung him down at his feet in the grass.

'Get up!' he growled, standing over the wreckage. 'Get up now, and I'll give you time to rest and breathe, and then you can fight a man to the death, without a dagger in your hand, instead of writhing through the undergrowth and stabbing him in the back, or carving up a defenceless girl. Take your time, I can wait to kill you till you've got your breath.'

Sioned flew to him, breast to breast, and held him fast in her arms, pressing him back. 'No! Don't touch him again! I don't want the law to have any hold on *you*, even the slenderest.'

'He tried to kill you—you're hurt....'

'No! It's nothing . . . only a cut. It bleeds, but it's nothing!'

His rage subsided slowly, shaking him. He folded his arms round her and held her to him, and with a disdainful but restrained jab of a toe urged his prostrate enemy again: 'Get up! I won't touch you. The law can have you, and welcome!'

Columbanus did not move, not by so much as the flicker of an eyelid or the twitching of a finger. All three of them stood peering down at him in sudden silence, aware how utterly still he was, and how rare such stillness is among living things.

'He's foxing,' said Engelard scornfully, 'for fear of worse, and by way of getting himself pitied. I've heard he's a master at that.'

Those who feign sleep and hear themselves talked of, usually betray themselves by some exaggeration of innocence. Columbanus lay in a stillness that was perfectly detached and indifferent.

Brother Cadfael knelt down beside him, shook him by the shoulder gently, and sat back with a sharp sigh at the broken movement of the head. He put a hand inside the breast of the habit, and stooped to the parted lips and wide nostrils. Then he took the head between his hands, and gently turned and tilted it. It rolled back, as he released it, into a position so improbable that they knew the worst even before Cadfael said, quite practically: 'You'd have waited a long time for him to get his breath back, my friend. You don't know your own strength! His neck is broken. He's dead.'

Sobered and shocked, they stood dumbly staring down at what they had hardly yet recognised for disaster. They saw a regrettable accident which neither of them had ever intended, but which was, after all, a kind of justice. But Cadfael saw a scandal that could yet wreck their young lives, and others, too, for without Columbanus alive, and forced by two respected witnesses to repeat his confession, how strong was all their proof against him? Cadfael sat back on his heels, and thought. It was startling to realise, now that the unmoved silence of the night came down on them again, how all this violence and passion had passed with very little noise, and no other witnesses. He listened, and no stirring of foot or wing troubled the quiet. They were far enough away from any dwelling, not a soul had been disturbed. That, at least, was time gained.

'He can't be dead,' said Engelard doubtfully. 'I barely handled him at all. Nobody dies as easily as that!'

'This one did. And now what's to be done? I hadn't bargained for this.' He said it not complainingly, but as one pointing out that further urgent planning would now be necessary, and they had better keep their minds flexible.

'Why, what can be done?' To Engelard it was simple, though troublesome. 'We shall have to call up Father Huw and your prior, and tell them exactly what's happened. What else can we do? I'm sorry to have killed the fellow, I never meant to, but I can't say I feel any *guilt* about it.' Nor did he expect any blame. The truth was always the best way. Cadfael felt a reluctant affection for such innocence. The world was going to damage it sooner or later, but one undeserved accusation had so far failed even to bruise it, he still trusted men to be reasonable. Cadfael doubted if Sioned was so sure. Her silence was anxious and foreboding. And her grazed arm was still oozing blood. First things first, and they might as well be sensibly occupied while he thought.

'Here, make yourself useful! Help me get this carrion back into the chapel, out of sight. And, Sioned, find his dagger, we can't leave that lying about to bear witness. Then let's get that arm of yours washed and bound up. There's a stream at the back of the hawthorn hedge, and of linen we've plenty.'

They had absolute faith in him, and did his bidding without question, though Engelard, once he had assured himself that Sioned was not gravely hurt, and had himself carefully and deftly bandaged her scratch, returned to his dogged opinion that their best course was to tell the whole story, which could hardly cast infamy upon anyone but Columbanus. Cadfael busied himself with flint and tinder until he had candles lighted, and the lamp refilled, from which he himself had drained a judicious quantity of oil before Sioned took her place under the draperies of the saint's catafalque.

'You think,' he said at length, 'that because you've done nothing wrong, and we've all of us banded together to expose a wrong, that the whole world will be of the same opinion, and honestly come out and say so. Child, I know better! The only proof we have of Columbanus' guilt is his confession, which both of us here heard. Or rather, the only proof we had, for we no longer have even that. Alive, we two could have forced the truth out of him a second time. Dead, he's never going to give us that satisfaction. And without that, our position is vulnerable enough. Make no mistake, if we accuse him, if this fearful scandal breaks, to smirch the abbey of Shrewsbury, and all the force of the Benedictine order, backed here by the bishop and the prince, take my word for it, all the forces of authority will band together to avert the disaster, and nobody, much less a friendless outlander, will be allowed to stand in the way. They simply can't afford to have their acquisition of Saint Winifred called in question and brought to disrepute. Rather than that, they'll call this an outlaw killing by a desperate man, a fugitive already, wanted for another crime, and trying to escape both together. A pity,' he said, 'I ever suggested that Sioned should call you in to wait in reserve, in case we had trouble. But none of this is your fault, and I won't have you branded with it. I made the plot, and I must unravel it. But give up all idea of going straight to Father Huw, or the bailiff, or anyone else, with the true story. Far better use the rest of this night to rearrange matters to better advantage. Justice can be arrived at by more routes than one.'

'They wouldn't dare doubt Sioned's word,' said Engelard stoutly.

'Fool boy, they'd say that Sioned, for love's sake, might go as far aside from her proper nature as Peredur did. And as for me, my influence is small enough, and I am not interested in protecting only myself, but as many of those in this coil as I can reach. Even my prior, who is arrogant and rigid, and to tell the truth, sometimes rather stupid, but not a murderer and not a liar. And my order, which has not deserved Columbanus. Hush, now, and let me think! And while I do, you can be clearing away the remains of the syrup bottle. This chapel must be as neat and quiet tomorrow as before we ever brought our troubles into it.'

Obediently they went about removing the traces of the night's alarms, and let him alone until he should have found them a way through the tangle.

'And I wonder, now,' he said at length, 'what made you improve on all the speeches I made for you, and put such fiery words into Saint Winifred's mouth? What put it into your head to say that you'd never wanted to leave Gwytherin, and did not want it now? That Rhisiart was not merely a decent, honest man, but your chosen champion?'

She turned and looked at him in astonishment and wonder. 'Did I say that?'

'You did, and very well you delivered it, too. And very proper and apt it sounded, but I think we never rehearsed it so. Where did you get the words?'

'I don't know,' said Sioned, puzzled. 'I don't remember what I did say. The words seemed to come freely of themselves, I only let them flow.'

'It may be,' said Engelard, 'that the saint was taking her chance when it offered. All these strangers having visions and ecstasies, and interpreting them to suit themselves, yet nobody ever really asked Saint Winifred what *she* wanted. They all claimed they knew better than she did.'

'Out of the mouths of innocents!' said Cadfael to himself, and pondered the road that was gradually opening before his mind's eye. Of all the people who ought to be left happy with the outcome, Saint Winifred should surely come first. Aim, he thought, at making everybody happy, and if that's within reach, why stir up any kind of unpleasantness? Take Columbanus, for instance! Only a few hours ago at Compline he prayed aloud before us all that if the virgin deemed him worthy, he might be

172

taken up out of this world this very night, translated instantly out of the body. Well, that was one who got his wish! Maybe he'd have withdrawn his request if he'd known it was going to be taken up so literally, for its purpose was rather to reflect incomparable holiness upon him while he was still alive to enjoy it. But saints have a right to suppose that their devotees mean what they say, and bestow gifts accordingly. And if the saint has really spoken through Sioned, he thought—and who am I to question it?—if she really wants to stay here in her own village, which is a reasonable enough wish, well, the plot where she used to sleep has been newly turned today, no one will notice anything if it's turned again tonight.

'I believe,' said Sioned, watching him with the first faint smile, wan but trusting, 'you're beginning to see your way.'

'I believe,' said Cadfael, 'I'm beginning to see our way, which is more to the point. Sioned, I have something for you to do, and you need not hurry, we have work to do here while you're away. Take that sheet of yours, and go and spread it under the may trees in the hedge, where they're beginning to shed, but not yet brown. Shake the bushes and bring us a whole cloud of petals. The last time she visited him, it was with wondrous sweet odours and a shower of white flowers. Bring the one, and we shall have the other.'

Confidently, understanding nothing as yet, she took the linen sheet from which she had unwound herself as from a shroud, and went to do his bidding.

'Give me the dagger,' said Cadfael briskly when she was gone. He wiped the blade on the veil Columbanus had torn from Sioned's head, and moved the candles so that they shone upon the great red seals that closed Winifred's reliquary. 'Thank God he didn't bleed,' he said. 'His habit and clothes are unmarked. Strip him!'

And he fingered the first seal, nodded satisfaction at its fatness and the thinness and sharpness of the dagger, and thrust the tip of the blade into the flame of the lamp.

Long before daylight they were ready. They walked down all three together from the chapel towards the village, and separated at the edge of the wood, where the shortest path turned off uphill towards Rhisiart's holding.

Sioned carried with her the blood-stained sheet and veil, and the fragments of glass they had buried in the forest. A good thing the servants who had filled in Rhisiart's grave had left their spades on the scene, meaning to tidy the mound next day. That had saved a journey to borrow without leave, and a good hour of time.

'There'll be no scandal,' said Cadfael, when they halted at the place where the paths divided. 'No scandal, and no accusations. I think you may take him home with you, but keep him out of sight until we're gone. There'll be peace when we're gone. And you needn't fear that the prince or his bailiff will ever proceed further against Engelard, any more than against John. I'll speak a word in Peredur's ear, Peredur will speak it into the bailiff's ear, the bailiff will speak it into Owain Gwynedd's ear —Father Huw we'll leave out of it, no need to burden his conscience, the good, simple man. And if the monks of Shrewsbury are happy, and the people of Gwytherin are happy—for they'll hear the whisper fast enough—why should anyone want to upset such a satisfactory state of affairs, by speaking the word aloud? A wise prince—and Owain Gwynedd seems to me very wise—will let well alone.'

'All Gwytherin,' said Sioned, and shivered a little at the thought, 'will be there in the morning to watch you take the reliquary away.'

'So much the better, we want all the witnesses we can have, all the emotion, all the wonder. I am a great sinner,' said Cadfael philosophically, 'but I feel no weight. Does the end justify the means, I wonder?'

'One thing I know,' she said. 'My father can rest now, and that he owes to you. And I owe you that and more. When I first came down to you out of the tree—you remember?—I thought you would be like other monks, and not want to look at me.'

'Child, I should have to be out of my wits, not to want to look

174

at you. I've looked so attentively, I shall remember you all my life. But your love, my children, and how you manage it—with that I can't help you.'

'No need,' said Engelard. 'I am an outlander, with a proper agreement. That agreement can be dissolved by consent, and I can be a free man by dividing all my goods equally with my lord, and now Sioned *is* my lord.'

'And then there can no man prevent,' said Sioned, 'if I choose to endow him with half *my* goods, as is only fair. Uncle Meurice won't stand in our way. And it won't even be hard for him to justify. To marry an heiress to an outlander servant is one thing, to marry her to a free man and heir to a manor, even if it's in England and can't be claimed for a while, is quite another.'

'Especially,' said Cadfael, 'when you already know he's the best hand with cattle in the four cantrefs.'

It seemed that those two, at any rate, were satisfied. And Rhisiart in his honoured grave would not grudge them their happiness. He had not been a grudging man.

Engelard, no talker, said his thanks plainly and briefly when they parted. Sioned turned back impulsively, flung her arms round Cadfael's neck, and kissed him. It was their farewell, for he had thought it best to advise them not to show themselves at the chapel again. It was a wry touch that she smelled so heady and sweet with flowering may, and left so saintly a fragrance in his arms when she was gone.

On his way down to the parsonage Cadfael made a detour to the mill-pond, and dropped Columbanus' dagger into the deepest of the dark water. What a good thing, he thought, making for the bed he would occupy for no more than an hour or so before Prime, that the brothers who made the reliquary were such meticulous craftsmen, and insisted on lining it with lead!

CHAPTER ELEVEN

Prior Robert arose and went to the first service of the day in so great content with his success that he had almost forgotten about the escape of Brother John, and even when he remembered that one unsatisfactory particular, he merely put it away in the back of his mind, as something that must and would be dealt with faithfully in good time, but need not cloud the splendour of this occasion. And it was indeed a clear, radiant morning, very bright and still, when they came from the church and turned towards the old graveyard and the chapel, and all the congregation fell in at their heels and followed, and along the way others appeared silently from every path, and joined the procession, until it was like some memorable pilgrimage. They came to Cadwallon's gatehouse, and Cadwallon came out to join them, and Peredur, who had hung back in strict obedience to his orders to remain at home until his penance was appointed, was kindly bidden forth by Father Huw, and even smiled upon, though as saint to sinner, by Prior Robert. Dame Branwen, if not still asleep, was no doubt recuperating after her vapours. Her menfolk were not likely to be very pressing in their invitations to her to go with them, and perhaps she was still punishing them by withdrawing herself. Either way, they were relieved of her presence.

The order of procession having only a loose form, brothers and villagers could mingle, and greet, and change partners as they willed. It was a communal celebration. And that was strange, considering the contention that had threatened it for some days. Gwytherin was playing it very cautiously now, intent on seeing everything and giving nothing away.

Peredur made his way to Cadfael's side, and remained there thankfully, though silently. Cadfael asked after his mother, and the young man coloured and frowned, and then smiled guiltily like a child, and said that she was very well, a little dreamy still, but placid and amiable.

'You can do Gwytherin and me a good service, if you will,' said Brother Cadfael, and confided to his ear the word he had in mind to pass on to Griffith ap Rhys.

'So that's the way it is!' said Peredur, forgetting altogether about his own unforgivable sins. His eyes opened wide. He whistled softly. 'And that's the way you want it left?'

'That's the way it is, and that's the way I want it left. Who loses? And everyone gains. We, you, Rhisiart, Saint Winifred —Saint Winifred most of all. And Sioned and Engelard, of course,' said Cadfael firmly, probing the penitent to the heart.

'Yes . . . I'm glad for them!' said Peredur, a shade too vehemently. His head was bent, and his eyelids lowered. He was not yet as glad as all that, but he was trying. The will was there. 'Given a year or two longer, nobody's going to remember about the deer Engelard took. In the end he'll be able to go back and forth to Cheshire if he pleases, and he'll have lands when his father dies. And once he's no longer reckoned outlaw and felon he'll have no more troubles. I'll get your word to Griffith ap Rhys this very day. He's over the river at his cousin David's but Father Huw will give me indulgence if it's to go voluntarily to the law.' He smiled wryly. 'Very apt that I should be your man! I can unload my own sins at the same time, while I'm confiding to him what everyone must know but no one must say aloud.'

'Good!' said Brother Cadfael, contented. 'The bailiff will do the rest. A word to the prince, and that's the whole business settled.'

They had come to the place where the most direct path from Rhisiart's holding joined with their road. And there came half the household from above, Padrig the bard nursing his little portable harp, perhaps bound for some other house after this leave-taking, Cai the ploughman still with an impressive bandage round his quite intact head, an artistic lurch to his gait, and a shameless gleam in his one exposed eye. No Sioned, no Engelard, no Annest, no John. Brother Cadfael, though he himself had given the orders, felt a sudden grievous deprivation.

Now they were approaching the little clearing, the woodlands fell back from them on either side, the narrow field of wild grass opened, and then the stone-built wall, green from head to foot, of the old graveyard. Small, shrunken, black, a huddled shape too tall for its base, the chapel of Saint Winifred loomed, and at its eastern end the raw, dark oblong of Rhisiart's grave scarred the lush spring green of the grass.

Prior Robert halted at the gate, and turned to face the following multitude with a benign and almost affectionate countenance, and through Cadfael addressed them thus:

'Father Huw, and good people of Gwytherin, we came here with every good intent, led, as we believed and still believe, by divine guidance, desiring to honour Saint Winifred as she had instructed us, not at all to deprive you of a treasure, rather to allow its beams to shine upon many more people as well as you. That our mission should have brought grief to any is great grief to us. That we are now of one mind, and you are willing to let us take the saint's relics away with us to a wider glory, is relief and joy. Now you are assured that we meant no evil, but only good, and that what we are doing is done reverently.'

A murmur began at one end of the crescent of watchers, and rolled gently round to the other extreme, a murmur of acquiescence, almost of complacency.

'And you do not grudge us the possession of this precious thing we are taking with us? You do believe that we are doing justly, that we take only what has been committed to us?'

He could not have chosen his words better, thought Brother Cadfael, astonished and gratified, if he had known everything— or if I had written this address for him. Now if there comes an equally well-worded answer, I'll believe in a miracle of my own.

The crowd heaved, and gave forth the sturdy form of Bened, as solid and respectable and fit to be spokesman for his parish as any man in Gwytherin, barring, perhaps, Father Huw, who here stood in the equivocal position of having a foot in both camps, and therefore wisely kept silence.

'Father Prior,' said Bened gruffly, 'there's not a man among us now grudges you the relics within there on the altar. We do believe they are yours to take, and you take them with our consent home to Shrewsbury, where by all the omens they rightly belong.'

It was altogether too good. It might bring a blush of pleasure, even mingled with a trace of shame, to Prior Robert's cheek, but it caused Cadfael to run a long, considering glance round all those serene, secretive, smiling faces, all those wide, honest, opaque eyes. Nobody fidgeted, nobody muttered, nobody, even at the back, sniggered. Cai gazed with simple admiration from his one visible eye. Padrig beamed benevolent bardic satisfaction upon this total reconciliation.

They knew already! Whether through some discreet whisper started on its rounds by Sioned, or by some earth-rooted intuition of their own, the people of Gwytherin knew, in essence if not in detail, everything there was to be known. And not a word aloud, not a word out of place, until the strangers were gone.

'Come, then,' said Prior Robert, deeply gratified, 'let us release Brother Columbanus from his vigil, and take Saint Winifred on the first stage of her journey home.' And he turned, very tall, very regal, very silvery-fine, and paced majestically to the door of the chapel, with most of Gwytherin crowding into the grave-yard after him. With a long, white, aristocratic hand he thrust the door wide and stood in the doorway.

'Brother Columbanus, we are here. Your watch is over.'

He took just two paces into the interior, his eyes finding it dim after the brilliance outside, in spite of the clear light pouring in through the small east window. Then the dark-brown, wood-scented walls came clear to him, and every detail of the scene within emerged from dimness into comparative light, and then into a light so acute and blinding that he halted where he stood, awed and marvelling.

There was a heavy, haunting sweetness that filled all the air within, and the opening of the door had let in a small morning wind that stirred it in great waves of fragrance. Both candles burned steadily upon the altar, the small oil-lamp between them. The prie-dieu stood centrally before the bier, but there was no one kneeling there. Over altar and reliquary a snowdrift of white petals lay, as though a miraculous wind had carried them in its arms across two fields from the hawthorn hedge, without spilling one flower on the way, and breathed them in here through the altar window. The snowy sweetness carried as far as the prie-dieu, and sprinkled both it and the crumpled, empty garments that lay discarded there.

'Columbanus . . . ! What is this? He is not here!'

Brother Richard came to the prior's left shoulder, Brother Jerome to the right, Bened and Cadwallon and Cai and others crowded in after them and flowed round on either side to line the dark walls and stare at the marvel, nostrils widening to the drowning sweetness. No one ventured to advance beyond where the prior stood, until he himself went slowly forward, and leaned to look more closely at all that was left of Brother Columbanus.

The black Benedictine habit lay where he had been kneeling, skirts spread behind, body fallen together in folds, sleeves spread like wings on either side, bent at the elbow as though the arms that had left them had still ended in hands pressed together in prayer. Within the cowl an edge of white showed.

'Look!' whispered Brother Richard in awe. 'His shirt is still within the habit, and look!—his sandals!' They were under the hem of the habit, neatly together, soles upturned, as the feet had left them. And on the book-rest of the prie-dieu, laid where his prayerful hands had rested, was a single knot of flowering may.

'Father Prior, all his clothes are here, shirt and drawers and all, one within another as he would wear them. As though—as though he had been lifted out of them and left them lying, as a snake discards its old skin and emerges bright in a new. . . .'

'This is most marvellous,' said Prior Robert. 'How shall we understand it, and not sin?'

'Father, may we take up these garments? If there is trace or mark on them. . . .'

There was none, Brother Cadfael was certain of that. Columbanus had not bled, his habit was not torn, nor even soiled. He had fallen only in thick spring grass, bursting irresistibly through the dead grass of last autumn.

'Father, it is as I said, as though he has been lifted out of these garments quite softly, and let them fall, not needing them any more. Oh, Father, we are in the presence of a great wonder! I am afraid!' said Brother Richard, meaning the wonderful, blissful fear of what is holy. He had seldom spoken with such eloquence, or been so moved.

'I do recall now,' said the prior, shaken and chastened (and that was no harm!), 'the prayer he made last night at Compline. How he cried out to be taken up living out of this world, for pure ecstasy, if the virgin saint found him fit for such favour and bliss. Is it possible that he was in such a state of grace as to be found worthy?'

'Father, shall we search? Here, and without? Into the woods?'

'To what end?' said the prior simply. 'Would he be running naked in the night? A sane man? And even if he ran mad, and shed the clothes he wore, would they be thus discarded, fold within fold as he kneeled, here in such pure order? It is not possible to put off garments thus. No, he is gone far beyond these forests, far out of this world. He has been marvellously favoured, and his most demanding prayers heard. Let us say a Mass here for Brother Columbanus, before we take up the blessed lady who has made him her herald, and go to make known this miracle of faith.'

There was no knowing, Prior Robert being the man he was, at what stage his awareness of the use to be made of this marvel thrust his genuine faith and wonder and emotion into the back of his mind, and set him manipulating events to get the utmost glory out of them. There was no inconsistency in such behaviour. He was quite certain that Brother Columbanus had been taken up living out of this world, just as he had wished. But that being so, it was not only his opportunity, but his duty, to make the utmost use of the exemplary favour to glorify the abbey of Saint Peter and Saint Paul of Shrewsbury, and not only his duty, but his pleasure, to make use of the same to shed a halo round the head of Prior Robert, who had originated this quest. And so he did. He said Mass with absolute conviction, in the cloud of white flowers, the huddle of discarded garments at his feet.

Almost certainly he would also inform Griffith ap Rhys, through Father Huw, of all that had befallen, and ask him to keep an alert eye open in case any relevant information surfaced after the brothers from Shrewsbury were gone. Brother Prior was the product of his faith and his birth, his training for sanctity and for arbitrary rule, and could shake off neither.

The people of Gwytherin, silent and observant, crowded in to fill the space available, made no sound, expressed no opinion. Their presence and silence passed for endorsement. What they really thought they kept to themselves.

'Now,' said Prior Robert, moved almost to tears, 'let us take up this blessed burden, and praise God for the weight we carry.'

And he moved forward to offer his own delicate hands and frail shoulder, first of the devout.

That was Brother Cadfael's worst moment, for it was the one thing he had overlooked. But Bened, unwontedly quick at the right moment, called aloud: 'Shall Gwytherin be backward, now peace is made?' and rolled forward with less stateliness and greater speed, and had a solid shoulder under the head end of the reliquary before the prior was able to reach it, and half a dozen of the smith's own powerful but stocky build took up the challenge with enthusiasm. Apart from Cadfael, the only monk of Shrewshbury who got a corner hoisted into his neck was Jerome, being of much the same height, and his was the sole voice that cried out in astonishment at the weight, and sagged under it until Bened shifted nearer and hefted most of the load from him.

'Your pardon, Father Prior! But who would have thought those slender little bones could weigh so heavily?'

Cadfael spoke up in hasty interpretation: 'We are surrounded here by miracles, both small and great. Truly did Father Prior say that we thank God for the weight we carry. Is not this evidence of singular grace, that heaven has caused the weight of her worthiness to be so signally demonstrated?'

In his present state, at once humbled and exalted, Prior Robert apparently did not find the logic of this nearly as peculiar as did Brother Cadfael himself. He would have accepted and embraced anything that added to his own triumph. So it was on sturdy Gwytherin shoulders that the reliquary and its contents were hoisted out of the chapel and borne in procession down to the parsonage, with such brisk enthusiasm that it almost seemed the parish could hardly wait to get rid of them. It was Gwytherin men who fetched the horses and mules, and rigged a little cart, spread with cloths, on which the precious casket could be drawn home. Once installed on this vehicle, which, after all, cost little in materials or labour, given the smith's benevolent interest, the casket need not be unloaded until it reached Shrewsbury. Nobody wanted anything untoward to happen to it on the way, such as Brother Jerome crumpling under his end, and starting the joints by dropping it.

'But you we'll miss,' said Cai regretfully, busy with the harness. 'Padrig has a song in praise of Rhisiart you'd have liked to hear, and one more companionable drinking night would have been pleasant. But the lad sends you his thanks and his godspeed. He's only in hiding until the pack of you have gone. And Sioned told me to tell you from him, look out for your pear trees, for the winter moth's playing the devil with some of ours here.'

'He's a good helper in a garden,' Cadfael confirmed judicially. 'A shade heavy-handed, but he shifts the rough digging faster than any novice I ever had under me. I shall miss him, too. God knows what I shall get in his place.'

'A light hand's no good with iron,' said Bened, standing back to admire the banded wheels he had contributed to the cart. 'Deft, yes! Not light. I tell you what, Cadfael! I'll see you in Shrewsbury yet. For years I've had a fancy to make a great pilgrimage across England some day and get to Walsingham. I reckon Shrewsbury would be just about on my way.'

At the last, when all was ready and Prior Robert mounted, Cai said in Cadfael's ear: 'When you're up the hill, where you saw us ploughing that day, cast a look the other way. There's a place where the woods fall away, and an open hillock just before they close again. We'll be there, a fair gathering of us. And that's for you.'

Brother Cadfael, without shame, for he had been up and busy

all night and was very tired, annexed the gentler and cleverer of the two mules, a steady pad that would follow where the horses led, and step delicately on any ground. It had a high, supporting saddle, and he had not lost the trick of riding through his knees, even when asleep. The larger and heavier beast was harnessed to draw the cart, but the carriage was narrow yet stable, rode well even on a forest floor, and Jerome, no great weight, could still ride, either on the mule's back or the shafts and yoke. In any case, why trouble too much about the comfort of Jerome, who had concocted that vision of Saint Winifred in the first place, almost certainly knowing that the prior's searches in Wales had cast up this particular virgin as one most desirable, and most available? Jerome would have been courting Columbanus just as assiduously, if he had survived to oust Robert.

The cortège set forth ceremoniously, half of Gwytherin there to watch it go, and sigh immense relief when it was gone. Father Huw blessed the departing guests. Peredur, almost certainly, was away across the river, planting the good seed in the bailiff's mind. He deserved that his errand should be counted to his own credit. Genuine sinners are plentiful, but genuine penitents are rare. Peredur had done a detestable thing, but remained a very likeable young man. Cadfael had no serious fears for his future, once he was over Sioned. There were other girls, after all. Not many her match, but some not so very far behind.

Brother Cadfael settled himself well down in the saddle, and shook his bridle to let the mule know it might conduct him where it would. Very gently he dozed. It could not yet be called sleep. He was aware of the shifting light and shadow under the trees, and the fresh cool air, and movement under him, and a sense of something completed. Or almost completed, for this was only the first stage of the way home.

He roused when they came to the high ridge above the river valley. There was no team ploughing down there now, all the ploughing, even the breaking of new ground, was done. He turned his head towards the wooded uplands on his right, and waited for the opening vista between the trees. It was brief and narrow, a sweep of grass soaring to a gentle crest beyond which the trees loomed close and dark. There were a number of people clustered there on the rounded hillock, most of Sioned's household, far enough removed to be nameless to anyone who knew them less well than he. A cloud of dark hair beside a cap of flaxen, Cai's flaunting bandage shoved back like a hat unseated in a hot noon, a light brown head clasped close against a red thorn-hedge that looked very like Brother John's abandoned tonsure. Padrig, too, not yet off on his wanderings. They were all waving and smiling, and Cadfael returned the salute with enthusiasm. Then the ambulant procession crossed the narrow opening, and the woods took away all.

Brother Cadfael, well content, subsided into his saddle comfortably, and fell asleep.

Overnight they halted at Penmachno, in the shelter of the church, where there was hospitality for travellers. Brother Cadfael, without apology to any, withdrew himself as soon as he had seen to his mule, and continued his overdue sleep in the loft above the stables. He was roused after midnight by Brother Jerome in delirious excitement.

'Brother, a great wonder!' bleated Jerome, ecstatic. 'There came a traveller here in great pain from a malignant illness, and made such outcry that all of us in the hostel were robbed of sleep. And Prior Robert took a few of the petals we saved from the chapel, and floated them in holy water, and gave them to this poor soul to drink, and afterwards we carried him out into the yard and let him kiss the foot of the reliquary. And instantly he was eased of his pain, and before we laid him in his bed again he was asleep. He feels nothing, he slumbers like a child! Oh, brother, we are the means of astonishing grace!'

'Ought it to astonish you so much?' demanded Brother Cadfael censoriously, malicious half out of vexation at being awakened, and half in self-defence, for he was considerably more taken aback than he would admit. 'If you had any faith in what we have brought from Gwytherin, you should not be amazed that it accomplishes wonders along the way.'

But by the same token, he thought honestly, after Jerome had left him to seek out a more appreciative audience, *I* should! I do believe I begin to grasp the nature of miracles! For would it be a miracle, if there was any reason for it? Miracles have nothing to do with reason. Miracles contradict reason, overturn reason, make game of reason, they strike clean across mere human deserts, and deliver and save where they will. If they made sense, they would not be miracles. And he was comforted and entertained, and fell asleep again readily, feeling that all was well with a world he had always known to be peculiar and perverse.

Minor prodigies, most of them trivial, some derisory, trailed after them all the way to Shrewsbury, though how many of the crutches discarded had been necessary, and how many, even of those that were, had to be resumed shortly afterwards, how many of the speech impediments had been in the will rather than in the tongue, how many feeble tendons in the mind rather than in the legs, it was difficult to judge, not even counting all the sensation-seekers who were bound to bandage an eye or come over suddenly paralytic in order to be in with the latest cult. It all made for a great reputation that not only kept pace with them, but rushed ahead, and was already bringing in awestruck patronage in gifts and legacies to the abbey of Saint Peter and Saint Paul, in the hope of having dubious sins prayed away by a grateful saint.

When they reached the outskirts of Shrewsbury, crowds of people came out to meet them, and accompany the procession as far as the boundary church of Saint Giles, where the reliquary was to await the great day of the saint's translation to the abbey church. This could hardly take place without the blessing of the bishop, and due notice to all churches and religious houses, to add to the glory accruing. It was no surprise to Brother Cadfael that when the day came it should come with grey skies and squally rain, to leave room for another little miracle. For though it rained heavily on all the surrounding fields and countryside, not a drop fell on the procession, as they carried Saint Winifred's casket at last to its final resting-place on the altar of the abbey church, where the miracle-seekers immediately betook themselves in great numbers, and mostly came away satisfied.

In full chapter Prior Robert gave his account of his mission to Abbot Heribert. 'Father, to my grief I must own it, we have come back only four, who went out from Shrewsbury six brethren together. And we return without both the glory and the blemish of our house, but bringing with us the treasure we set out to gain.'

On almost all of which counts he was in error, but since no one was ever likely to tell him so, there was no harm done. Brother Cadfael dozed gently behind his pillar through the awed encomiums on Brother Columbanus, out of whom they would certainly have wished to make a new saint, but for the sad fact that they supposed all his relics but his discarded clothes to be for ever withdrawn from reach. Letting the devout voices slip out of his consciousness, Cadfael congratulated himself on having made as many people as possible happy, and drifted into a dream of a hot knife-blade slicing deftly through the thick wax of a seal without ever disturbing the device. It was a long time since he had exercised some of his more questionable skills, he was glad to be confirmed in believing that he had forgotten none of them, and that every one had a meritorious use in the end.

CHAPTER TWELVE

It was more than two years later, and the middle of a bright June afternoon, when Brother Cadfael, crossing the great court from the fish-ponds, saw among the travellers arriving at the gate a certain thickset, foursquare, powerful figure that he knew. Bened, the smith of Gwytherin, a little rounder in the belly and a little greyer in the hair, had found the time ripe for realising an old ambition, and was on his way in a pilgrim's gown to the shrine of Our Lady of Walsingham.

'If I'd put it off much longer,' he confided, when they were private together with a bottle of wine in a corner of the herb-garden, 'I should have grown too old to relish the journey. And what was there to keep me now, with a good lad ready and able to take over the smithy while I'm gone? He took to it like a duck to water. Oh, yes, they've been man and wife eighteen months now, and as happy as larks. Annest always knew her own mind, and this time I will say she's made no mistake.'

'And have they a child yet?' asked Brother Cadfael, imagining a bold, sturdy boy-baby with a bush of red hair, rubbed away by his pillow in an infant tonsure.

'Not yet, but there's one on the way. By the time I get back he'll be with us.'

'And Annest is well?'

'Blossoming like a rose.'

'And Sioned and Engelard? They had no troubles after we were gone?'

'None, bless you! Griffith ap Rhys let it be known that all was well, and should be let well alone. They're married, and snug, and I'm to bring you their warmest greetings, and to tell you they have a fine son—three months old, I reckon he'd be now—dark and Welsh like his mother. And they've named him Cadfael.'

'Well, well!' said Brother Cadfael, absurdly gratified. 'The best way to get the sweet out of children and escape the bitter is to have them by proxy. But I hope they'll never find anything but sweet in their youngster. There'll be a Bened yet, in one household or the other.'

Bened the pilgrim shook his head, but without any deep regret, and reached for the bottle. 'There was a time when I'd hoped. . . . But it would never have done. I was an old fool ever to think of it, and it's better this way. And Cai's well, and sends you remembrances, and says drink down one cup for him.'

They drank many more than one before it was time for Vespers. 'And you'll see me again at chapter tomorrow,' said Bened, as they walked back to the great court, 'for I'm charged with greetings from Father Huw to Prior Robert and Abbot Heribert, and I'll need you to be my interpreter.'

'Father Huw must be the one person in Gwytherin, I suppose, who doesn't know the truth by this time,' said Cadfael, with some compunction. 'But it wouldn't have been fair to lay such a load on his conscience. Better to let him keep his innocence.'

'His innocence is safe enough,' said Bened, 'for he's never said word to bring it in question, but for all that I wouldn't be too sure that he doesn't know. There's a lot of merit in silence.'

The next morning at chapter he delivered his messages of goodwill and commendation to the monastery in general, and the members of Prior Robert's mission in particular, from the parish of Saint Winifred's ministry to the altar of her glorification. Abbot Heribert questioned him amiably about the chapel and the graveyard which he himself had never seen, and to which, as he said, the abbey owed its most distinguished patroness and most precious relics.

'And we trust,' he said gently, 'that in our great gain you have not suffered equally great deprivation, for that was never our intent.'

'No, Father Abbot,' Bened reassured him heartily, 'you need have no regrets upon that score. For I must tell you that at the place of Saint Winifred's grave wonderful things are happening.

More people come there for help than ever before. There have been marvellous cures.'

Prior Robert stiffened in his place, and his austere face turned bluish-white and pinched with incredulous resentment.

'Even now, when the saint is here on our altar, and all the devout come to pray to her here? Ah, but small things—the residue of grace....'

'No, Father Prior, great things! Women in mortal labour with cross-births have been brought there and laid on the grave from which she was taken, where we buried Rhisiart, and their children have been soothed into the world whole and perfect, with no harm to the mothers. A man blind for years came and bathed his eyes in a distillation of her may-blossoms, and threw away his stick and went home seeing. A young man whose leg-bone had been broken and knitted awry came in pain, and set his teeth and danced before her, and as he danced the pain left him, and his bones straightened. I cannot tell you half the wonders we have seen in Gwytherin these last two years.'

Prior Robert's livid countenance was taking on a shade of green, and under his careful eyelids his eyes sparkled emerald jealousy. How dare that obscure village, bereft of its saint, outdo the small prodigies of rain that held off from falling, and superficial wounds that healed with commendable but hardly miraculous speed, and even the slightly suspicious numbers of lame who brought their crutches and left them before the altar, and walked away unsupported?

'There was a child of three who went into a fit,' pursued Bened with gusto, 'stiff as a board in his mother's arms, and stopped breathing, and she ran with him all the way from the far fields, fording the river, and carried him to Winifred's grave, and laid him down in the grass there dead. And when he touched the chill of the earth, he breathed and cried out, and she picked him up living, and took him home joyfully, and he is live and well to this day.'

'What, even the dead raised?' croaked Prior Robert, almost speechless with envy.

'Father Prior,' said Brother Cadfael soothingly, 'surely this is but another proof, the strongest possible, of the surpassing merit and potency of Saint Winifred. Even the soil that once held her bones works wonders, and every wonder must redound to the credit and glory of that place which houses the very body that blessed the earth that still blesses others.'

And Abbot Heribert, oblivious of the chagrin that was consuming his prior, benignly agreed that it was so, and that universal grace, whether it manifested itself in Wales, or England, or the Holy Land, or wheresoever, was to be hailed with universal gratitude.

'Was that innocence or mischief?' demanded Cadfael, when he saw Bened off from the gatehouse afterwards.

'Work it out for yourself! The great thing is, Cadfael, it was truth! These things happened, and are happening yet.'

Brother Cadfael stood looking after him as he took the road towards Lilleshall, until the stocky figure with its long, easy strides dwindled to child-size, and vanished at the curve of the wall. Then he turned back towards his garden, where a new young novice, barely sixteen and homesick, was waiting earnestly for his orders, having finished planting out lettuces to follow in succession. A silent lad as yet. Maybe once he had taken Brother Cadfael's measure his tongue would begin to wag, and then there'd be no stopping it. He knew nothing, but was quick to learn, and though he was still near enough to childhood to attract any available moist soil to his own person, things grew for him. On the whole, Cadfael was well content.

I don't see, he thought, reviewing the whole business again from this peaceful distance, how I could have done much better. The little Welsh saint's back where she always wanted to be, bless her, and showing her pleasure by taking good care of her own, it seems. And we've got what belonged to us in the first place, all we have a right to, and probably all we deserve, too, and by and large it seems to be thought satisfactory. Evidently the body of a calculating murderer does almost as well as the real thing, given faith enough. Almost, but never quite! Knowing what they all know by now, those good people up there in

Gwytherin may well look forward to great things. And if a little of their thanks and gratitude rubs off on Rhisiart, well, why not? He earned it, and it's a sign she's made him welcome. She may even be glad of his company. He's no threat to her virginity now, and if he is trespassing, that's no fault of his. His bed-fellow won't grudge him a leaf or two from her garland!

BOSTON PUBLIC LIBRARY

3 9999 00749 370 1

Boston Public Library

CODMAN SQUARE
BRANCH LIBRARY

FICTION

PZ3
.P2163MO

88072084

The Date Due Card in the pocket indi-
cates the date on or before which this
book should be returned to the Library.

Please do not remove cards from this
pocket.

DERCO